A Secret Edge

A Secret Edge

Robin Reardon

KENSINGTON BOOKS
http://www.kensingtonbooks.com

KENSINGTON BOOKS are published by

Kensington Publishing Corp.
850 Third Avenue
New York, NY 10022

All Kensington titles, imprints and distributed lines are available at special quantity discounts for bulk purchases for sales promotion, premiums, fund raising, educational or institutional use.

Special book excerpts or customized printings can also be created to fit specific needs. For details, write or phone the office of the Kensington Special Sales Manager: Kensington Publishing Corp., 850 Third Avenue, New York, NY, 10022. Attn. Special Sales Department. Phone: 1-800-221-2647.

Kensington and the K logo Reg. U.S. Pat. & TM Off.

ISBN-13: 978-0-7582-1927-5
ISBN-10: 0-7582-1927-X

First Kensington Trade Paperback Printing: June 2007
10 9 8 7 6 5

Printed in the United States of America

For Jody Thomas, 1951–1993

In 1983, across a table at a New York City sidewalk café, my friend Jody Thomas told me in hushed tones about the "gay plague." I'd never heard of it before. Neither of us knew then that within ten years it would claim him.

Jody made me believe that, for him, gay pride was not pride in being gay but pride in being himself.

Jody, this is my square in the quilt for you.

Chapter 1

Dream a Little Dream

It's like most of these dreams, when I'm lucky enough to have them. The other boy is a little taller than me, dark hair where I have blond, and deep brown eyes where mine are blue. His touch electrifies me, and my back arches in response to the kisses he plants on my neck, my shoulders, my belly.

And then I'm sitting up, alone.

I throw myself back down onto the bed, embarrassed, wanting to cry. Wanting to dream it again. The boy had been no more recognizable than any of the others. So I guess he was no more or less attainable.

I hate what happens when I'm determined to dream about girls. Which of course I should be doing if I'm trying to be like the other guys I know. Girls are what they dream about. But no matter how hard I try, the girl always turns out to be David Bowie. I barely know who David Bowie is! Just from a couple of tunes and that weird movie I saw at the retro theater last year. But there he is in my dreams, sharp bones of his face, lank hair, scrawny body, calling up feelings every bit as strong as the dark-eyed boys who haunt me.

I'm sixteen years old, for crying out loud! Shouldn't I be

having normal dreams by now? I don't mind the sexiness of the dreams, but the sex of the people in them is making me crazy. I'm dying to ask someone about this, but there's no one I can think of to talk to. Not Aunt Audrey, that's for sure. I can just imagine her response.

"It's called a wet dream, Jason."

"Yes, Aunt Audrey, I know that. I've been having them for years. But why is it always boys in them?"

"Don't worry about that. It will pass. It's just a phase you're going through. Did you take the sheets off the bed?"

But I do worry about it. I think it means I'm gay.

Really, you could ask Aunt Audrey anything, she's so gentle, so even tempered. And there's something about the fluffy style of her "prematurely" (she's careful to stress that when she mentions it) gray hair that gives off a soft warmth.

But if I tell Aunt Audrey, there's no way not to tell Uncle Steve as well. And then I'd have to be prepared for a no-nonsense answer. Matter-of-fact doesn't come close to how he approaches life and everything in it. I don't want a no-nonsense approach to this question. No-nonsense makes it seem like nothing is more important than anything else. Even me.

But that's not fair. All right, they won't let me have my own cell phone ("When you can afford to pay the bills yourself, young man . . ."), but I know they care for me. I mean, if they didn't, would they have kept me? I was dumped on their doorstep at the ripe old age of two, after my parents died in the car wreck that didn't do more than scrape my tender baby skin in a few unimportant places.

Aunt Audrey has told me that I'm like the child she and Uncle Steve couldn't have. But we have an understanding, he and I. I don't bring him anything that isn't really important, good or bad, and he doesn't make me feel silly for bringing something to him.

Aunt Audrey may be easier to talk to, but she can be tough as nails when she needs to be. Even a crisis wouldn't faze her. I know she's cool in a crisis, because the surgeons at the hospital want her more than any of the other nurses when they're in the operating theater. But—I need more than her usual cool reaction, so I don't bring this question to her.

So she wields a knife, in a way, where she works, and—unbeknownst to her—I wield one where I work as well. School.

Okay, wielding a knife is overstating it. I just carry the thing around. I'm probably giving the impression that my school is a dangerous place, which it isn't. We don't even have metal detectors, or I couldn't carry it. But I decided a long time ago that I wasn't going to run all the time, away from the bullies and the tough kids who think I'm easy prey just because I have this baby face and I'm not very tall. If they believed I was gay, it would be even worse.

Anyway, dream over, I massage myself into something resembling calm and roll away from the wet spot. And before I know I'm asleep again, the alarm goes off.

The day begins like any typical day, despite how important it will turn out to be. Despite the fact that it will change my life. Aunt Audrey has already left for the hospital and Uncle Steve is still in the shower by the time I'm dressed—his schedule at the vocational school where he teaches math is later than Aunt Audrey's—so I grab something from the kitchen and gnaw on it while I'm dressing. I could catch the bus that picks up kids who live over a mile away from school—I'm a mile and a half—but unless it's pouring rain, I walk. And I walk superfast, to keep my breathing in shape for my favorite "subject." Track. It's spring-training time. I don't pretend I'm Olympic material. I just love it.

I love the long-distance run, when you feel like you're about to die and if possible you'd hurry it up because you feel like crap, and then suddenly you reach this place where your mind and body are the same, no difference, no boundaries, and you feel like there are no boundaries for you anywhere. I also love the short dashes, the sharpness of my senses as I wait for the signal, the huge burst of energy that the signal releases, the feeling that, once I'm under way, no one can catch me. Most guys are much better at one or the other—distance or dash— and it's true I'm faster on the dash. But I love all of it.

Most of all I think I love it because now, now that my knife and I have scared most of the goons away, I run because I want to. Not because they want to make me.

Today after school the trials for track intramurals start. One thing I'm competing in is the hundred-yard dash, but my real goal is to be anchorman for our relay team. Anchor is the last of four runners, always the fastest. So, yeah, I want to be picked for best.

My last class of the day is English Lit. We have this teacher who seems to think everyone should be able to write. But, you know, some people just don't have it in them. Not every- one who can construct complete sentences is a writer, and many kids can't even do that. I guess Mr. Williams is trying to improve this situation, and I wish him luck, but—really.

Take that kid who always sits halfway down the room be- side the wall like he's trying to avoid being noticed. If you sit at the front, you look too eager; at the back, you're hiding and really begging the teacher to pick on you. So Robert Hubble sits halfway down. But he can't bring himself to sit in the middle of the room. He has to hug the wall, like if he were put to it he'd know what was behind him.

Actually, he looks like the kind of guy who'd know what to do if he were up against it. He's tall, heavy in a powerful way, with a face so homely it's almost attractive. Not your typical A student. And he can't write, that's certain. I've heard some of his attempts. But he seems like an okay guy, just not someone I have much in common with.

I glance at Robert as Williams is giving us today's in-class essay assignment: write a character sketch of Jesus. Robert's jaw falls, and he fixes a kind of empty stare at Williams. I can imagine him saying to himself, "What? You want me to do what?"

I dig in. I love this stuff. I might be a writer when I finish college. Who knows?

I stop at my locker on the way to the trials to pick up books I'll need for homework tonight. As I slam it shut, I'm greeted with the unpleasant grin of Jimmy Walsh.

Once upon a time, in a far-off land, I was pretty good friends with Jimmy Walsh. Most of the kids in class liked him. He had this really confident air about him, he was good in sports, and some of the girls thought he was cute.

He used to read over my shoulder to get my math answers in fifth grade; that's how I first got to know him. At first I didn't like that, but then one day he stood up for me when this other kid (whose name I've forgotten, which is fine with me) deliberately threw a softball right at me. It was between innings, and I'd just made it to home base and put our team ahead. The guy pitching for the other team was pissed because he'd thrown too late to put me out. The catcher threw the ball back to second base, where the batter was headed, and put him out, but I'd made it. There was this signal that went between the pitcher and the second baseman just as the teams were starting to exchange positions. I didn't think anything of it until the ball came smacking into my ribs.

"Hey!" I heard through a fog of pain. "What d'you think you're doin'?" It was Jimmy's voice. I turned a little, saw him throw his hat on the ground, and then he launched himself bodily into the pitcher. The coach broke it up pretty quickly and wasn't any too pleased with either of them, but he'd seen me get hit so he knew what it was about.

I had no objection to letting Jimmy cheat off my math assignments after that. And we were friends, sort of—considering that we're pretty different people—for a couple of years before it started to cool off. He used to come over to my house for dinner and stuff, and I was at his sometimes. His parents and my aunt and uncle never made friends in any particular way, probably because they didn't have even as much in common as Jimmy and I did.

The beginning of the end was when Dane Caldwell moved into our school district. Dane had to make a splash right away, I guess, because it didn't take him long to start looking for people to pick on. You know the type? It's like he's got to prove he's a man by pushing real hard at anyone or anything that doesn't measure up to some masculine standard in his head. I guess I didn't measure up, because it wasn't long before he started pushing at me.

I'll never forget the day he turned Jimmy against me for real. I was fourteen and starting to look good as a runner. Starting to be competition for Jimmy, actually, and I'd just proven it by beating him in a race during phys ed. And Dane was smart. He didn't taunt me. He taunted Jimmy.

"Walsh, you gonna let that sissy boy beat you like that?"

There was a little more exchange between them that I don't remember now, and nothing happened right away. But on my way home from school that day, they followed me. Both of them. If memory serves, I put up a pretty good fight; I'd been in a few scuffles in years gone by, and maybe I'd never be a fighter, but I was no chicken, either. But finally Dane got my arms behind me and held me.

"Give it to him, Jimmy!" he shouted.

I looked right at Jimmy's eyes, panting through gritted teeth, and said, "Don't let him do this to you. Don't let him turn you into a bully."

He plunged his fist into my stomach. And again. And I'm not sure what happened after that, except that some lady came out of nowhere and yelled at them. They ran, and she half carried me down the street and into her house.

"Who were those boys?" she demanded. "What are their names?"

I was in a hell of a lot of pain at this point, but I managed to say, "Never saw them before." Even today I'm not sure why I lied. Some misplaced loyalty to Jimmy, maybe. Anyway, she made me give her my home phone number, and Aunt Audrey came to get me.

And the demands for information started all over. "Jason, I insist you tell me! Those boys have to be punished."

By now there was no doubt in my mind that I had to keep quiet. I mean, think of the terror campaign they'd have gone on if I'd ratted! Thank God Uncle Steve reacted differently; I think he understood.

"Audrey, if the boy doesn't know them, he doesn't know them." Then to me, "You okay, son? How bad are you hurt?"

"I'll be all right. Really. It hurt a lot before, but it's better." And it was better, sort of; but what hurt the most was knowing that Jimmy had let Dane make his dark side too powerful to be my friend anymore, probably forever.

The next day at school it was like Jimmy had never stood up for me for anything. From then on, every time I saw him or Dane, and especially if they were together—which was the case more and more—they'd make these smirky faces. Pretty soon they started calling me sissy and wuss, and they'd do things like push my tray off the table in the cafeteria. The school year was almost up, and I knew I wouldn't have either of them in many of my classes next year, but I was starting to get a little worried. It was bad enough when I was little, getting picked on and slugged occasionally. But a ten-year-old can hurt you only so bad. When the bully is fifteen, it raises the stakes. It wasn't out of the question for me to get really hurt. And I was beginning to feel afraid, which of course is like waving raw steak under the nose of a hungry dog.

That's when I decided to arm myself. I searched eBay until I found someone willing to let me pay for a switchblade with a bank check. Now it goes with me almost everywhere. Not many people know about it, but I do. And that's what counts.

The look on Jimmy's face right now as we stand here by my locker, like he thinks I'm the scum of the earth, makes me glad that knife is with me. It gives me the courage to look blankly at him, like I don't give a shit what he thinks of me, as I give my locker combo a few turns. I'm about to walk away when he decides he'll have to speak first.

"Running today, are ya?"

I don't answer, so he has to try again.

"Think you'll beat me? Think again."

I turn my back on him and walk—saunter—away. He's in the competition for short dashes. Not relays. But I'm trying out for short dash as well, and I'll beat him if I can. He's fast, but his performance is inconsistent.

On my warm-up jog around the track, I pass by the high jump. There's only one guy there, practicing, someone I don't recognize. At first I think he's black, but as I get closer I see he's more likely from India or something. His hair has a beautiful gloss to it, and his face—intense with concentration—

transfixes me. It's a big school, over three hundred in my year alone, and there are lots of guys in my class year I don't know. But I'm surprised I've never noticed this fellow before.

I slow to a walk and watch as he starts his run. He's so graceful, it's almost like slo-mo. There's no doubt he knows just where he wants to take off from, and there's no doubt he does it. And then he's soaring. I'm motionless now, except for my eyes, which are following him in this incredible flight. His body twists slowly, gently, and when he lands, every part of him is where it should be.

I'm still there, staring, when he walks around from behind the jump. He sees me. He just stands there, poised and perfect, staring back at me. It's like he wants me to admire him. Maybe he does.

I shake myself out a little and jog back to where Coach Everett is gathering the runners. But I can't shake the face of the high jumper. The arched black eyebrows, the curve of the full lips—these stay with me.

There will be only one relay team from our school in the intramural competitions, so only four of us will be picked as finalists. But there are about seventeen guys waiting to compete, so we do a few elimination heats.

We're down to eight guys in no time, which means that we'll race four and four against each other. Then Coach will mix us up and we'll do it again to get the final team. In relay, it isn't just speed that counts. If you drop the baton in the handoff—well, it's pretty much over. You still pick it up and run, but just so you can say you did.

For the first of these final heats, Coach puts me in the starting position. Not what I want, but it's the second fastest, and you have to get off to a good start, so there's some glory in it. We win.

Mixed up again, I'm anchor this time, but we don't have

the inside track. This means we start farther ahead, but it's harder on the curves anyway. Maybe it's just a psychological thing, but it seems real. Those of us in nonstart positions jog off at angles toward our posts to wait for the baton.

Since I'm anchor, I see the whole race as it happens. Denny Shriver is our start, and he gets a really good launch, exploding from the line like a champagne cork. He's handing his baton off to Paul Roche ahead of the other team's hand-off, so we're in great shape. I almost don't want this, because I shine better if we're a little behind, but I'd rather have a sure win than risk wishing for a slow runner.

For some reason Paul is in some kind of frenzy and he runs like I've never seen him. He gets to Norm Landers way ahead of the other team. Paul is about to hand off just as I'm starting to dance a little so that I'll be ready to pace with Norm when he approaches me, and suddenly the baton is on the ground. I can't tell whose fault it is. It doesn't even matter. What matters now is how quickly Norm can pick it up and how fast I can run. Our lead is gone.

I don't even look at the other team's runner. I don't allow myself. Right now the baton is everything. In a minute, the finish line will be everything. Norm's pumping toward me, grimacing with effort. And then all I can see is that baton.

I don't even know when my feet start moving, but by the time Norm reaches me we're like two parts of the same machine, two pistons working in tandem, and the engine is smooth. Our hands are together on the baton only as long as it takes for me to relieve him of it, and I'm off.

It's all mine now. It's all my race. Denny, Paul, Norm—they've done their part, but from here on it's up to me. Somewhere on the edge of my vision I can see another boy, running, ahead of me. I can just make out the motion of his arms flying forward and back, the whipping motion of his jersey. But I'm not looking at him. I'm looking at the finish line.

There's no thought. My concentration moves my arms, my arms move my legs, and I'm flying.

A split second before I cross the line, I pass the other guy. A split second. But it's enough. It's fantastic.

I hold my arms up as I run forward, slowing down, opening my mouth wide to get as much air into my lungs as possible. I can hear cheering behind me, and I turn, a grin on my face.

And then I see him again. The high jumper. He's in the bleachers this time, standing, watching me, his face expressionless. I shake my hands in the air once, still clutching the baton, looking right at him. I want to shout, "Yes!" But his look has silenced almost everything. I can't hear cheering now. But I can hear myself breathing. And if he even whispers, I'm sure I'll hear him.

And then he smiles. Suddenly I can hear clapping again. I do shout now. That "Yes!" I'd wanted to. I do. And it feels great.

He turns and moves away. I stand there for a second, grinning after him, and then lope back to my team.

Paul is pretty upset; he feels it was his fault the baton dropped. It seems the coach agrees with him, or maybe there's some other reason, but Coach doesn't put him on the final team. Paul's performance is a little like Jimmy Walsh's; some days he does great, some days he doesn't. But I like Paul. Too bad, though; this isn't a friendship team, and we want to win. So the final team is me, Denny, Norm, and the anchor from the other team, Rich Turner. But I'll anchor ours. I'm soaring now, as high as that fellow over the high jump.

Speaking of Jimmy Walsh, I know I'm up against him in

less than fifteen minutes, when we do short dashes. A number of us from the relay competition will try for dashes too, so Coach gives us a few minutes' rest. I look at the tryout sheet posted on the side of the bleacher: high jump next.

Everyone is moving that way, so I fall in. I'm fully expecting to see that Indian fellow again, and I'm expecting he will outshine everyone else there.

I'm not wrong. He's fifth in a group of nine contestants. Coach Everett calls out something unintelligible, stumbling over the unfamiliar syllables of my Indian's name. But I know it's going to be him. And he does, in fact, soar every bit as gloriously as he'd done before the relays. It's the sort of thing that's so studied, and yet so effortless, that you know it will be the same every time. Until it gets even better.

It doesn't get better today, but it doesn't need to. He beats everyone else hands down. But we get to send two jumpers, so Dane Caldwell will also represent us. Remember Dane? The one who turned Jimmy into my enemy? He does okay, I have to admit grudgingly.

I watch to see who goes up to congratulate the Indian. I'm not the most popular kid in school, but a lot of guys clapped my back after that relay. But no one moves toward the high jumper. So I do. I reach out my hand. He looks at me a second and then takes it. His eyes are such a deep color I feel like I could fall into them.

"Jason Peele," I tell him, trying not to sound as breathless as I feel. "You were fantastic."

"Thank you. Nagaraju Burugapalli," he says in the most lilting, undulating tones. Seeing my blank stare, he adds, "You Americans usually find it easier to call me Raj."

I hear Coach shouting for the dash contestants, so I just say, "Anyway, great job." And I turn and jog back to the starting line.

Again we have to go through a few elimination runs. I'm sort of watching how Jimmy is doing and sort of watching to see where Raj has gone. Jimmy is doing well; Raj is nowhere in sight. I guess he decided not to stay and watch the other trials, and I'm disappointed. It means he didn't want to stay and watch me.

As luck would have it, I'm up against Jimmy in the final heat. He grimaces at me before falling into his starting position, and I swear he growls, but I could be making that up. I've done well so far, or I wouldn't be in this last heat, but there's no denying I'm tired. I have to call on all my concentration not to let Jimmy's ill will affect me. So I try to imagine something great at the finish line that I want to beat him out of. But what?

The signal goes before I come up with something, but I'm ready to run. So's Jimmy. We're neck-and-neck for a good seventy-five out of the one hundred yards. I can hear him breathing through clenched teeth, occasionally grunting with strain.

And then I see my goal. Or, rather, I don't. It's a mirage, I'm sure of it, and yet there's Raj standing just past the finish line, his deep eyes full on me. I know it's my mind doing this, he's not really there, but I sure don't want Jimmy to get there first.

He doesn't. Again, it's a split-second-or-two win, but it's a win. But there's something dark in it; I don't feel like shaking my hands in the air and shouting, so I just run forward a ways and bend over, hands on knees, panting. That's done it; I'm in the dashes.

Jimmy's time is still good enough to qualify him, so he's on the final team. But I can tell he's pissed that I beat him. He's punching at nothing and scowling as he gulps for air; it's a funny picture, but I'm not in the mood to laugh, and I don't have the breath.

I decide to ignore him. I turn and walk toward where the other runners are standing. Once I'm there, someone in the bleachers catches my eye. But this time it's not Raj. This time it's Robert Hubble, the guy from English Lit. I'm standing there, hands on hips, puzzling over this, when he grins and waves. So I shrug and wave too. Guess he just wanted to watch the trials and congratulate someone, and I was looking at him. That's cool.

There are a few more trials—shot put, running long jump, things like that—but I decide not to hang around. I just want to hit the showers and go home, where I can find something sugary to eat before Aunt Audrey can stop me.

There are a few runners in the showers, but a lot of guys are still trying out for other events. I don't see Raj; he must have left already. But I don't see Jimmy or Dane either, and I didn't think they were competing for anything else. Never mind.

The main gate to the athletic field points you back toward the school, but there's a side gate that leads to a small wooded area next to the road that makes for a shorter walk home. I'm ready for a shorter walk. I work the latch, a rusty, cantankerous old thing, until it gives. I shut it behind me, test it, and turn to walk toward the road.

Suddenly there are two other guys there: must have been behind trees or something. It's Jimmy and Dane, of course. I freeze. They're still in track getup, and I'm back in jeans and my leather jacket, not to mention the heavy backpack. No chance of outrunning them, and forget opening that old gate again. Seems like old times.

"So, you think you're pretty hot stuff, eh?" is Jimmy's snarling contribution.

There's no good response, so I don't try. They begin to separate a little, each of them slightly to one side of me.

Dane goes next. "It would be such a shame if you couldn't run, wouldn't it? Like if you had a broken leg or something."

Slowly I shift my pack off my shoulder, but before I set it down I reach into an outer pocket and grab my folded switchblade. I've never had to use it on anything that was alive, but it seems like this might be the time to consider it. Or at least make it look like I would. I pop it open.

They both see it and stop moving, their eyes glued on it. We're standing like that, as though we're waiting for some slow photographer to capture the image, when I hear running feet on my right. All three heads turn.

It's Robert Hubble.

He stops running and sort of lumbers forward. He looks at me, at my knife, and then at Dane, who's nearest him.

"What's going on?" he asks. It's not entirely clear what his own intentions might be.

Jimmy decides to try and co-opt him. Hands on hips, doing his best to look confident, he says, "We're just going to teach this little faggot here a lesson."

Faggot?

Robert stares at him for another few seconds and then moves over toward me, facing the others.

"Seems to me," he says in a drawl that challenges contradiction, "there's not a lot you jokers could teach him. Why don't you try teaching me?"

Robert faces off against Dane, and I turn my full attention to Jimmy, knife still at the ready. But they decide they aren't up for this kind of fight, so they back away several paces and then turn and run toward the road.

When I'm sure they're gone, I refold the knife and tuck it into a pocket, trying to put Jimmy's accusation out of my mind and trying to keep my hand from shaking. That was a close one.

"You, my friend," I say to Robert, hand up for a high five, which he gives me, "are a lifesaver! Where the hell did you come from?"

"I was looking for you. After the trials. But you didn't come out the front door, so I thought maybe you'd gone the other way. And I saw you guys down here. Didn't look friendly, so I just thought I'd see what was going on."

"Looking for me? But why?"

Robert makes a few grimaces, seemingly not sure where to start, and finally leans his shoulder against the fence, hands in his pockets.

"Well, you always seem—it always seems like you understand that stuff. In Williams's class. You always know what the book is really about, not just what the words say—you know. And I'm lucky if I even get all the words. And forget writing about it. So—I dunno, I was hoping maybe I could talk you into giving me a few pointers. I can't afford to fail another class. I already got kept back last year, and my dad'll kill me. Plus, you know, it's embarrassing."

I'm thinking, uncharitably, that's probably the most words the fellow has strung together in one speech in his life. He's looking sheepishly down at his shoes now. I can't help grinning.

"And did you set those two goons on me just so you could rescue me and I'd owe you?"

He looks horrified. "What? No, I—no!"

I chuckle at the expression on his face. "Look, I'm only kidding. When do we start?"

We start that night after dinner. Aunt Audrey has this policy that I don't go anywhere with friends she's never met, so we decide it's easier if he comes to my house. Plus, he says his little brother is a bit of a pain. So when he shows up, we head for my room, and I think about what music to play. Call me weird, but it helps me to think if I play something really old like Bach or Mozart. Aunt Audrey says she got me started, putting that stuff on when I was little whenever I was doing something like drawing or practicing reading, that sort of thing. I guess it stuck.

I start the CD player, put on a disk, and sit on the floor with my back to the bed.

"What's that you're playing?" Robert is halfway across the room before I answer.

"Bach."

"Well, no," he says, picking up the jewel case and scowling at it. "Says here it's somebody called Brandenburg."

It's a good thing I'm on the floor already, or I'd have hurt myself falling. I can barely speak for laughing. Robert just stares at me, not getting what's so funny, and I'm wiping tears off my face and trying to explain.

"That's the name of the guy who asked Bach to write the concertos," I manage finally. "Some nobleman of Branden-burg, in Germany. He commissioned them, and they were named for him. Johann Sebastian Bach wrote them. Look again."

I decide this is our first lesson. Robert had just seen the large text and stopped looking. He scowls now at the cover, and soon his face relaxes and goes a little red. Maybe he wouldn't be embarrassed if I hadn't laughed at him, but—really.

"Hey," I call to him, "bring it here. Sit." I pat the floor beside me.

Together we go over the labeling, and he agrees that his misinterpretation is a lot like how he reads our English Lit assignments. He doesn't take things in, just reads enough to get a superficial understanding of something.

Next I reach for my copy of *A Handful of Dust*, our current assignment. I hand it to Robert and ask him to read the opening quote and first paragraph.

"Okay," I say when he's finished, "now try and tell me, in your own words, what that first paragraph says, and where you think it might lead. Pretend you're telling me the story."

He looks at it, glaring. I can practically smell the wood burning, he's thinking so hard. Finally he says, "Well, I think it might be saying—"

"No, wait. Don't tell me what you think it says. See if you can construct your own story and have it say the same thing, but in different words, and then go on with what might happen next." He's silent so long that I ask, "Would it help to write something down?"

"Are you sure this will help?"

"It's not something you're going to do a lot of, but it's a test of how well you're internalizing what you read. If you can't do that, you can't see between the lines. And if you can't do that, then the only point of reading fiction is momentary entertainment."

While he's digging through his bag for pen and paper, I ask, "Robert, was there a particular reason you decided to take English Lit? It's an elective, after all."

"Sure there was. I can't do advanced math, that's certain. I hate Civics, and I'm not smart enough for French. I figured, y'know, I can read." He shrugs. Obviously, he didn't know what he was getting himself into.

He sits back down next to me. "What did you write today? About Jesus?"

"The character sketch. I enjoyed that. I took the position that Jesus of Nazareth was a very gifted and spiritual person who was convinced by desperate people around him that he was the fulfillment of this biblical prophecy. And because he was convinced of it, he did everything he could think of to make it work, but there were too many people who had differing ideas of what that would mean. He wanted nothing more than for everyone to understand God the way he did. But he couldn't quite bring himself to bend his image of God to fit what was expected of him, and that was his undoing."

About ten seconds of silence later, Robert says, "You put all that into one paper?"

"I write fast."

I'm tempted to ask him what he wrote. But now that I've told him about my paper, I'm not sure that's a good idea. So we go back to the first paragraph of *A Handful of Dust*.

He makes some progress, but pretty soon that wears thin, so I decide we should start a character sketch he can finish on his own. At first he wants to do his favorite football player.

"You can do that if you think you know enough about him personally. Mr. Williams today made an assumption we all had enough information about Jesus to do the assignment."

"What would I have to know?"

"What factors do you think went into his decision to play football? Did he have a father who was physically handicapped and this is like a gift for him, or a father who always made him feel like a loser and this is a way to prove himself? Did he have a sister who made him feel like he could do anything he really wanted to do? Or is he just some dumb lunk who can't do anything else? Does he have an interest outside of football that inspires him or has taught him lessons he brings to the game? Does he—"

"Okay, okay. Maybe I don't know enough. So who then?"

"Santa Claus." I don't know where this comes from. It isn't even Christmas season, and I haven't believed in Santa since I was four. An early skeptic, if you will. But I can smell cookies baking, and Aunt Audrey used to leave cookies out on Christmas Eve.

"Santa Claus?" he echoes.

"Sure. Why not? I mean, maybe you don't know who his

father is either, like you don't with the football player's family, but in this case you could make it up. In a way, this is a double exercise. First you have to construct the person, and then you have to put together the reasons why he ended up in that career."

He's still looking blankly at me.

"Tell you what. We'll work together to get some background down, and then you can take that with you and work on it for a character sketch. If you get stumped, we'll work on that part together as well. Okay?"

I can tell it isn't, really, but he's asked for help, and it seems he's determined to take it.

Just before we're done, Aunt Audrey knocks on the door and opens it.

"Boys, I have some chocolate chip cookies if you'd like some. Keep up your energy. In the kitchen, whenever you're ready."

She disappears again. I really could have done a lot worse than Aunt Audrey.

Robert gets this determined look on his face, like he's trying really hard not to be distracted by the thought of those cookies. He leans over the notebook and scowls. While he's scribbling away, my mind goes back to one of those times when I'd been practicing drawing and Aunt Audrey was playing one of these old classics. I was using my brand-new, gorgeous set of colored pencils. That set was huge; not a color in the world was missing from it. I loved the feel of the pencils, the way they moved over paper, the way you could use water to make the color intensity change. I was never much good at the drawing itself, but I really got into the colors.

We'd bought that set of pencils together. I was just starting second grade, and after a few sessions in Art it was obvious the pencils in class were lousy. So the teacher said we could bring in our own if we wanted to. I told my aunt and uncle this, and Uncle Steve asked if I wanted my own set.

"I dunno. There's pencils there. I can use those."

Aunt Audrey went next. "But are there enough to go around? And do you enjoy using them, or are they all chewed and broken?"

It was like she could see them herself, like she'd gone to the class and had seen how grungy they were. I just shrugged, but that weekend she took me to an art store. I'd never known places like that existed. Man, there was nothing they didn't have! I was running around looking at everything, but especially the paints and pencils, anything with color.

If there was one thing Uncle Steve had made me understand, it was that we weren't poor, but we didn't have money to throw around. So when it came time to decide on some pencils, I picked up the smaller set. Aunt Audrey grinned at me, tousled my hair, and put it back. She handed me the larger set. The huge set. The one with more colors than I had names for.

"Now, young man, these are pencils, and you'll be using them in water sometimes, and they'll get dull very quickly. Let's find you a good sharpener you can carry."

And again, going for cheap, I picked up a black plastic one. But Aunt Audrey went to find a sales clerk.

"I'm considering pencil sharpeners, but I want to make sure of the quality. Is there a pencil I can test with?"

We stood there with our test pencil and tried every sharpener we could see. And the one that worked best was not the plastic one, and it was not the cheapest one. It was metal with a really cool gold matte finish.

"We'll take this one, and these pencils. And while we're at it, we'd like a tablet of your best drawing paper."

I took them to school the very next day, really excited

about all my new stuff. During Art, I was working away at a long wooden table with my beautiful new pencils, sharpening them from time to time with the gold matte sharpener, and really getting into the drawing. The pencils made it easy, and the paper was the best, and the sharpener was there whenever I needed it.

I was sitting beside a girl named Kristi. Everyone knew her parents were really rich. She was nice, didn't lord it over anyone, but they had lots more money than my family. So there we were, working away, and Kristi kept clicking her tongue like she was disgusted about something. At one point she sat back hard and threw her dark green pencil onto the table. I watched it clatter across the wood.

She looked at me, I looked at her, and then she looked at my pencils. Then we both looked at hers. It wasn't a very big set, and it looked like there were some colors missing. Most of the pencils that were there were broken and chewed, just like the ones Aunt Audrey hadn't wanted me to have to use.

I offered her one of my two kinds of dark green, and she ran it across her paper. Then she said, "No wonder my mom said I could have these old pencils. The color part is all crumbly!"

You know, I don't think I ever told Aunt Audrey about Kristi's pencils. I think I'll have to do that. I think I'll have to let her know that I realize she's always treated me more like a son than a nephew. And that if I'm like that son she and Uncle Steve couldn't have, then she's like the mother I can't really remember.

Suddenly Robert throws his own pen down in disgust. He's ready to get up right now, but I want to see what he's written.

"Hang on," I say as I lay a hand on his leg to stop him getting up. He reacts by trying to pull away from me while he's in the process of lifting from the floor, and he falls over heavily.

"You all right?" I ask, trying not to laugh at him again.

"Yeah." He sits up, rubbing an elbow. "I think I have enough, you know. I'll take this with me." He nods toward his notebook, which we've been writing in.

I can sense there's something else going on, but I don't know what. "That's fine. Are you sure you're okay?"

He slides over to lean against the wall, a few feet from me. "Yeah. I just—well, I guess I just need to be sure of something."

He stops. I wait.

I give up. "Like what?"

"Those guys today. Jimmy and Dane. Jimmy called you— he called you a faggot."

I try not to let my cringe show. "So? He calls everyone a faggot. He thinks it's this big insult." I stop, hoping that will do it, but—no. "Are you asking me if I'm gay?" He says nothing, but the look on his face tells me that's it. "So when I touched you just now, that made you nervous, right?"

Maybe a year ago I would have laughed as hard as I'd laughed at the Brandenburg error. Maybe, if I hadn't been dreaming those dreams.

He shrugs. "Well, I mean—sure, he probably says that to a lot of guys. But you . . . I've heard some of the girls say how cute you are. Maybe that kind of boy thinks you're cute too."

On one hand, I like this. I do have a nice build, even if it's not supermuscled; I'm a runner, not a football player. And I spend as much time looking in the mirror as anyone else. So it's nice to know that others like what they see. But—that kind of boy, eh? "That kind" might be me.

But this isn't something I want to deal with here. I attack from the side. "Do you have a girlfriend?"

Now he looks scared, and I do laugh. I can't help it. "Robert, will you chill? I was going to suggest that we double-date this weekend. I'm going to ask Rebecca Travers out, and in the past she's had an easier time getting permission if it's not just the two of us. What do you say?" I hadn't really been planning to ask her out this weekend, but I may as well.

He's grinning a little sheepishly now, still rubbing his elbow absentmindedly. "I, uh, I—honestly, Jason, I've never asked a girl out."

If I weren't afraid of offending him, I'd try to turn the tables and ask if maybe I'm the one who should be afraid he's gay. At least I've been dating for a year, even if it was just for show.

I collect the stuff we've strewn all over the floor as I tell him, "That, my friend, will be another lesson, then. Tomorrow after school, you and I will go to the mall, and I'll teach you how to talk to girls."

I stand and hold my hand out. He grins and then takes it, and I haul him to his feet. Or at least I provide a balance point; he's too big for me to haul anyplace. And then we go massacre half a batch of cookies.

That night, as I'm trying to fall asleep, I'm haunted by my deceit, by what I've done to mislead Robert. To mislead everyone. Even me.

It's true that I'm not the least intimidated talking to girls. I feel like I've got nothing to lose. But most of my dates have been with Rebecca, someone I've known all my life, someone who lives in the next block from me. In fact, I'd started asking her out almost by default. And partly out of a sense of—I don't know, maybe expectations. Other people's expectations. I mean, wasn't I supposed to *want* to ask girls out? Wasn't I supposed to want to touch them and kiss them and have them touch me and kiss me?

Rebecca and I have been kissing since we were six, and although it's true the kisses have, well, matured, they haven't led to much else, and so far I haven't been tempted to get them to. I was a little surprised, actually, the first time she opened her mouth when I was kissing her. After all, I was just practicing; wasn't she? But then I decided this was practice too. If I was expected to do this, I'd better learn how. But it felt wrong somehow. I don't mean like we were doing it wrong; how would I know that? But I knew it wasn't what I wanted. What I want. What I want is something I can let myself have only in my dreams.

I shake my head to clear it; those dreams are scaring me. In the dreams, I'm not in control. Because then, when I can't stop myself, that's when it's a boy I want touching me. A boy I want kissing me.

But that isn't an option!

Is it?

What really scares me is that it might have to be Rebecca for me, or someone like her, which is to say someone female. I guess when I asked her out the first time, I was thinking, you know, believe it and you will see.

And I tried. I tried really hard. I started to pay more attention, watching TV or at the movies, when a man and a woman would kiss or more. When some girl in a song would gush about some boy or some boy would wail if some girl wouldn't notice him. I paid attention to the way kids at school would talk. Even guys who don't admit to being afraid of anything can't hide when they aren't really sure a girl will go out with them. Heck, if the girl will even talk to them!

I never felt that fear. Partly it's because there was never any girl who made me want her. So I never worried about whether a girl would go out with me—at least, not in terms of having anything really personal at stake. And I also never felt those butterflies you hear so much about. You know the kind? When you think of the person you want to be with, and something fluttery happens inside.

And since it was so obvious everyone else *did* have these feelings, it started to make me feel isolated. Separate. Like not only was there something wrong with me, but also I couldn't join in. I wasn't part of the club. So I started asking out Rebecca, because it was easy. Because I didn't want anyone else any more than I wanted her. And despite her parents' concerns, I've never wanted to do anything they wouldn't approve of. Caressing shoulders and even the roundness of her backside doesn't seem to count for much when you consider the other treasures I'm supposed to have intentions about.

My mind drifts kind of automatically from what I don't care about when I'm with Rebecca to something I used to love when I was little. When I spent as much time as I could with Darin, one street in the other direction from Rebecca's house. Darin, who used to hide with me in his mother's walk-in closet in the dark, shining flashlights onto each other's naked groins. Darin, who got really brave one day and reached out a hand and touched me for real. Just thinking of that now sends these jolts of something through me, makes me breathe oddly.

It didn't end there, either. Well, I mean, we didn't do much, you know? We were kids. Sometimes we'd shut the door to his room when his mom was someplace, maybe out sunbathing in the backyard, and we'd lie on the bed and hold each other's dicks. We'd press them together and giggle wildly.

I still remember the time he kissed me. It was just before his family moved away, when we knew we probably wouldn't see each other anymore. We were nine. And we weren't even doing anything. We were fully dressed, sitting on the floor in my room. It was August, and hot, and if we'd been "normal" boys we would have been outside playing tag or ball or something.

Hell, we were normal! It's just that . . . It's just that when he left that day, I knew he'd be gone. Sure, there was e-mail, but what's that compared to having someone touch you where no one else does? To feeling about someone the way you never feel about anyone else?

I was looking at his face, trying not to cry. He reached out and touched my shoulder, caressed it a little, and then pulled me toward him.

His lips were so soft. And it felt so right. So fucking *right*.

Darin never liked Rebecca.

I toy with the idea of trying to dream about girls tonight, but I'm not in the mood for David Bowie. Finally I begin to drift off.

And then I'm having one of those dreams again. Only this time I know who the other boy is. This time, it's Raj.

We don't actually do anything in the dream. He's standing at a distance, and he's looking at me. There's something about his eyes that makes me believe he would come to me if he could. It's like he's begging me to come to him. I try, but he never seems any closer. And there's this feeling I get. It's—I guess it's a longing, more than anything else. I want to know if his skin feels different, it's such a different color. I want to touch his arm, his shoulder, his hair, his face, his eyebrows. I'm breathing shallow breaths, faster and faster, and then—well, the usual. And it's over.

I'm almost awake, but even though I'm still asleep I know I don't want to wake up. I want to stay in the dream, where it seems right to feel this way about Raj, where no one is going to call me a faggot. So I struggle to stay under. I imagine touching his face again, but it seems even further away than before. I reach for his hand, but there's nothing to grasp.

When I finally have to admit I'm awake, I'm furious. I couldn't hang on to the dream, the feeling, and now I'm back where I have to let go of it. I'm half sitting up, pounding on my pillow.

"Jason?"

It's Aunt Audrey, with the door open just a crack. I can't speak. She comes in farther.

"Jason, are you all right? Have you had a nightmare?"

She sits down on the side of the bed. I wrap my arms tight around my pillow and bend my head over it, and Aunt Audrey strokes my hair. I want to tell her. This is important now. This is my life.

But all I say is, "I'm okay."

"Are you sure?"

"It's all right," I lie.

And I hate myself for doing it.

Chapter 2

At the Mall

Robert finds me between second and third periods the next day. He says, "Y'know, it occurs to me that those guys might tell somebody about that knife."

"Yeah. I thought of that too. I left it at home today."

" 'Cause, I mean, I didn't really see it. You know?"

Is he saying he'd lie for me? "Are you telling me that's your story, if you're asked?"

"Yeah. What's yours?"

"I guess I didn't really see it either." I punch his shoulder. "We still on for the mall?"

He reddens a little. "I'm game. I just don't know what I'm supposed to do."

"We'll figure that out when we get there. That's part of the fun. Reacting to the situation. It's kind of like playing ball, when the scheme falls apart and you have to improvise."

His grin says he likes that analogy.

He's lost it, though—the grin—by the time I see him after school. We hop a city bus to get to the mall and then kill a little time looking through a sporting goods store, waiting for a good selection of girls to show up. I'm trying to decide whether it's a better idea to scout for girls we know, or if total strangers would be safer test subjects. I decide we aren't going to ask anyone out right away, so I opt for strangers.

We head to the food court and get a couple of drinks.

"No food?" Robert asks.

"We're not here for food. You can get some later as a reward, if you want. But right now we want to stay mobile. It's easy to move around with a can of Coke in your hand. But a tray full of meatball sub, and sauce dripping all down your chin . . . I'm sure you get the picture."

He sighs, but he's still with me.

Over in the corner there's a round table with three girls. They look about our age, and they're huddled to one side of it, giggling. There's nothing terribly appealing about giggling girls, but I nudge Robert.

"See that table?" I ask. He nods. "They've left one side of it open, so there's room for us to sit. We can—"

"There's only one more chair."

"You going to let something like that stop you?"

He shrugs.

I go on from where I was interrupted. "Now, I don't think any of them will really turn out to be a good date for either of us, but we can practice. We'll just talk to them, okay? We don't know them, so even if things don't go well, we don't have to face them in the cafeteria at school. Get it?"

He takes a gulp of his drink and moves forward.

I grab his arm. "No, wait. We'll both approach slowly— stay with me. And then you'll hold back and look shy. Listen to what I say and watch their reactions. Then if we decide we don't want to sit, we don't."

"Right."

As casually as possible, we make our way toward the girls. They see us at about ten paces and stop giggling, watching our approach. At six feet or so, Robert stops as instructed. I turn, wink at him, and move forward.

"Pardon me, ladies," I say, smiling at each one in turn. I lower myself, one knee on the floor, as sweet as possible a look on my face. "That fellow I'm with was wondering if we might join you. I'd ask you myself, only I'm really nervous about talking to girls I don't know."

These girls are a little older than they looked from across the room. The one to my left looks right into my eyes, and she says, "My name is Doreen. And now that you know me, are you still nervous?"

I hold her eyes as I stand and reach for a chair from the next table. This is a game, and it's fun. I set the chair facing away from the girls and sit with my legs on either side of the plastic back supports.

"Not at all." I turn to Robert and indicate the other chair. "And neither is my friend. I'm Jason, and this is Robert."

I can't quite tell if we're being toyed with, or if there's really some interest there, but I get Robert talking by telling the girls things about him that aren't true, so he has to contradict me, and pretty soon we're laughing and flirting. I'm having a great time, and so is Robert.

We don't even try to make arrangements to meet the girls again. After a while they say they have to leave. I stand as they do, and Robert follows my lead. As they're saying good-bye, Doreen lets her hand brush really close to me, slips something into my rear jeans pocket, and then presses her hand against my backside.

In my ear I barely hear her words: "In case you're serious. You're cute."

I try to look like nothing happened as Robert and I watch them leave. No way am I going to reach for what's in my pocket while they're still in sight. Come to think of it, no way do I even want Robert to know there's anything in there; he needs to think he's done as well as I have.

Robert is more confident now. He's scouring the room with his eyes, a male animal on the make.

"That was fun," he says without looking at me. "Who's next?"

We walk around a little, and Robert actually rejects a couple of possibilities. Finally we see two girls we know. Robert pulls me to the side of the room.

"Jason, look. I think I'm ready. I really want to ask someone out. Do you think we could ask Debbie and Meg? Oh— but you were going to ask Rebecca."

I glance at the girls. Debbie is a bottle-blond cutie (eyebrows are the clue about the bottle) with curls, mascara, rouge. Meg wears her dark brown hair in a sleek bob, looking out from under feathered bangs with eyes that seem to take everything in, a feeling of quiet reserve about her. I imagine I know the answer to this question, but I ask it anyway: "Which one would you rather ask out?"

He thinks for a moment. I'm getting a little concerned that they'll see us. Finally he says, "Meg. She's taller and not as pretty. I think I might have a better chance with her."

Too bad; I'd kind of hoped he'd go for Debbie; Meg's smarter, and I think I'd have more fun talking with her. "Well, I haven't said anything to Rebecca yet, and it's not like we're going steady or anything. Why don't we go and talk to Debbie and Meg and see how it goes? You might end up with Debbie, you know; let's not make the decision for them. What do you think?"

"Debbie might go out with me?"

"We'll see how it goes. If you feel it's hopeless, pull on your ear, the one closer to Meg, when I'm looking at you, and I'll take the lead from there."

They don't spot us until we're close to their table. Meg's face says she's surprised to see us together.

"Hey," I greet them. "Fancy meeting you here. Listen, is it okay if we sit down?"

Debbie looks a little amused. "Sure."

I opt for casual conversation rather than the ready-for-anything approach I'd used on the three other girls. "So, are you shopping or just here to hang out with friends?"

Meg answers, her tone making it seem she doesn't think we'll like the answer. "I'm killing time until a poet I like gets to the bookstore for a reading."

I glance at Robert, he looks at me, and then he turns to Debbie. He says, "What about you?"

Debbie lets her eyes rest on Robert's broad shoulders for a minute. "I'm shopping. But I saw Meg, so we came here to get something to drink."

"Going to the poetry reading?" he asks.

She gives her head a shake, and the curls bounce a little. "I don't think poetry is my thing, really. What about you?"

I can tell they're off to a start at least, and I like poetry. So I talk to Meg about the reading, keeping an ear trained on Robert's progress. At one point I think I hear Debbie say something about some other boy, and then Robert's low voice says, "Well, in the meantime, how would you like to see a movie with me?"

Meg is in midsentence. She stops, but I don't want Robert to feel awkward, so I say something to get her to continue. I barely hear Debbie say, "That might be okay."

Meg stops talking again, looks at Robert, looks at me. "Did you guys come over here to ask us out?"

I shrug and flash a lopsided grin at her. "Sure. How would you like to see a movie with me?"

It takes us a while to figure out what movie we might all

like to see, and finally we settle on *The Return of the King*, the last of the "Lord of the Rings" cycle. There's a marathon of all three of them showing, but we can see just the third one. I haven't seen the first two, but I've read the books, so I think I'll be okay.

Debbie nearly squeals when I admit this lack in my cultural education. "How could anyone not have seen them?"

I treat the question as rhetorical, and we move on to logistics. We decide on an early Saturday show, with dinner at a hamburger place nearby afterward.

Robert is flying when we finally get up from our chairs. I'm tempted to stay for the poetry reading, but it seems a little like I'd be trying too hard. And anyway I have to talk to Robert about the date; I have no idea if he knows how to handle himself in this kind of social situation, and it seems unfair to throw him into the water without teaching him a few swimming techniques. We go hang out on some benches near a fountain at the center of the mall.

He's not as unschooled as I'd feared, so I really don't say much—just ask a few questions to make sure he has an idea what he's in for. The really good news, something I hadn't counted on, is that he can borrow his dad's car. Aunt Audrey lets me use hers from time to time, but it's a VW bug. Not much good for double dating. And Uncle Steve's is off-limits, not because it's anything special, but because—or so I suspect—there's enough room in it for a pair of determined teenagers to have sex more comfortably than in the bug.

We do some people watching—Robert eyeing the girls, and me surreptitiously following a few boys with my gaze—until we need to leave. On the way through the mall, we pass by a small boutique, and I'm looking through the glass at a leather jacket when I see two kids in the store. My breath stops. One of them is Raj.

He's standing with his side to me, hands in his pockets,

watching a girl do a little spin to show off the skirt of a dress she's trying on. He's smiling at her, a little possessively it seems. She looks Indian too. Could she be his girlfriend?

My heart is in my throat. I have to know.

Robert has stopped several feet away, waiting for me to follow him. I try to speak, but I have to clear my throat first.

"I'll just be a minute" finally emerges a little hoarsely.

I stroll in, doing my best to look unconcerned, and pretend to examine a few things hanging on a rack, working my way slowly to where Raj and the girl are talking.

She's saying, "But do you think it's too much money?"

"You like this boy, yes?" She nods. He adds, "I like him too, and Mum and Dad. This is a special event." His smile makes his whole face glow.

I'm staring right at him when he sees me. The smile fades, but the eyes—well, the eyes pull me forward.

I try to fake serendipity. "Raj? It's Raj, isn't it?"

"Yes. I—yes." He seems flustered. In a way, this is a good thing. I move over to him, knowing that he'll either introduce me to the girl or take me aside and tell me to get away from him. Whoever speaks first . . .

He does. "This is my sister, Anjani. Anjani, this is Jason Peele from school. He's on the track team. A runner."

Anjani's deep eyes sparkle as she holds her hand out for mine. "How do you do?"

How do you do? Can't remember when anyone has said that to me.

"Delighted to meet you," I say, and—I can hardly believe I'm doing this—I bow over her hand. I decide to throw caution to the wind. If I can make friends with his pretty sister, who knows what else might happen? "I hope you don't mind if I tell you how charming you look. This outfit—you're trying it on? It suits you."

"Thank you so much! Yes, I do think I'll take it."

She turns to her brother—her brother!—and laughs, a musical sound. She's older than Raj, I decide; at first I had thought the opposite. She dances away, presumably back to the dressing room, and leaves Raj and me alone.

This is awkward. He's not saying anything, just looking at me with those eyes. Pretend you're with a girl, I tell myself. It almost works; at least I can talk, even if I can also hear my heart pounding.

I say, "She's lovely. And what a wonderful brother you are, to take her shopping."

He clears his throat. I feel a strange gratification. "She trusts my judgment. I won't tell her something looks good if I don't think it does."

I nod slowly, trying to look wise. "Honesty is rare. I like it."

Another moment goes by, awkward again, but neither of us makes a move to end things, to break off the meeting. I'm thinking there's something about him that seems unusual. Not just that he's from India; it's like he has some special knowledge, or something like that.

Finally he breaks the silence. "How did you do in the dash?"

I tilt my head at him. "How did you know I was trying out for it?"

If someone with a complexion as dark as his can blush, he blushes. "I saw your name on the list."

It's everything I can do not to laugh. I feel giddy, foolish, happy to the point of ridiculousness. He looked for me. On the list. He remembered my name. He knew it well enough to tell his sister. And it makes him blush to admit it to me.

Gradually I grow calm enough to speak. "I did fine. I'm on the team."

"And the relay," he adds.

I'm breathing oddly, but there's nothing I can do about it. "Can I ask a personal question?"

He shrugs one shoulder and inclines his head.

"Would you say your whole name slowly? I want to know how to pronounce it correctly. All of it."

In my peripheral vision I can see Robert heading my way. Must have grown tired of waiting. I ignore him. So does Raj.

Raj smiles. Finally. He says his first name slowly, and I repeat it. "That's good," he says, and I'm thrilled. We move on to the last name, which I have to try twice, and then I put them both together by myself. Just in time, for Robert can be ignored no longer.

I turn to him. "Robert Hubble, meet Nagaraju Burugapalli." I grin at Robert's face, which probably looks a lot like mine the first time I heard that tongue twister. "I don't think he'll mind if you call him Raj."

They shake hands a little awkwardly. Raj is looking hard at Robert, and suddenly it occurs to me that there's no way I can say why Robert and I are here. I don't want Raj to think Robert is "with" me, but I also don't want him to know we were picking up girls. I need to take the lead now, and then get out of here.

To Robert: "Raj is our lead high jumper on the track team." I turn to Raj. "Robert was helping me decide about a pair of running shoes, but I didn't buy anything today."

Before the puzzled look on Robert's face is any more obvious, I say, "Well, I need to get home or my aunt will send out the Saint Bernards looking for me."

"You have dogs?" Raj asks.

I smile at him, as sweetly as possible. "No. Just an expression."

I've been careful not to say "We need to leave" or "We need to get home." I hope that registers. I look at him for just a few more seconds. "See you."

He raises his chin a little, his eyes still on mine, and I turn toward the door. Deliberately, I stop to let Robert go out first, and I turn back toward Raj. He's still looking at me. I pause just long enough to let him know I've taken this in and then disappear.

I'm flying as high as Robert now. It was Raj's sister with him, not a girlfriend! He looked for me on the track roster! He let me know he watched me win the relay!

If only there were something I could do with this feeling. Something other than dream.

Chapter 3

Moving Fast

The date is a total disaster. At least, from my point of view.
For everyone else, I think it's a huge success.

It's easy for me to follow the plot of the movie, as I'd predicted. I know all the characters, what their roles are, and
what's going to happen. This turns into a problem for me; if I
were distracted by the tension of not knowing the outcome
already, maybe I wouldn't be so affected by the Frodo character. As soon as I see him, I'm lost. He pulls at me, pulls at my
head, my heart, my—well, all of me. I was fidgeting so much
Meg probably thought I was trying to get my arm behind
her, but that was not on my mind at the time. Elijah Wood,
playing Frodo, had my full attention.

I recover a little over dinner, forced into conversation by
the fact that Robert is so overwhelmed at the idea of being
on a date with a cutie like Debbie that he can't think of anything to say. I keep feeding him lines, asking him questions.
He warms up after a while, once I start teasing him about his
size, making sure what I say is actually flattering. And Debbie
smiles at him a lot, which helps.

At one point, Meg whispers in my ear that she hasn't seen

the first two movies, and she hasn't read any of the books either. This sends us into a private fit of the giggles.

But all this congeniality leads to my biggest problem.
Robert, driving, takes it upon himself to stop in a rather deserted area near a ball field. I can see the side of Debbie's face
in the front seat, pretending astonishment and gentle outrage,
really wanting Robert to reach for her. He does.

So Meg and I sit in the back, and I can't tell what she
wants. My mind is back on Frodo. I look at Meg, though it's
hard to see much in that light, and her dark hair and very
light skin send my mind flashing to the scene in the movie
where Samwise Gamgee is trying to free Frodo from the spi-
der cocoon he's in, and all you can see is that sweet, sweet,
very pale face and the very dark eyebrows and eyelashes. I
open my mouth and lean toward Meg's face, and she leans toward me. I don't want to do this. It feels strange, wrong. And
it's not fair to Meg. I mean, how would I feel if right this
minute, she were imagining not me but—I don't know—
Orlando Bloom leaning toward her? Actually, maybe that
would be okay. And the truth is, it isn't Elijah Wood I want.
It's Raj. But—hell, Meg's here. Raj isn't. And I'm in the backseat of a car, on a date with a terrific girl, the air thick with
expectations. I have no choice here.

At first it seems okay, kind of like kissing Rebecca. But
then things change. Rebecca and I really are practicing. Who
knows, maybe she's a lesbian, and she's using me for cover
same as I'm using her. Whatever, I don't remember ever feeling anything like passion from Rebecca. But Meg wants me.
I can feel it.

Her fingers go into my hair, and I think: *Oh yeah, that's
right, I'm supposed to reach for her too.* So I do. I say to myself,
Pretend you're with Rebecca. And it kind of works, except that
after a few minutes, things kind of stall out. For us, anyway.

Robert and Debbie are not experiencing any shortage of ideas, based on the sounds coming from the front seat.

What the fuck am I supposed to do now? How do you fake passion when you don't even know what you're supposed to do if it's real?

I start to panic. This makes my breathing quicken, which Meg—bless her heart—misinterprets. She takes my head in her hands and looks into my eyes. She smiles and says, "Are you okay?"

No. Yes. How do I answer that?

Think, Jason; pretend you're writing this scene. Pretend it's fiction. I say, "I don't want to get carried away. I don't want to take advantage of you." This second statement is true enough.

She lifts a lock of hair off my forehead with a finger. "That's sweet. Why don't you sit back and close your eyes for a minute."

This seems like a terrific idea to me, so I do. Meg cuddles up next to me and leans against my chest, stroking my face, my shoulder, my neck. After a minute, I'm calmer; this could be worse. I open my eyes and look down at her, and she looks up at me, and then we're kissing again. But it's not passionate. It's not desperate. It's just sweet.

We get a little more into it for a bit, but then we back off again. I'm feeling really, really grateful to Meg by now, but I'm also starting to wonder how much longer the front seat will be bouncing around.

My voice low, I ask Meg, "Do you want to walk for a bit?"

She glances toward the front. "They might like to be left alone, but I'm not sure they should be."

She's right. I decide it's time to be a man, time to do something decisive. So I lean forward, rest my arms on the back of the seat in front of me, and take in the sight of Debbie's sweater pushed up around her neck and one breast barely showing from under Robert's large hand. Her bra is in there someplace, but it's kind of tangled. I clear my throat.

There's a frantic rush to get themselves together. I can hear Meg trying to smother giggles. Once Robert and Debbie are in some semblance of order again, Robert running a distracted hand through his hair, I ask, "How about a short walk around the ball field before we head home?"

It's kind of hard to tell whether they think this is a good idea or a lousy one, but they sort of say, "Sure. Fine." And we all tumble out of the car.

Nobody says much as we walk. I take Meg's hand, and she smiles at me. And suddenly it hits me that this is the first date I've been on with a girl other than Rebecca. It's like I've taken some kind of step, and I'm pretty sure it's the wrong one. So it's scary for that reason, but it's also scary for another: this step involves someone other than me.

In one sense, tonight has been a rousing success. Robert not only gets his first real date, but also he makes out with someone he likes. I have to say it looks like Debbie has enjoyed herself. And Meg and I—well, we've done whatever it is we've done. But I feel like a real shit, like I'm just using Meg. And not in a way that's fair.

I'm not being very fair to myself either. I got through this evening by pretending. First by pretending Meg was Elijah. Then pretending Meg was Rebecca. Then pretending the whole thing was a fictional scene I was writing. To be fair to me, what I should have been pretending was that I was with Raj.

Yeah. Right. Like that's fair? If I'm going to be fair to myself, it would have to *be* Raj.

Once around the field is enough to bring everyone back to earth. I'm the only one who seems to have landed with a thud, but there's not much I can do about that. Robert drives to Meg's house first, not because it's closer, but I think because he wants Debbie beside him as long as possible.

I walk Meg to her door. The overhead light is on, and it's bright, and there's a light on inside too. I imagine we're being monitored, even if it's only because they know we're here.

What I want to say is this: "I'm so sorry, Meg. I like you so much. You are a really terrific girl, and you deserve the best boyfriend in the world. And I wish it could be me, but it can't. Please don't hate me."

But this is what I say. "You're terrific, Meg." I kiss her forehead. She smiles, real sweet, and squeezes my hand. I watch as she turns and opens the door, and as she's about to close it she turns her smile on me again.

The message from her is pretty clear, isn't it?

Idiot, I tell myself later as I lie sleepless in bed. What did I expect would happen? In a car? Two teenaged couples? And what would I have done with Raj anyway, even if he'd been there? What do I know about making out with another boy? Plus, I don't even know if he feels the same way. I don't know whether he dreams about me.

I torture myself all Sunday, wondering how I'm going to behave toward Meg this week in school, how she'll behave toward me. Robert and Debbie I have no doubts about. At one point I realize I'm wearing the same jeans I'd had on when Robert and I had been cruising at the mall. I reach into my back pocket and pull out a piece of paper. No name, just a telephone number. Doreen had said I was cute. If I called this number, what would I say? What would I do? But I don't fret too much over Doreen; she's probably not really my type anyway.

But Meg could be. I know I like her. But how much? In what way? I enjoyed kissing her, but I didn't do much else, and I don't really think she wanted me to. Not on the first date. But will she expect a second? There's not much doubt in my mind about that, either. And then, what else? I can barely focus on the book I'm reading as I lie on my bed and try to pretend I'm not obsessing about this situation.

Finally I can't take inactivity any longer. I put on some track duds, add some warm-up pants and a sweatshirt, and call to my aunt as I'm heading for the door.

"Going for some practice runs, Aunt Aud. What time is dinner?"

"The usual. Around six."

Uncle Steve calls from his easy chair, long legs extending from under the newspaper that hides his face: "Finished your homework?"

"All but a few math problems I'll do after dinner. See you later."

I've done about five laps around the school track almost before I know it, my mind's so busy. But suddenly I have no more energy. Interesting: I'm right at the high-jump pit. I walk around it a few times, cooling down, and then go and sit off to the side of where the jumpers land. Right in front of me is where Raj's body had settled so gracefully.

After maybe fifteen minutes there are scores of shredded grass blades on the ground bordered by my crossed legs, where I've been dropping them after tearing them up. I'm looking sightlessly before me, creating my own images, when I see another boy. He's under the trees on the other side of the chain link fence that surrounds the track field. He looks like Raj.

"Yeah, right," I say to myself, believing it to be a mirage like last time, like the dash where I barely beat Jimmy Walsh. But then I refocus my eyes.

It *is* him. It's Raj. He's really standing there, and he's looking right at me. There's this timeless moment, and then I
stand. And then I'm moving.

As I get closer, I can see his hands are on the fence, fingers
curling over the wires. We're so close now. I have to look up a
little to see his eyes; he's taller than me. And then I reach my
hands up, on my side of the fence, and I curl my fingers over his.

He doesn't move.

We don't speak. There's no need. What would we say?

Slowly he pulls his hands away, his eyes still on mine, and
he backs off a little. And I find my voice.

"Raj!"

He stops.

"Wait," I tell him. "Just stay there."

I run as fast as I can to where I've dropped my outer
clothes and then back. He's still there! I throw my things over
the top of the fence. As I'm struggling up the chain links, I see
him bend over to pick up my clothes.

I don't think I've ever climbed as fast as that. Raj holds
out my pants to me, and I lean against him as I struggle to
work my track shoes through the cloth. One leg through, I
start on the next, and then I slow down, feeling the warmth
of his body, knowing he's feeling warmth from me as well.
Never climbed so fast; never dressed so slowly.

Eventually I have to admit I've finished this task, and he
hands me the sweatshirt. Putting it on, though, my vision is
blocked and I can't see him, so I want to hurry again. In my
haste I get the hem all caught, but this has an advantage; Raj
laughs and then reaches around behind me, his face mere
inches from mine, to pull the resisting cloth into place.

I don't dare do it. But I do it anyway. My arms are around
him before I can stop them, and we stand there in an embrace
so sweet I could die and be happy about it.

We walk for a few minutes, aimlessly, not speaking. We're pretty hidden from the road, and from the track, among the trees. By some silent arrangement we sit down and lean against the trunks of two trees that are so close their bodies have grown together. My thigh and Raj's touch.

He speaks first. "How long have you known?"

I panic. Known what? Known how I feel about him? Or about myself? I parry. "I'm not sure what I know."

"No?" He sounds almost amused. "I've known for a long time."

So he means about being gay. He thinks I'm gay. I guess I know I am, really. I inhale deeply and let the breath out, calming myself. If being gay means being with Raj, well, that's something I can take. But it's not necessarily something I want to talk about.

I ask, "Why haven't I seen you before?"

"I keep a low profile."

"Why?"

I feel him shrug. "It's hard to make friends. And I'm not into a lot of things the other guys seem to like."

"You mean girls?"

He laughs, and I love the sound. "I was referring to things like video games, contact sports, drinking beer, talking trash."

I could listen to him talk all day. His voice sings, and he makes consonants sound like something he's trying to taste with just the tip of his tongue.

And then he speaks again. "Have you ever been with a girl?"

My chuckle comes out more like a snort. "I've never been with anyone."

"Who is Robert?"

Robert? So he really had thought that Robert and I were together. I almost laugh, but I don't want Raj to think I'm laughing at him. "He's a friend, that's all. I'm helping him. With English Lit. It's one of my favorite subjects."

"Why are you helping him?"

I glance at the side of Raj's face; he doesn't turn toward me. I think he's still trying to figure out if he should be jealous. I reach for a dead pine twig and decide to tell him the story.

"He saved my ass. After tryouts the other day, these two goons were waiting for me. Just over there." I point with my twig to where I'd been accosted and then rescued, and Raj looks that way. "Robert had been looking for me to ask for my help. But I needed his first, and he gave it."

He looks at me. "Which goons are those? There are so many."

"Jimmy Walsh and Dane Caldwell. Two of my favorite goons."

"Dane jumps like a dog."

I have this image of a clumsy Saint Bernard throwing himself through the air and trying to land without hitting his heavy head on the ground.

I reply, "And Jimmy runs like a rabbit. Ever notice how a rabbit stops and starts, and stops again? Jimmy's fast, but—" I don't have to finish. I can see Raj's head nod in agreement.

"You're good," he says.

"You're fantastic," I counter, looking at him.

He turns toward me, and then his hand reaches behind my neck. I can't breathe. I can't think. I can't move. He kisses me. Lightly, sweetly.

Something pops inside my head. Just as strange and wrong as it had felt kissing Meg last night? It feels every bit as perfect and right and oh, so fucking wonderful when it's Raj's lips on mine.

Why couldn't it have been you *in that car last night?* This is what I want to ask him. *Where were you when I needed you? Where was your mouth, your face? Why wasn't it your hand reaching for me?*

And then, alongside the tension, underneath the butterflies (yes, there they were!), there's this feeling of relief. No more pretending.

But I don't know what to do with this. It's what I've dreamed about, but now that it's here . . . I hide behind words.

"You move fast."

"We have to. We won't get much time, and we won't get any encouragement."

He waits just long enough to see if I have anything else to say, and then he pulls my face to his again. Before I know it, we're lying on the ground, breathing hard, hands everywhere.

I have to pull away. I'm not ready for this. I lean against the tree again, feeling shaky.

"You okay?" he says, still lying on the ground near my feet.

I try a smile, but it wobbles. "Yeah."

"Is this a new idea for you?"

I shake my head. "No. Just a new reality."

"Sorry. I guess I thought you were—you know. Ready. You seem so confident."

"What?"

"Like just now, at the fence. And in the tryouts. And when I saw you in the store. It was like you knew exactly what you were doing, what you wanted. I felt like the shy one." He half sits up, leaning on an elbow. "And I'm not shy."

I laugh out loud. "No. I can tell. But if I seem confident, it's because I've had to. It's either that or run away all the time."

He nods, and I can tell he understands. "I chose aloof."

"You don't seem aloof now."

He gets up onto his knees and moves toward me. "No." He leans forward but stops before he touches my mouth, his lips so close I can almost feel them move. "Do you want me to be?"

"No."

This time the kiss isn't just a light, sweet test. This time he doesn't wait to see what I'll say, to see what I want. He knows.

It's funny, but when you're in the right place with the right person doing something like this, it's so different from how it had been for me last night. I'd had to remind myself that I was supposed to reach for Meg. With Raj, I don't think about reaching. I just reach. I want him as close to me as I can get him. Did I open my mouth, or did it just land against his that way? Did I reach for him with my tongue, or has it always been twisted together with his like this?

He pulls his mouth away from mine, and at first I want to shout *No! More!* But then he buries his face against my neck and kisses and bites and moistens every inch of skin he can reach. Somehow I've pulled his clothing open at the back of his waist, and one hand moves up while the other moves down.

And then his mouth is on mine again. Hell, it's practically *in* mine.

This is joy. *This* is rapture. This is the way it's supposed to feel.

In the end we don't do much more than lie on the ground, touching each other's faces, kissing from time to time. I don't want the sun to set. Or the temperature to fall. Or my dinner to be ready, or my aunt and uncle to be waiting. I chuckle.

"What?" he wants to know, smiling at me.

"It's my aunt. She has this policy where she meets my friends before I'm allowed to go anywhere with them. But she doesn't know about you!" I'm laughing now, holding my sides, rolling around. Bits of twigs are poking at me through my clothing, and it feels good. Everything feels good.

Raj waits until I'm still and then kisses me again. "Should she?"

"I don't know. I don't know what I'd say. 'Aunt Audrey, I'd like you to meet Nagaraju Burugapalli. Now may I go and roll around in the woods with him?' Can you see it?"

His face is hovering over mine. I can barely see it in the dusky light. But I can see he's smiling.

"Kiss me again," I beg.

He does.

Chapter 4

Sword vs. Knife

We hold hands in the darkening light after our romp in the woods, parting with only a look when we come to the first corner. I run all the way home, partly from euphoria, partly because I know I'm late. I don't know when I'll see Raj again. I don't remember our paths crossing before tryouts, and it was just chance that we were both at the track on Sunday.

The next week is a torture, sometimes sweet, sometimes bitter. I'm friendly to Meg when I see her, but I don't go out of my way to make her think I'm taking any special notice of her. She seems to take this in stride. I like her even better for it.

Robert and I have lunch on Monday, and between mouthfuls he tells me about how much he likes Debbie, how he wants to ask her out again.

"Is it too soon, d'you think?" he wants to know. "I mean, can I ask her out for this weekend?"

I try hard to focus on his problem. "Why don't you ask her out this week for next weekend? That way she'll know you're interested, but it won't seem so much like you're pushing her. You don't want the girl to think you can't live without her, you know."

"How do you know all this stuff?"

I laugh. "See, if you'd pay more attention to the literature we have to read, you'd get a really useful portrait of human nature. And you'd know that mostly no one wants to be with someone who wants to be with them too much."

He stares at me a minute and then nods. I can't tell if he's really got it, but probably he does, and I'm too busy trying to apply this maxim to my own thoughts about Raj that I don't have a lot of attention left over. Then he startles the heck out of me.

"It's like that Woody Allen line. You know the one? About not wanting to belong to a club that would have him as a member?"

I slap the table. "Robert, my friend, you've got it. Make her want you a little too." He's got the credit wrong. It's really a Groucho Marx quote, but I'm not going to correct him— it's the concept that's important.

He nods again. "Then I won't call her until Friday. For next week, like you said. Can we double-date?"

With Raj? Right. "I think you're ready to head out on your own, don't you?"

He grins at me. "So, when can we go to the mall again?"

This won't do. I'm never going to the mall again. Not for that. "I think we'll go to the library next time."

"Library?"

"Sure. We can practice some more internalized reading, and you can do a little girl-watching at the same time. If you see someone you want to get to know, we can decide the best action plan. How does that sound?"

We're due for another practice session anyway, so we agree to go that night.

I decide to walk rather than ask Aunt Audrey for the car. All day something's been nagging at me, and I haven't had a quiet moment to let it really speak. And I think I need to know what it wants to say.

At first I don't think about anything, just let my mind acknowledge the drop of each foot so there's this *ump, ump, ump* thing going on, like a metronome. Or a mantra. But then the *ump* changes to another syllable. Now it says *Raj, Raj, Raj.* Then the two feet make a song together: *Raj and me. Raj and me. Raj and me.*

And then it changes again.

Gay. Gay. Gay. Gay. Jason's gay. Jason's gay.

Suddenly I'm leaning against a tree. Really, I sort of fall against it. My head spins, and I'm gasping so hard my breath feels like it's shredding my throat. Before I know it, I'm sinking, and then I'm on the ground.

My head hits the rough bark behind me so hard it hurts. I can't see; why can't I see?

Oh. My eyes are clenched shut. But I don't open them. I force myself to take a few deep breaths. Can you force calm? It's what I'm trying to do.

And then something's on my hand. I yank it toward me and open my eyes to see the big brown eyes of a collie staring at me.

"Here, boy! Siddhartha, come!" I don't know the woman calling to him.

Siddhartha looks at me another moment, and at first I think he's sad, but then I swear he smiles at me. And then he's off.

"Sorry!" the woman says to me. But she shouldn't be. Her dog made me smile too. Plus, Siddhartha was from India. He was the Buddha.

Back on my feet, I try to make some sense out of my feelings. What does it mean if I'm gay? Does it mean I'm not normal? Does it mean I have to run with my feet going out to the sides like a girl and call myself Jessica?

Do I even know anyone who's gay? Who would tell me if he were?

Raj. Raj is gay. Suddenly I want to talk to him. But I don't know what I'd say.

At the library I pick out a table that's strategically placed so that Robert and I can see as much of the floor as possible, and we settle down with notebooks and pens. He stays put while I go into the shelves, scouring them for likely candidates for our literature examination. They need to be books I know, so that I'll be able to find places that are good for him to work on. I want him to get writing the way he got the Groucho Marx line.

I'm rounding the end of one set of shelves, and just as I start down the next there's someone behind me.

It's Raj.

My intake of breath is so loud I'm surprised no one tells me to keep quiet. He takes a quick glance behind him to make sure no one can see us, and then he puts a finger under my chin, and I melt. I think he's going to kiss me.

Will it be like on Sunday? Or will it be long and lingering and will my heart ever be still again and will my pants ever fit right at the crotch again and do I want them to? I take a breath in, and it's nearly a gasp.

Please kiss me, I beg silently. But he doesn't. He drops his hand.

Shit.

"You're with Robert again," he says, keeping his voice low.

Is he jealous, really? "Does that bother you?"

"You seem . . . incompatible."

"We're friends. He helped me, I'm helping him." I shrug.

I don't know how I'm supposed to feel. Should I sulk like he's accusing me of unfaithfulness? Should I play up the Robert card to make Raj want me even more? Does any of that make any sense at all?

My mind is full of things I want to ask. Say. Beg. Like, I have to talk to you. When will I see you again? I think about you all the time, every minute. When can we roll around under the trees again? Do you know what to do, and will you teach me? Do you know what this damn thing is all about?

"Can you be here tomorrow night?" he asks. "Alone?"

I nod. He nods. He moves away. We won't have much time, he'd told me. We need to move fast. No waiting till the end of the week to ask if I'll see him a week after that.

Forcing myself to concentrate on literature, I pick out a few books. Only when I get them back to the table do I realize that I've pulled one by mistake. It must have been next to the one I'd wanted, and it was misfiled anyway; it's a collection of essays about sports.

Robert of course is thrilled. "Jason," he whispers, "you're all right."

So we work on those. For a while he's having such a good time that he forgets to look around for girls. I remember, though partly it's because I'm also looking for Raj, whom I don't see again. Just as well.

Finally Robert sits back and rubs his face. "This is hard work," he says. He sort of shakes himself out like he's run a long distance and then glances around.

I point out a couple of possibilities to him. One of them is a girl he knows from school, Carol Morgan.

"I like her," he says. "She was nice to me when I had a broken arm. I dropped my books, and she stopped to pick them up for me."

"Want to talk to her?"

"Yeah."

"Okay, so here's the plan. You go over there and pretend you're looking for something in the shelves behind her. Whether she sees you or not, you go over to her and say, 'Excuse me, I'm looking for a book, and I'm wondering if you might be using it. Do you mind if I check?' She has some books in front of her, see?"

He nods. "What if she asks what book I'm looking for?"

"No problem. You act a little shy and say, 'All right, you caught me. I really came over here to talk to you. Is it okay if I sit down?' If she says no to that, well—you're wasting your time anyway, but you know it right away. And if she doesn't ask that, then you admit it anyway, because you really do want her to know it. It's okay if she thinks you went to a little trouble to arrange things."

He punches my shoulder. "You're going to be married before I am, you know that? You know everything about this stuff."

He heads toward the shelves behind Carol, and as I watch him go I think about marriage. I've never given it much thought before. But now—I guess it's out of the question for me. I mean, you hear about two guys getting married, sort of, but it seems a little far-fetched to me. And suddenly a lot of things most people take for granted seem a little far-fetched for me. Living with someone you love. Having kids. Heck, just hanging out with friends. Just being with Robert tonight makes me feel like I'm lying to him. I've led him to think I'm as interested in girls as he is, that Jimmy Walsh was wrong to call me a faggot.

My mind goes back to the day Robert had rescued me. That's sort of why I'm here with him anyway, right? He'd rescued me, and I'm teaching him about reading and girls.

In my head, I say, *Take that, Jimmy Walsh. Maybe I could teach you a thing or two about girls. Maybe I could teach you what happens when you call me a faggot.* Absentmindedly I reach toward my pack, to the little pocket where my knife lives. I pinch the nylon so I can feel the outline of the knife. It's almost like a dick. A small one, sure, but still. It's an effort not to take it out, to hold it in my hand.

I close my eyes. It feels larger, somehow. Maybe it's Raj's. I haven't actually touched that yet, not really, but oh I want to.

But would that make Jimmy right? Would that make me a faggot? He'd never said that before. Not to me. I'd heard him say it to other kids. And although I have no reason to think this, what I think is that Jimmy never called me that out of some nearly buried memory of friendship. Guess that's gone for good. And now I'm a faggot.

My breathing is odd. A little ragged. And suddenly I realize I'm near tears.

What the fuck? I snatch my hand away from the knife and plant it firmly next to the other one on the tabletop. They're both fists before I know I've done that. I clench my eyes and force my breath to be calmer.

Such an ugly word, "faggot." At least the way I'd always heard it used. Printed words float suddenly inside my eyelids, and when I open my eyes it comes to me that I've seen the word "faggot" in the orchestral descriptions of some of the CDs I play. What was that about?

I look around the room. There's a dictionary someplace, a huge one on a stand, waiting like an open Bible at a pulpit for someone to step up and read.

There it is. I walk casually toward it, pretending (yes, that again) not to be in a hurry. I shield it as much as possible with my body so anyone passing by won't see what I'm looking up.

"Faggot," it seems, has a number of meanings, such as a stick or small branch, something used to kindle fires. And because a bassoon is three long pieces of wood bundled together, it's often referred to as a faggot. Or, in Italian, *fagotto*. Okay, this makes sense. But . . .

I'm standing there struggling to come up with some reason sticks have anything to do with being gay. All I can think of is that a stick and a dick are similar shapes. Like my knife. It doesn't make a lot of sense, but I don't want to hang out here any longer. I flip the pages away from where I'd been reading to cover my tracks and head back to the table.

At least I'm calmer now. But I'm still left with the other puzzle. Did Jimmy know something I hadn't figured out yet? Is there some way he could have known I was gay before I did, and it made him scared to think that we'd been even a little close? Do gays glow in the dark so we can find each other when it matters, and had Jimmy seen this at some point? Or has he just crossed some point of no return, and it doesn't matter anymore what he does to me?

I'm feeling like *I've* crossed some line of no return. And it's like the whole thing started when Jimmy called me a faggot.

I'm staring into space, holding up some book propped on the table that I'm not even looking at, when Robert appears next to me. He's got a date for this weekend, thanks to me (see, Jimmy?), and I do my best to act enthusiastic.

But he's a little nervous. "Jason, can't we double again? I really feel better when you're there. You help me."

What can I say? I'm not going to do it again. I'm not going to lie to some girl and then make out with her in the back of Robert's dad's car. So I lie to Robert instead.

"Can't. I have plans already."

"What plans?"

I slap his back. "I think you've accomplished enough for tonight. Do you want to check out this essay book and take it with you?"

I'm on tenterhooks all day Tuesday. Just the idea of seeing Raj makes me feel all jittery, but I can't tell if it's good or bad. I don't even know what he wants to see me for. I mean, in the library? On one hand, I hope we'll do some research together on what it means to be gay. On the other, I'm not as sure as I was that I'm ready to talk about it with him. Plus, we'll have to act like we're nothing more to each other than classmates. He won't kiss me. We won't hold hands. Sometimes when I think about what we can't do, it makes me angry. If one of us were a girl, we might get a scowl from the librarian if there's too much "Public Display of Affection." But as it is . . .

By the time I've washed the dinner dishes and packed up my books so that it looks like I'm doing my homework at the library, it's already seven o'clock. Raj is there, books spread out all over a large table. I stand across from him, holding my breath, until he looks up. He smiles. I beam, I'm sure of it.

"Please." He indicates the chair beside him.

This might be better than I'd thought. But our legs don't touch, our hands don't touch, nothing touches but our eyes.

"Do you have much work?" he asks, glancing at my backpack.

"Not a lot. Looks like you do, though."

"Actually," he says as he starts sifting through things, "some of this is for you."

"For me? What? Why?"

"This is something that's very important to me. I want you to understand it. And I need to know if it can be important to you too."

I pick up the nearest book. It's a biography of Mahatma Gandhi. So much for talking about homosexuality.

"Do you know who he was?" Raj asks.

"Of course. I mean, I don't know a lot about him, but I know about how he used pacifism for civil disobedience. Everyone's heard about his starvation techniques."

"He was a man of God. A man of peace. A man of love. Those are all the same things." He looks hard at me, scowling. "Do you understand?"

"I think so. Does this have anything to do with your not liking contact sports?"

Raj chuckles. "I like your sense of humor, Jason." I feel his hand on my thigh. "I like you. Very much. And I want you to know who I am, just as I want to know who you are. I'm taking this risk, showing you first. Is that okay with you?"

The hand withdraws before I can place mine on top of it. But there's a warm spot where it was. Or a cool spot, really, from the removal of his warmth.

"More than okay. Somehow I think it's going to be very different getting to know you, different from how I've been helping Robert get to know girls."

He blinks at me, startled. "Would you say that again?"

Wow. That was dumb. How can I get out of this one? I can't. Honesty; I'd told Raj I liked it. "It's a little awkward," I say. I decide not to tell him about Robert wanting to know if I was gay, so I work around that and just tell him that meeting girls was something else Robert had confessed he needed help with. Something besides English Lit.

Raj is trying not to laugh. I'm relieved; he thinks this is funny. He says, "And he's getting help about girls from you?"

I shrug. "I'm pretty good at talking to girls, you know." I shoot him an arch glance. "I've got nothing to lose."

Raj's head goes down into his hands as he tries to smother

his laughter. When he's recovered enough, he says, "That's rich. And are you able to help him?"

"He had his first date last weekend. And he has another this weekend and possibly another the weekend after that. It's part of why we were here last night, actually. And at the mall."

"The mall? I thought you were—you devil. You are some character, do you know that?"

God, I want to kiss him. His face is so beautiful. He puts a hand on my shoulder.

"You are a good friend to him, aren't you? I like that." His hand drops. "Okay, so you know a little about Gandhi. I hope you won't mind knowing a lot more."

I know a lot more before we leave the library that night. One of the things Raj shows me is a quote, one of his favorites. It has special meaning for me for reasons I can't share with Raj. It goes, "I know the path. It is straight and narrow. It is like the edge of a sword. I rejoice to walk on it. I weep when I slip."

Nonviolence. Gandhi was huge on nonviolence, and the image in Raj's favorite quote leaves little room for error. Despite the sword metaphor, I feel sure this means no knives.

On our way out, standing on the steps of the library and reluctant to go our separate ways, Raj says, "Is it time for me to meet that aunt of yours?"

I swallow. How to answer that? "Actually, I also have an uncle. Steve. But what should I tell them about you? I mean, they don't know about me. You know."

"Tell them I'm helping you prepare for a paper on Gandhi. Maybe you don't have a paper due yet, but you will. Would you be willing to write it about him?"

He's as clever as I am. But he's more careful about lying. Stretching truth, maybe, but this doesn't have to be a lie. "Yes," is all I say.

"Someday you will tell them. About you. You're not ready yet; that's understandable. But you will be."

I guess he doesn't see a need to talk about this thing. Can't say that I blame him; I haven't exactly been playing hard to get, so why should he think I have reservations? All I can think of to ask is, "Do your folks know? About you?"

"Yes. They aren't happy, but they know."

"So I suppose they wouldn't want to meet me."

"Actually, I think they would. They try not to judge me, but they're very disappointed that I won't marry the girl who was promised to me, that I won't have children for them to spoil."

"You have a girl promised to you?"

"Sort of. At least, that's what our parents were hoping for. In India. She's been told. It will be easy for her parents to find another boy when she's ready. So, how about if I come over tomorrow after dinner?"

Honesty. Would I ever tell them at home? I want to ask about the girl in India; why would her parents need to find the boy? But that will have to wait for another time.

Raj reaches for my hand, gives it a quick squeeze, and walks away.

"Wait!" I call after him. "You don't know where I live."

"Yes, I do."

Chapter 5

Love and Philosophy

Raj is coming over on Wednesday evening. Tomorrow! He'll be in my house. He'll be in my bedroom! God. I can't wait to see him, to be alone with him.

But he'll be full of Gandhi. *Cool your jets, Jason,* I tell myself. *You're already moving fast. Don't rush this.*

I clear things with my aunt and uncle when I get home that night, not that I expect any resistance.

"Is it okay if a friend comes over tomorrow night after dinner?"

Uncle Steve, the disciplinarian, asks, "It's a school night. Is this schoolwork?"

"I want to do a term paper on Gandhi, and this friend knows a lot about him."

Aunt Audrey wants to know more about Raj. "Really? Has he studied Gandhi?"

"Yes."

"What's his name?"

"Raj. Nagaraju, really. Burugapalli." I'm so nervous talking about Raj that I nearly stumble over his name.

"Say it again?"

She makes me repeat it until she's comfortable saying it by herself. She even tries to get Uncle Steve to do it, but he keeps breaking up, laughing. Finally he comes close enough.

I feel guilty, knowing they're taking this interest because of me and I'm not leveling with them about who he really is. I promise myself that Raj is right; I will tell them one day.

"I'll make cookies again, if you like. By the way, how is your friend Robert doing?"

"Aunt Aud, you won't believe this. I accidentally pulled out a book for him that he loves reading! It's a collection of sports essays."

She looks thoughtful. "He seems like an odd friend for you to have, Jason. So different from you."

"You're right, really. He is different. That's what makes it good. I'm teaching him, and he's teaching me."

Uncle Steve chimes in. "What's he teaching you?"

Aunt Audrey looks expectant, and her smile tells me she believes what I've said and thinks he's just testing me to see if I can identify something specific.

"Humility," I shoot back. "And courage."

So I've cleared the way for Raj. Cookies means Aunt Audrey will sit down with us, as she had with Robert, to get to know him a little. Despite my guilty feelings, I'm sure she'll like him. Both of them will like him.

He rings the bell, and I let him in. I've been watching for him for fifteen minutes at least.

"Hey," I greet him.

"Hey, yourself."

Uncle Steve is in his study, so I introduce Raj to Aunt Audrey. She's gracious, as always, and Raj is so polite that she likes him immediately. You'd have to hate all Indians not to like him. Just before sending us up to my room, she says, "I'm looking forward to talking with you later, Raj. There'll be cookies for you before you leave. I hope you would like that."

"I would. Thanks." He gives her a sweet smile and follows me out of the room.

As soon as he's in, I shut the door. We stand there for a minute, and then I take his pack and set it down. Before I'm upright again, his arms are around me. We hold each other so tightly, it's like the world is about to end. Then he takes my head in his hands and kisses me. And kisses me. I start to move toward the bed, but he stops me.

"No," he says, his voice husky. "Don't do that. We can't."

"Why not?"

"I might not be able to stop. When I should."

Stop? I don't want him to stop. And then it hits me what he means. Okay, he's right. We can't do that. I can't do that. So I go back to where he's standing and hold him again.

And, honest, we do spend some time on books and Gandhi. But I need to know more about being gay. Raj is the only gay person I know, and I have so many questions. I start with parents.

"You said your folks aren't happy that you're gay. Are they angry? Do they try to convince you to go straight? Do they think it's some kind of perversion, or sin, or—"

"Slow down, there!" He laughs.

"Well, do they? Think it's terrible?"

We're on the floor, but we're sitting, much like Robert and I had been. Only really close to each other. Raj sets down the book he had picked up, leans back, and exhales. He looks thoughtful for a minute, as though he's trying to figure out where to start.

"My family are Hindu," he opens and then comes to a halt again. I wait, and finally he goes on.

"There is a very rich Vedic tradition around what's referred to in the ancient texts as the third sex. This is a category into which ancient Hindus believed I would have fallen. It had subcategories, like men who are with men but take the active role, or the passive role, and women with women, and so on. And it carried no negative connotations at all."

"You mean it was okay to be gay back then? How long ago was this?"

"Centuries ago. And it was more than okay; it was not only widely accepted, not only a natural way to be, but in certain situations—like the birth of a child—we would have been sought out because our presence was considered good luck."

A kind of half laugh, half snort escapes me. "So why don't your parents—"

"Ah, Jason, things have changed. The ancient texts are the same, but as with many things about my country, my culture, we have allowed Western attitudes to dictate what's appropriate. What's worth striving for. My parents—especially my father—have been convinced to think along these lines. He still pays lip service to his Hindu roots, but his attitudes are Western. And in most of India today, gays are treated much as we are here. Outcast. Pariahs. At the very least, a little sick in the head."

We both stare for a minute at the empty space between my bed and my desk. "Western" means here. Home. Aunt Audrey might react okay, or at least not fly into a rage. But I've never heard Uncle Steve say anything about his opinion when it comes to homosexuality. Would he think I'm sick in the head?

Finally I dare to ask, "So your folks are more than unhappy. Do they try to convince you to change?"

"My father thinks it's an option, yes. He's angry that I

won't make the effort he demands of me. There have been a few—scenes."

I look at his profile. The way he's clenching his jaw tells me he doesn't really want to talk about his father. "And your mother?"

His face softens. "I think she wishes I could be what my father expects, what she expected, but mostly I think she's just trying to hold the family together. But she's actually tried to get my dad to be more reasonable. One Saturday she ran into me in town. I was with a boy I'd been seeing, and she invited him to the house for an afternoon snack. I could tell it was a huge effort for her, and it was really uncomfortable for the boy and for me. And for Dad; he was home, and he knew what was going on, though he didn't come into the kitchen with us. At the time I didn't appreciate it very much. But later, I thanked her."

Another boy. Down, Jason; jealously is not a good color for you. The operative phrase is "had been seeing." But I can't stop myself asking, "How long ago was that?"

"Last fall."

"So your dad wouldn't be very happy that you're here with me."

He laughs, a short barking sound. "Not exactly." Then he shrugs. "I think he's getting used to it. But he still hates it. We actually talked about it over winter holiday."

I notice he didn't say "Christmas holiday."

I ask, "Did you agree to disagree or something?"

"Or something. He still doesn't understand that it's an orientation, not a choice. I don't think he's convinced that I'm not just being willful. But at least our relationship is on a more even keel these days." He picks up the book he'd dropped, obviously ready to go back to Gandhi, but I have a question I'd been holding onto since our parting on the library steps.

"When you mentioned the girl your folks wanted you to marry, you said her parents would find her another boy. Why wouldn't she find him herself?"

Raj chuckles. "That must have sounded strange to you. For most people in India, when a child is ready for marriage—and this is something he or she decides together with the parents, usually—the parents start looking. Many times they already have someone in mind, as was the case for me. You almost never hear of anyone being forced to marry someone they don't want, but the introductions are typically a family affair, with lots of people present, and if you and your, um, prospect don't want to meet again, you don't. If you both do, then the courtship begins." He shrugs. "It seems to work pretty well."

I look at him from the corners of my eyes. "Do parents ever find a boy for their son?"

Raj laughs and then kisses me. "I think you know the answer to that one." And again he holds the book up. "Shall we?"

I guess my other questions will have to wait for another day. And Raj can't tell me what kind of a reaction I'd get at home.

By the time Aunt Audrey knocks on the door with the good news about cookies, Raj and I are deep into Gandhi's biography.

"Boys? Ready for a treat?"

Now, I love cookies. Don't get me wrong. But the idea of leaving this paradise, where Raj's mind and mine are meeting as intimately as our lips had earlier—and a few times since then—is almost unpleasant. It is getting late though, and I really want Aunt Audrey and Raj to have a chance to talk.

They talk. And talk. I know Aunt Audrey is interested in philosophy, but she's evidently been keeping the extent of her knowledge from me. As I listen now, the times we've talked about it in the past seem to have been almost juvenile. I'm thinking that's probably my fault, not expressing enough interest, and I'm laying plans to dig in a little deeper when I notice that Uncle Steve is standing in the doorway, leaning against the frame. Sometimes it surprises me how good-looking he is: tall, slender, steely blue eyes over a nice smile.

I get the impression he's been there a few minutes. Raj sees him and stands politely. It takes me a minute to realize the next move is supposed to be mine.

"Uncle Steve, this is Raj Burugapalli."

They shake hands. Uncle Steve reaches for a cookie as Raj sits again, then takes an empty chair. And changes the subject. Radically.

"How old are you, Raj?"

"Seventeen."

It's an effort not to snap my head toward him. So that's it; he's a year older than me. I knew there had to be something essentially different, and maybe the fact that he's from India fogged things, made me think that was the extent of it. It had seemed like wisdom, the first time I'd noticed it. Maybe it still is.

Uncle Steve says, "So you aren't in the same classes as Jason."

"No, but I am in the same school year. When my family moved here from India, I had medical problems that kept me out of school for some time."

"I see. And when did you meet?"

"As it happens, it was only last week. You know, of course, that the track intramurals are coming up, and tryouts were last week?"

"I certainly do. I was a short dash runner in my own youth, and I keep an eye on Jason's progress."

"Well, I was practicing my high jumps when the relay races started. Jason may not have told you how impressive he was, but when the second man on his team dropped the baton, they were seriously behind. Jason flew like the wind and managed to win for his team anyway. Everyone cheered like mad. So after the high jump tryouts, when he came over to me to say how well he thought I'd done, I decided he might be someone worth getting to know."

"That was just last week . . ."

"Yes. We've bumped into each other a couple of times since then, including Monday night at the library when he was helping Robert Hubble learn to read."

Aunt Audrey chuckles in spite of herself.

"And last night," Raj adds, "as it happened, I was reading a new book about Gandhi. Or new to me, at least. And Jason, it seems, has an interest."

"Well, this is very kind of you, to help out a younger classmate."

"Jason is not your ordinary younger classmate. I'm sure he owes that to the two of you."

Uncle Steve gives Raj a look that's hard to gauge. But Aunt Audrey blushes! She blushes, sure as I'm sitting there.

That night I can't sleep. No surprise. On one hand, I'd love to; maybe I'll dream about Raj. On the other, I never want this feeling to end. But it's sobering to remember how the evening started, when I'd tried to pull him toward this bed.

To say I'm overwhelmed at what might have happened with Raj is a huge understatement. All I was thinking was that the bed would be more comfortable than a forest floor. I guess it comes of my not having ever considered not being able to stop with a girl; unless you count Darin's farewell kiss I've never even kissed another boy before, so . . .

Raj must have though. He seemed to know just what might happen, and since he knew when to put a halt on things, he must have—you know: been there, done that. I mean, he seems so amazingly comfortable in his own skin. As gay. I'm even more in awe of him.

Suddenly I want to know who else has kissed him. Who has done other things with him.

Jealous again, Jason? How absurd can I be? I shake my thoughts out and let them settle again on how marvelous he is.

And thank God he is. Marvelous, and thoughtful. Conscientious. Whatever it takes to consider someone else's feelings, someone else's needs, to care for someone—me!—so much that he wouldn't allow something that wouldn't be good for the other person, no matter how much he might want it himself.

I think I'm falling in love with him.

"No. I have already."

There. I've said it out loud, even if it's only in the darkness of my own room.

Chapter 6

Watershed

Track training starts Thursday after school. There won't be many free after-school times until the intramurals are over next month, so Robert is going to stop by after dinner one or two nights a week to work on his writing while I do my homework.

During the first training session, I have to concentrate deliberately so that I don't keep thinking about Raj and wondering how I'll get to see him again, other than from the distance of half the track. He does some warm-up laps, and it's agony not to watch him, but Coach has us on the side practicing baton handoffs. Then, when the high-jump practice begins, Coach has an upperclassman work with us on dash starts, so I can't watch Raj then either. We do heats, we do laps, we climb ropes for upper body strength, we just don't stop. I'm exhausted over dinner.

"Aunt Aud, don't let me drown in my soup, will you?"

"They're working you pretty hard, it seems. Are you getting better?"

"Ask me in a couple of weeks. If I'm still alive."

Later, sitting on my bed doing my homework, I fall asleep. When Uncle Steve knocks on the door to tell me how late it is, I realize I wasn't even dreaming about Raj, and I'm so tired it doesn't bother me.

What bothers me is how much time I seem to be spending with Jimmy Walsh. Track practice is every Monday and Thursday after school for the next three weeks, and he's right there. Training for intramurals means racing the other guys from my own school for now. Jimmy growls whenever we race together. Occasionally he beats me, but not often. But he never has the grace to acknowledge that he and Dane were ready to beat the crap out of me, and I'm not about to call his attention to it.

The weekend is a killer. I spend as much time as I can hanging around the school, not knowing where else to look for Raj. I'm not exactly going to wander around his neighborhood, assuming that the only Burugapalli I'd found in the phone directory is his family.

But I don't see him. And he doesn't call me. So much for moving fast. What are the rules, anyway? Am I allowed to call him? Will he think I'm being too forward, too eager? Christ! Maybe I should go and ask Robert how to talk to boys.

The next Thursday we spend a long time working on baton handoffs. Coach has us try every conceivable hand position so we can see what doesn't work and why; he's seen too many guys forget what they're supposed to be doing at that critical moment. Even so, I really don't think we need to spend so much time on what won't work. I'm getting frustrated, and I'm turning around to calm down when I see someone in the bleachers. Someone looking at me.

It's Meg. I've barely spoken to her since that night out with Robert and Debbie. There's no escape, so I wave as though everything's cool. She doesn't wave back. I wonder how long she's been up there, watching all this. Watching me. Has she been there before today? I just can't say.

She's still there as we're about to leave the field and hit the showers. I decide to go and talk to her. It's the least I can do. Maybe—I'm hoping against hope here—she's actually watching someone else.

I sit on the bench above her. It's a mean trick, I realize after I've done it; she'll have to look up to see me. So I move down and sit near her. But not too near. I try to look nonchalant, elbows on knees, hands dangling together.

She doesn't say anything. So I do. "Thinking of trying out?" It's lame, but—what the heck?

Wisely she ignores this. "I don't know what to say to you. I mean, I thought we had a good time that night. Now you don't even say hello. Are you, like, waiting for me to call you or something evolved like that?"

I look down at my hands. "I don't know what to say either."

"You can say 'Yes, Meg, we had a good time, and I would have called you, but I've been so busy with track.' Which would be at least an attempt, even if it's not quite credible. Or you can say, 'It meant nothing, and I don't know why you're talking to me at all.' Which would be hard to hear, but if it's the truth, I guess I want to hear it."

I clear my throat a few times, thinking, *Or I could say, "Meg, it's like this. I'm gay, and I've been busy with a boy."* But I can't say that, and I'm silent too long, it seems, because she interrupts my unpleasant contemplation.

"Or you could just sit there like a lump and make me feel like a total idiot for caring enough to talk to you at all. You do realize, I trust, that I have nothing in common with Debbie and wouldn't have been talking to her that day except that she wanted to pump me for information about my brother. And as for Robert, he's a sweet kid, but the only reason I agreed to that date . . ."

She takes a breath. "The only reason was because it was you who asked me. Honestly, Jason, I thought you were different." She stands, turns, and starts to walk away.

If only she knew just how different. And if she hadn't said that word—"honestly"—maybe I'd have just sat there and watched her leave.

"Meg, I—" I what? What on earth am I going to say? She turns and looks at me.

I say, "I'm sorry."

It's all I can get out. And it's not enough. She nearly runs away from me.

I don't get up right away. I don't want to go into the locker room and see Raj with all those other guys around. Monday had been so weird for me, when I'd seen him naked in the shower. There he was, twenty feet away. All that beautiful brown skin, glistening with water, untouchable. I had to lean against the nearest wall for support before I could go in there myself.

I thought I was okay at that point. In control.

And then he saw me.

All the other boys disappeared—no one in the world but Raj and me. He was looking at me over his shoulder, so that from where I stood I could see the profile of his body. All of it. Including the part of him that was pointing away from his body, wanting me.

Without really knowing what I was doing, I started padding my way across the shower area, not toward a free showerhead, where I should have been headed, but right toward Raj. My eyes lifted from his penis to his face, and his eyes were still boring holes into me. I can't say what would have happened if someone else hadn't collided with me.

"Watch where you're going, Peele! Jesus."

All those other bodies were suddenly around us again. Anyone might have seen what I was doing, where I was going, what

I wanted. Frantically I looked around for a free showerhead, as far away from Raj as possible.

After that, the only thing I noticed about him was that he had turned away from me. And the only other thing I remember about the next several minutes was how desperate I was to hide my own hard-on.

I don't want to repeat that scene. So here I am, sitting high above the track field, having just been told off by the most interesting girl I know, and I'm remembering this shower scene. And thinking of Raj. We haven't talked since he was at my house, over a week ago now. I want so badly to be alone with him.

Fifteen minutes after Meg leaves me, I'm still sitting there, cursing my cowardice and the lot that fate has dealt me. Coach Everett comes out from somewhere, sees me, and climbs up toward me. He stands a few feet away. I look up at him, thinking how I'd decided not to make Meg do that.

"Everything all right, Peele?"

I shrug. What does he think, I'm going to unburden my soul?

He sits down beside me and we both stare out across the field. Finally he says, "Something going on between you and Walsh?"

At first my head is still so full of Raj, I can't quite think who Walsh is. But it comes back to me. I shrug again, but I know that won't cut it. "He's a little competitive."

Coach laughs. "Like you're not? Come on, Jason. Talk to me."

What I want to say is that it might be a little less tense if Jimmy and his fellow hoodlum hadn't threatened to break my leg so I couldn't run. But all I say is, "We don't like each other. That's all."

"Yeah. I guess not. But see here, I don't want anything to

jeopardize our chances. If you guys are going to get into it, do it after the meet, will you?"

I look at him, not quite believing what he's said. "What makes you think I have any control over that?" Other than wielding my knife, which I now carry with me again.

"Look, Jason, you're head and shoulders smarter than he is. I know that, you know that, he knows that. Now, I'm here to help you, but I can't if I don't know enough about what's going on."

"All I can say is he wishes I weren't running, and I wish he weren't. If you want to help, it might be better if we didn't have to race each other. It only makes things worse."

He thinks about this a minute. Then, "Okay. Done. Usually I like to pair my two fastest runners to see if it spurs them on even more. But you're right, I've made a mistake with you two. Competition is one thing; hatred is another. I don't want to use that as a tool, no matter what. Anything else?"

"Yeah. You know a good counselor?" This comes out of nowhere.

He looks at me. "Girl problems?"

It's hopeless. "You could say that. Never mind; it'll work itself out. It's not that bad." I stand up.

"Peele, hang on. You haven't got Meg Warner in trouble, have you?"

So he'd seen her up here with me. It's all I can do not to laugh. I manage to shake my head. "No, Coach. Nothing like that. Just a few hurt feelings, that's all. Guess I was a little insensitive about something. Um, thanks. For caring enough to ask. I'll be okay."

He stands and slaps my shoulder. "Attaboy. Glad to hear it. I like Meg; sensible girl. Smart too. Guess I should've known better than to think—you know. I'll see what I can do to keep you and Walsh apart, if you promise to let me know if there's something else I can help with. Or if you just want to talk. Deal?"

I hold out my hand, and he takes it. I say, "Deal." Adults like that. When you offer to shake their hand first. They take it as a sign that you've drunk the Kool-Aid or something.

He says, "Now get down there before they lock up the place, or you won't be able to get your clothes until tomorrow." He goes one way, I go another.

There's no one in the locker room. I'm not sure whether to stay and shower or just head home. But I strip and head into the huge space. It feels eerie to be in here alone. The sound the water makes echoes on the tile walls.

I'm almost done when I sense someone else. Terrified it's going to be Walsh, I wheel around to see a naked Raj standing there. He moves forward until we're both under the pelting hot water, and he uses his hands like they're washcloths. He caresses my arms, my back, my ass, my legs, the insides of my thighs until I'm embarrassed by the obvious effect he's having on me. It feels so wonderful and so terrible all at once.

Then he's behind me, holding me, leaning his face into the back of my neck. I've had the same effect on him, it seems, but he doesn't do anything about it. He just holds me. I swear I'm ready to faint.

When he finally lets go, I do collapse a little, leaning with both hands against the tiles, breathing hard. I feel his hand on my shoulder and then—nothing. By the time I look up again, he's nowhere in sight. I turn the water off.

"Raj?" I call out.

No answer, just echo. I race toward the lockers, slip and stub my toe painfully, looking frantically around for him. Nothing. Not a sound.

What the hell? It was like he was a ghost. But he was sopping wet from the shower! Did he just throw on his trousers over soaking skin and run? It's what I do. Pants and sneakers barely in place, I stuff everything else into my backpack except my shirt and jacket, which I scramble into as I dash outside. Once there, though, still no sign of anyone.

By the time I get home, I've decided I don't much like wearing jeans without underwear. At least, not if I'm going to walk a mile and a half. I'd stopped to put socks on at one point, but I couldn't very well do much else on the sidewalk.

At home they're waiting for me. Aunt Audrey says, "What took you so long? Why didn't you call?"

I just want to get to my room and change. "Sorry. Really. It was a long practice, and I was talking to Coach Everett afterward. I, uh, I need to go change. Couldn't find any towels in the locker room."

"Dinner's getting cold," she calls after me.

As if I care. If only she knew. If only I could tell someone. Anyone! God! I can't even talk to my friends about this. I can't tell Robert, I can't tell Coach Everett, I can't tell Meg. And now, it seems, I can't even talk to Raj! He just sneaks up on me, makes me nearly sob for wanting him so much, and then disappears.

I pull on fresh underwear and a clean pair of jeans. God, but I'm mad at him. Who does he think he is that he can just do that to me? Doesn't talk to me for days, and then he's all over me, making me crazy, and then—poof! I laugh, a bitter sound, at that: poof. Poofta. Faggot.

Faggot!

I hurl myself on my unsuspecting pillow, pounding it, pulverizing it. I don't even realize I'm making this horrid, grunting, animal sound until I hear Aunt Audrey's voice.

"Jason! Stop it this minute!"

I don't look at her, I just curl down over the edge of the bed, kneeling on the floor, drenching my pulverized pillow with tears.

She kneels next to me, and I feel her arm across my bare shoulders, which are shaking uncontrollably. I can't stop. I don't even really know why I'm crying.

Aunt Audrey waits until I've settled into sniffles and then strokes the back of my head. Finally she says, "Please. Tell me. There's nothing that will surprise me, you know."

I turn around and slump onto the floor, my back to the bed, exposing my misery. My red eyes. My running nose.

"I'll bet you're wrong," I manage.

"How much?"

"What?"

"How much do you want to bet? Anything up to fifty dollars."

I know this is a trick to get me to spill my proverbial beans. But somehow it works. I let it work. It's like she's given me a platform to present this to her on. "You're on. Fifty."

She sits on the floor next to me, knees up, arms crossed on them, looking expectantly at me. "Fine. Fifty dollars says you can't surprise me. So try."

"I'm gay."

I watch her face. I expect the eyes to widen, or at least flicker. Maybe her jaw will drop, or her chin will wobble. Something to give it away. And she does open her mouth, but it's to speak.

"I know."

She's not lying. There's no sign of it. She just looks soft, gentle. I can't remember ever seeing her look at me like that. And then she moves closer and wraps her arm around me again. I lean against her, and then I'm sobbing once more, but quietly this time.

Dinner's really cold now, I'll bet. Bet! I've just lost fifty bucks. I don't speak, haven't a clue what to say. But she does.

"Why do you think I always want to meet your friends,

hmmm? Have I ever asked to meet the girls you go out with? It's just the boys I'm concerned about."

"Me too. The ones in my dreams. It's always boys, you know." I decide not to mention David Bowie. "I guess I should have realized this a long time ago."

She's shaking her head though. "It isn't just dreams, Jason. That's only a clue. A lot of boys dream about other boys or men, but it doesn't mean they're gay. What's more important is how you feel about the people in your life when you're awake. And I have a pretty good idea how much Raj means to you. Is he why you're upset now?"

"No. Yes. I—I guess so. But it's not just him. Jesus! How could this happen?" I pull away so I can see her face. I really want an answer.

"Oh, Jason, I've wanted to bring this up so many times. But it's not the sort of thing one can just say to a child. Even if you believe someone is gay, you can't tell them that; they have to figure it out for themselves."

She sighs and then rubs her face. "I wanted so much to let you know it would be okay, that you were okay, regardless. But I was afraid even to say things that were obviously accepting. Of homosexuality, I mean. I was afraid you might think I was pushing it on you. So I decided you'd have to discover it for yourself, and then there'd be something to talk about."

She takes my hand, squeezes, and lets it go again. "It is okay, you know. And you are the same boy you always were. Are you just seeing it now?"

I nod; it's all I can do. But what I'm feeling is gratitude.

"Want to tell me what's upset you today?"

No; that, I don't want to do. I can't describe that shower scene to her. But there are other things I can say. "It's so horrible, having this huge secret from everyone. I can't talk to anyone about it! Except you, I guess, now that you know. Now that I know you know. How did you know, anyway?"

She smiles. "Can't really say, Jason. It's just a feeling I've had for a while, probably from seeing the way you react to different people. So, Raj is the first boy who's made you feel like this?"

"Yeah."

"Are you angry with him?"

"It's like—it's like he knows all about this thing, and I don't know anything, and he's just giving me little bits at a time. It's like if I'm keeping this secret from everyone else, he's keeping parts of it from me." My leg hurts, and then I realize I've been pounding on it.

"So you haven't had a quarrel?"

Quarrel. Ha. We didn't even speak. "No. I don't even think he knows I'm mad at him."

Aunt Audrey chuckles, and I look at her like she's committed some heinous sin. How can she chuckle when I'm in agony here?

"Well, you haven't mentioned any particulars, so I don't know what he's done or hasn't done, but the approach sounds like generally a sound one to me. He's older than you, probably more experienced, and he's trying not to go too fast. Or too far."

Uh-oh, I'm thinking, here comes the medical speech. I'm right.

"Jason, just because neither of you can get pregnant doesn't mean you can throw caution to the winds. You know this, yes?"

I'm beet red; *that* I know. "Yes."

The phone rings. Saved by the bell. I glance toward it, but Aunt Audrey pretends there's been no sound. I look at her, begging for permission to pick up the receiver just a few feet away. It might be Raj. I don't know why I think this; we've never spoken on the phone.

Aunt Audrey sighs. "Go ahead. But be quick, and then come down to dinner. Your uncle has already started his."

She gets up as I'm diving for the phone. She hears me say "Hello? . . . Raj . . . ," and she shuts the door behind her.

His voice is strained. "Jason, I—I need to apologize to you."

I'll say he does. But does he know why? Do I? I wait.

"I was watching you. I saw you go up to talk to that girl, and then you just sat there, and I couldn't imagine why. You looked so troubled. I was almost going to go to you, and then Coach Everett went up. And then I saw you go into the showers, and—well, and I . . ."

His voice trails off. But I don't give in. I don't say a word. Finally he breathes once into the phone and says, "I had to go to you. I had to. I couldn't stay away. Knowing you were alone in there, knowing you'd be—in the shower."

Another breath, shakier this time. "But once I was with you, it was too much for me. I couldn't stand it."

A long pause, and then, "I'm sorry. I'm sorry I just left like that, after—well, you know. You must be angry."

Must I? I was, yes. But it's gone. It's disappeared, as quickly as he had earlier. Just gone. Finally I say, "How did you do that, anyway? Disappear so fast?"

His laugh is a little unsteady, but I can tell he's hoping he's forgiven. "You have no idea. I have no idea. I don't think I could do it again. I ran for blocks, barefoot. I have bone bruises on my feet. High-jump practice will be agony."

"I thought you were deliberately trying to be mysterious. Keep me guessing. Keep me thinking about you. You disappear for days and then sneak up on me. It seemed like you were manipulating me." I'm getting a little angry again just thinking about it, and it shows in my voice.

"I know. I really am sorry. It's just that I'm such a fool for you. I've never felt this way about anyone before. And it—well, it scares me. I've never lost control before."

So I'm not the only one who's scared. But I'm not altogether ready to relent.

"Listen, they're waiting dinner for me." I'm debating whether to tell him that I've talked to my aunt, but his next words take my breath away.

"Will you go out with me?"

"What?"

"You know. On a date? Will you?"

"What are you talking about?"

"I'll come and get you tomorrow after school. We'll come back to my house and have dinner—my folks want to meet you—and then we can see a film."

I'm stunned. Stunned into more silence.

"We can sit in the dark theater and hold hands. It'll be great. You'll see."

"You've done this before?"

"Jason, I've known I was gay for years. Yes, I've been out with other boys. It—well, it takes courage. But we don't have to advertise anything, you know. If you aren't ready to come out, then we're just a couple of friends out for the evening. That's not so weird."

"Are you out?"

"In a way. Some people know."

"So if they see us . . ."

"They'll know, yes. But, Jason, it's not like they're going to dance around us and call us names in singsong children's voices or anything."

I'm silent again, not convinced. I can see that happening, as a matter of fact.

"Jason, please say yes."

"God . . ."

"Tell you what. Let's just plan as far as you coming over for dinner. Then you and I can decide what we want to do after that. I'll let you make the call. How's that?"

"I thought your folks didn't like that you're gay."

"What I said was they're not happy about it. But they don't want me to be miserable, and they know there's nothing they can do about it. So—please? Say you'll come?"

"I told Aunt Audrey." Maybe I'm trying not to answer his question. I don't know.

"You mean about you? When?"

"She was with me when you called. I was so angry with you I just ran up to my room and pounded on my pillow and yelled obscenities until she couldn't ignore it any longer."

"And? How are you? How is she?"

I take a deep breath and let it out slowly. "We're okay. She says she knew. She says she understands who you are. To me. I owe her fifty bucks."

"What?"

I chuckle a little; it is funny, really. "She said I couldn't surprise her. I said I bet I could. She said how much. But she wasn't surprised."

Raj is laughing. "I knew I liked her. Jason, that's great! She won't mind at all, then, will she? If you have dinner here tomorrow?"

A thought occurs to me suddenly. "Tomorrow's Friday. Why Friday? Why not Saturday?"

It's Raj's turn to be silent. Finally he says, "It looks less like a date."

I don't know why this hurts, but it does. "So this isn't really a date."

"No, that's not it. I mean, it's for your sake."

Oh. What a dunce. "Sorry. I guess being angry with you earlier makes me forget how thoughtful you are."

"I want to hear the word 'yes,' Jason. Now. Please."

I'm grinning foolishly. "Yes."

"Hallelujah! Now go have your dinner. Tomorrow night will be great."

I want to say, "I love you." But all I say is, "Bye."

My euphoria, or whatever this feeling is, doesn't last long. Uncle Steve has always been a bit of a stickler when it comes to family dinnertime, so I'm already in the doghouse by the time I show up downstairs. He looks up from his now-empty plate as I approach the table, and I freeze. They're both just sitting there, looking at me.

Has Aunt Audrey told him? Just how angry is he?

But his expression tells me he's just irritated. I sit down.

"Sorry to be late," I mumble, hoping my face doesn't still look like I've been crying like a baby. I'm kind of hoping he'll punish me by leaving the table to go watch some TV or correct student papers in his study, but instead he stays.

"How is track practice going, Jason?"

Safe territory, anyway. I wash a mouthful of dinner down with some milk and respond, "Great. I think our relay team is the best yet."

"And your progress on the dash?" Short dash had been his thing, as he'd told Raj, when he was in college and he'd been the star of the team.

"I think I'm still ahead of Walsh."

"Walsh? You mean Jimmy Walsh? You want to beat your friend?" His smile is humorous, lopsided, like he's teasing me. Which he is; on the track, in competition, you want to beat everybody. And Uncle Steve knows this.

" 'Course I do. I wouldn't want to play second fiddle to that one." But I like Uncle Steve's word better. Yeah, I'd like to beat him, and gay or not, I'm not talking about sex.

Uncle Steve's face has changed. "I thought you two liked each other."

There's a stab in my throat. I'm ready to swallow, but I can't. Mouth full, I shake my head. I concentrate on relaxing. When I can speak, I manage to say, "That was a long time ago. Elementary school. He's become a total jerk."

"Oh? Like what?"

How much do I want to tell him? I guess I could leave out the part about the knife, so I tell him how Jimmy and Dane had accosted me after tryouts, and how Robert had saved my ass. Oh, and I leave out the part where Jimmy called me a faggot.

Aunt Audrey is horrified. "Jason, why didn't you tell us this before?"

I shrug. "Nothing you could do. It's past, and it hasn't been repeated. Plus, he probably knows Robert will cut him down to size if he tries it."

There's a silence I can't quite read at this point. Aunt Audrey is looking at Uncle Steve, and finally he says, "Well, Jason, I don't want you to think I want you fighting, but why does Robert have a role in this? Can't you take care of yourself?"

Well, this stings. I'd left out how ready I'd been—sort of—to take on both those goons alone, if I had to. I wasn't about to turn tail and run, or scream for help, for Christ's sake.

Aunt Audrey tries to come to my rescue. "Stephen, don't be absurd!"

But I know this isn't the way to go, with her protecting me. "Of course I can. But alone I'm hardly a match for both those bullies. As long as they know Robert is on my side, they'll leave me alone. What do you think, I'm some kind of chicken?"

It's almost like he'd wanted me to stand up to him. Like that was the right response. He says, "No, son. I don't think you're a chicken." He smiles at me. "I'm sorry if it sounded like that."

My plate is empty now, and Uncle Steve pushes away from the table. "It's late. Why don't you take your dessert up to your room so you can start your homework?"

He doesn't call me son very often. It has the usual effect, and I feel kind of goofy. It makes me want to do what he's asked. So I grab another glass of milk and take the slice of cake Aunt Audrey has cut for me upstairs.

I'm deep into something—history, maybe—when I hear Uncle Steve's voice. It's loud, and it gets louder by the word until a door closes. It sounds like he and my aunt must be in his study or something. This is what the voice is saying: ". . . mean to say that this is a good thing? That the boy I think of as my son . . ." and the door shuts, but I'm sure the last two words are "is gay?"

Christ. She's told him. There's this almost painful sensation going up my back, like pinpricks or needle jabs. I can't move. Hell, I can't breathe. I'm listening for more, but I don't want to hear it.

Then something in me snaps, and I throw aside whatever I'd been working on. I take the stairs as quickly and as quietly as I can, stopping every few steps to see if I can hear more. And I do, but I have to keep moving down farther.

"I did tell you I thought it might be the case, Steve. Last year. Remember?"

"I didn't give it much credence then, and I'm not sure I give it any more now. He's only sixteen, for God's sake! How can he know what he wants?"

Aunt Audrey's voice softens, and I have to move farther down the stairs to hear it. "Didn't you know what you wanted when you were his age? Didn't you know you wanted a girl-friend?"

"Sixteen is a very confusing time, Audrey."

"All the more reason why we should support him. If he thinks he's gay, we have no choice but to believe him and accept him. If in a year he decides he isn't, it will be a lot easier for him to admit he's made a mistake if he doesn't expect us to say 'We told you so.' We need to accept him, Steve."

There's a long silence. My ears are straining for any clues at all.

Finally Uncle Steve says, "I've failed." It's so quiet I almost can't hear. But I'm nearly outside the door now, so I don't dare move again. Then, "I couldn't give you children, and when fate gave us Jason—I've let my brother down, Aud. I've failed him, and I've failed Jason."

Aunt Audrey sounds like she's about to cry. "You've failed no one! We both love Jason as much as we would have loved our own child, and we've raised a son to be proud of. Jason is a wonderful boy! Smart, considerate, thoughtful, brave, clever, athletic—there's nothing wrong with him. There's no failure here. Can't you see that?"

A sudden loud thump takes my breath away. No, evidently Uncle Steve can't see that, and he's taking it out on his desk.

"I don't want that life for him." His voice is still quiet, like he's really depressed. "No one should have to live like that. He'll be hated, ostracized. He won't be able to marry or have children . . ." At this point his voice fades away, and afterward it sounds husky. "I know what it's like not to be able to have children. But at least my reason isn't something everyone around me disapproves of. They don't think it's what I de-serve."

At this point I start my silent trek back up the stairs. I don't what to hear him say that again. Any of it. It makes me feel like there's something evil inside me, something worse than cancer that can't be cut out or treated in any way. Something everyone will hate. Something that makes Uncle Steve feel like a failure.

Something that makes me feel as though I've failed him too.

I've just crawled into bed, sure I won't sleep, when Aunt Audrey knocks and comes in. I prop myself up against the wall. One look at my face tells her I'd heard enough. She sits down on the side of my bed.

"I guess you can tell that your uncle and I talked."

"Why did you tell him?"

"Jason, you're starting to want to spend time with boys like Raj. You'll want to go places with them, and I don't want you to feel like you have to pretend they're just friends."

"Some of them will be. And now Uncle Steve won't believe that."

She smiles. "Yes, he will. He's not an ogre, and he loves you very much."

I sit back hard and cross my arms over my chest. "As it happens," I tell her in a pouty tone I hate even as I hear it, "I'm going out tomorrow night. With Raj. I'm going to his house for dinner, to meet his parents. *They* want to meet *me*, even if Uncle Steve—"

"Jason, you know you're supposed to ask permission before you arrange for a date."

"Jesus, Aunt Audrey, that was last year. I'm sixteen now. And it's not like you don't know Raj. Even Uncle Steve has met him."

She looks torn. I can't tell if she's considering whether to hold me to last year's dating policy or if there's something about Raj she's trying not to say. In the end she just says, "Are you planning to do anything after dinner?"

"Yeah. We'll probably see a movie. A film." Raj had said *film*.

"Which one?"

"Don't know yet."

She sighs. "I'll tell your uncle. In the meantime, he may make himself scarce; I don't think he's figured out yet how to respond to the news."

Oh, I'm thinking, he's figured it out. We're both failures. We have that much in common.

Like "father" like "son."

Chapter 7

The Reluctant Student

All day Friday I'm sure Friday night will never come. And I almost don't want it to. I'm frantic about meeting Raj's parents for more reasons now than I would have had two days ago. Maybe I wasn't in the room with Uncle Steve when he'd found out about me, and maybe our paths didn't cross (I made sure of that) this morning, and maybe he'll hide so he won't have to witness the ugly scene of me leaving the house with my male date. But the idea of having to face Raj's father, who almost certainly will feel like my being with his son is a bad idea, makes me shiver.

But Raj said his folks want to meet me. And I never thought to ask what he's said about me. But one thing is sure: they'll know we're together. It will be the first time I've been with Raj with anyone who knows. It feels freaky just thinking about it.

I survive Friday's daylight hours somehow, and the worst part is English Lit. We've read this story about a man who is treating a woman rather badly, and Williams has Meg read her report on it. Aloud. Standing in front. Every word hurts. At least it gets my mind off dinner.

My aunt is home when I get there after school, and she doesn't say much about the date with Raj, just gives me a lecture about using protection.

"Aunt Aud, what do you think we're going to do? Honestly!"

"Jason, I may never have been a teenaged boy, but I do have a pretty good understanding of what this time of your life is like. Don't forget I'm a nurse. And I happen to know that you, my dear, won't always know what's going to happen. I'm not suggesting you do anything. But you should be prepared for anything."

Upstairs I find a packet of condoms on my bed. There's a note too.

> *Just in case. Besides, won't it feel kind of cool just having them?*

I have to laugh. She really is great. It almost makes up for Uncle Steve.

Raj picks me up right on time. He parks the car, a real gentleman, and rings the bell. Aunt Audrey lets him in this time, and it feels so weird having her let my date in, greeting him, telling him I'll be right there. I'm hovering in the hall, listening. I've been ready for half an hour. Uncle Steve hasn't come home yet from work—unusual for a Friday, but about what I expect tonight.

My aunt is into some light conversational topic with Raj when I decide to make an entrance. Raj barely looks at me. He's in the middle of a sentence, which he finishes before turning to me.

"Ready?" He sounds so calm! I just nod.

Aunt Audrey gives my hair a stroke. "Back before midnight, Jason."

At least he doesn't open the car door for me; that would have been way too much. He looks at me before he turns the key.

"How are you doing?"

I shrug. "Okay, I guess. Feels weird."

He nods. "Yeah. I know."

We're quiet for a few blocks, and then I tell him, "My uncle Steve knows."

"Ah. Who told him?"

"My aunt. I heard them arguing last night."

"Arguing? About what?"

"He's ashamed, I think." I take a deep breath. "At any rate, he doesn't like it. He doesn't usually stay at the school this late on Fridays. I think he didn't want to see us together. You and me."

Another few silent blocks go by. Then Raj says, "This was hard for him to learn. It might help you to remember that. Perhaps he will grow to feel better about it."

"Your dad didn't."

"Well, in a way he did. We've sort of agreed to disagree, as you put it. But we had to talk a lot—yell a lot—to get to that point. I'm hoping it will be easier for you."

"Why should it be?"

Raj shrugs. "It's just a hope. And maybe a feeling. Your uncle doesn't seem like as rigid a man as my father. But time will tell. Meanwhile," he reaches over and squeezes my left hand, "it will do you no good to worry about it. Just be yourself, and let him be himself."

Suddenly he pulls into a side street, a dead end. There's a wooded lot with no house, just what once may have been a bit of road. He stops and pulls on the emergency brake, and then he reaches for me.

God, but it feels so right to kiss him. To have his hands on my face, to grip his neck with my hands. Just before we reach a point of no return, Raj pulls away. We breathe hard for a minute, and then he laughs. And I laugh. I feel giddy, silly, euphoric and sad at once, and oh so in love.

He moves back behind the wheel, this huge grin on his beautiful face. "You know, I feel a little ashamed telling you this, but I can't resist. It doesn't apply so much to your uncle, perhaps, as it does to my father. The truth is that the biggest problem most straight men have with us, with gays, is that they're terrified of us. They can't admit it even to themselves, but the more violent their response, the greater their fear. It's like we have some kind of secret edge over them."

"Why would you be ashamed about liking that? I think it's really cool—a secret edge."

He shrugs. "I guess because I'd like everything to be more direct. More—pardon the contradiction, given the topic— straightforward. I wish it weren't necessary to be secretive, partly because it's usually not something we choose, but something that's forced on us."

"So . . . why not use the advantage when it's handed to us like that?"

He grins again and turns the car around.

I'm really glad I've practiced his last name. Imagine saying, "It's a pleasure to meet you, Mrs. Burugapalli," without at least a week's notice, while you're thinking to yourself, *My God, she knows I'm gay and that I want her son!*

At least I've met Anjani before. She's as sweet to me tonight as she'd been in the store, weeks—years—ago. She seems to be taking this dinner event very much in stride. Raj's father, on the other hand, seems stiff, formal. I can't tell if he's always like that or if he's reacting to his son bringing a boy home.

There's this haunting sort of music playing quietly in the background. Making conversation, I ask about it. Raj brings me the jewel case. Sitar.

"Ah, yes," I say, trying to sound sophisticated. "Like Ravi Shankar."

Raj's mom isn't dressed in one of those bright silk getups—a sari, I think they're called—but she is very nicely dressed. And it looks like silk. Her skin is beautiful, a lot like Raj's.

The house is filled with unfamiliar aromas. I say something complimentary, and Anjani responds.

"Mum decided to give you the Indian treatment," she says. "You'll have some of the dishes that they serve back where we come from."

Much of the dinner conversation is me asking questions about India, about the Andhra Pradesh state where the family once lived. Both Anjani and Raj were born there, Raj's mom tells me. There's a tense moment I can't quite figure out when Anjani says they moved to the U.S. five years ago, like there's a whole world of stuff they aren't saying, but I cover it with a comment that turns out to be stupid.

"I can't believe how good your English is. All of you. I mean, since you've been here only five years!"

Raj's mom smiles at me and looks like she's about to say something when his dad chimes in.

"You Americans are often surprised when someone knows more than one language. In India, my wife and I were expected to speak English, and so were our children."

He doesn't sound mean, exactly; maybe just a little crusty. And he's right, really. We're pretty bad about that here.

"Daddy," says Anjani, "you know, we're Americans too, now." She's sitting next to him, and she leans over and wraps a hand around his wrist. She gives him a fond smile, and he seems to soften a little.

"Yes, yes. Of course, dear. I know."

I decide it's time to make friends with Raj's dad. I ask, "What kind of work do you do, Mr. Burugapalli?"

At first I think I've made some awful gaffe, from the glare on his face. But no one else seems to be reacting badly, so I brazen it out. I tell myself, *He puts his pants on one leg at a time, just like you, Jason.* I take a forkful of saffron rice, my eyes on his face, like it's the most casual thing in the world.

He reaches out for a drink of water before he answers, but finally he says, "My brother and I own a software company."

He stops there, like that's all he's going to say, but I want more. I'm not taking any shit from father figures.

"Is that why you came to the U.S.? To do that with him?"

"Yes."

Everyone else at the table is studiously silent, waiting to see—what? If the man will explode? As I glance toward Raj, his gaze trained fully on his plate, I catch some movement of Anjani's in my peripheral vision. But it's Mrs. Burugapalli who speaks.

"Raj's uncle had moved here some years ago, Jason. My husband managed the India portion of the company while the U.S. side was getting on its feet, but we decided to move here too. We hired a cousin to manage the India operation so we could devote more attention over here. Fortunately, we've been quite successful."

There's this feeling kind of like a collective sigh that goes around the table, and it seems to help everyone but me. But the tension is past, and I'm not about to say anything to increase it again.

If I weren't nervous, I'd be enjoying the food more. I think I have an affinity for curry.

After dinner Raj says he wants to show me his room. No one seems to think this is a bad idea, so I follow him upstairs. The house is beautiful; lots of windows, a huge open staircase. His room is huge too.

I'm expecting an embrace immediately, kisses, caresses, like when he'd come to my room. But that doesn't happen. Instead he just opens the door and stands there, hands behind his back, watching me look around.

The room is like a miniature temple. I walk from spot to spot, picking up things, setting them down. The smell of incense lingers from some recent burning, or maybe from so many burnings that it doesn't go away. And there's this huge poster of Gandhi on the wall beside the bed. I turn to Raj at last.

"Wow," is all I can think of to say.

He's trying not to grin. "A bit much?"

I shrug. "I don't know. I guess it depends. Do you spend a lot of time here?"

"Yes."

"Then maybe it's not too much. I mean, you've surrounded yourself with things that are important to you."

He holds out a hand, and I move over to him so I can take it. He says, "If you surround me with your arms, that will be even more true."

I rest my head on his shoulder and hold him. Eyes closed, I breathe in the scent of incense, the scent of curry, the scent of Raj.

I try for an appropriate comment. "It's nirvana."

He chuckles; not the response I'd wanted. He pushes me gently away, hands on my shoulders. "That's Buddhism, Jason. For the Hindu, it's moksha that releases us from the cycle of rebirth."

"So, can I say it's moksha?"

He shakes his head. "Not exactly. But we can talk about that another time. It's enough for me to know you're happy here with me."

And that's when he kisses me. But it's not like any of his other kisses. It's tender, and slow, and deep. Nothing frantic. It's almost not even sexual. More spiritual, if I had to describe it. And it's amazing.

It makes me brave enough to ask, "Did I say something wrong at dinner? Your dad seemed almost angry or something."

He shakes his head. "No. It wasn't about you. It's—kind of private, that's all." I'm considering asking him if he'll ever explain it to me, but then he strokes my face with his hand and says, "Would you like to go out with me?"

I'm not sure I ever want to leave this room again. For anything.

We haven't talked about what movie we'd go to. I feel sure *The Return of the King* isn't going to come up, though this time maybe I could allow myself to enjoy Frodo.

All I say is, "Let's go."

Raj doesn't even ask what I want to see. He's already got something picked out, evidently. So he drives downtown and scouts out a parking spot, and he finds one on a side street. He turns to look behind him, his arm on the back of my seat to help him see as he's parallel parking. I scan his profile, and all these butterflies suddenly take up residence in my stomach.

It's funny how something so simple, an action that means nothing in itself, can take on a completely different dimension under certain circumstances. I mean, all that's happening is Raj is parallel parking while I watch his face. But my emotions are nearly sending me through the roof. *I'm on a date,* says something inside my head. *This boy, this gorgeous, intelligent, mysterious boy, is taking me out on a date!*

I get out of the car, but I still don't know where we're going. I'm just walking along beside Raj, too overwhelmed to speak. Suddenly I panic. I stop moving.

Raj asks, "What is it?"

I gulp. How can I even ask the question? I mean, who's paying? He asked me out, but—what are the rules? I just don't know. I decide to let him get to the box office first. But meanwhile I'm standing here, and he's waiting.

I fudge. "What are we going to see?"

"It's a surprise." He puts a hand on my shoulder. "Trust me?"

I nod. I don't really care; I just want to sit in the dark next to Raj. His hand slides down my arm, takes my hand, squeezes, and pulls me forward. Suddenly he ducks into an alley. It's wide enough for one vehicle, but there's no sidewalk. I'm guessing it's a shortcut, and as it turns out, it is. But first, it's a place where no one can see us.

Raj stops partway in and turns to me. His hands go to my face, and I wrap my arms around his waist. We stand there forever, just kissing, and then his hands are on my hips. He pulls me hard against him.

By the time he lets go of me, I'm wishing I could pull him over to that bed he turned down at my house. All I can do is tug on my jeans with the hand he's not holding.

On the other end of the alley, I can see where we're headed. It's the retro theater. The one where I'd seen *The Man Who Fell to Earth,* with David Bowie. I've just never approached it through this alley before. Tonight, it's *La Cage aux Folles.*

There's no problem having Raj get to the box office first, 'cause I've stopped moving again. He's bought two tickets before he realizes that I'm not next to him.

"Jason?" he calls, smiling at me. "Come on." He pushes the door open and goes in.

I have little choice but to follow. All right, I do like the idea of sitting there toying with his fingers in the dark, and if anyone had asked me five minutes ago whether I cared what we'd see, I'd have said, "Nope!"

But now I care. I mean, I've seen *The Birdcage,* so I have some idea what *La Cage* is about. But I saw *Birdcage* with Rebecca, in her living room. I could chuckle and even guffaw and generally enjoy the silly things the two old gays got themselves into, but I didn't have to identify with any of it. Now, though, my safety barrier is gone. Shot. Kaput. The scene where Robin Williams's son runs a finger down Williams's face and then wipes it on the wall to demonstrate how much makeup is on it is flashing in and out of my mind, alternating with the image of the swishy, lisping, muscular houseboy who's wearing frayed jean short-shorts and a T-shirt that says "Straight Looking." That was funny, then. But not now.

So I have little choice. It's true I could turn and leave. I could get home from here on my own; the buses are still running, there's the taxi option, or in a pinch I could call Aunt Audrey.

But Raj is in there.

I take a quick glance to either side of me; no one I know is in sight. I go in.

He's waiting by the concessions. "Want anything?"

I just shake my head and look for the door we're supposed to go through. I want to spend as little time as possible here, in the light. Raj isn't with me; he's getting candy or something, so I find a couple of seats off to the side and hunch down, wondering how long it will take him to find me, wondering if he'll want to sit somewhere else. The place is about half full, and I'm grateful not to see anyone I know. Not that I'm making an effort.

Raj is there very soon, just plunks himself down, grins at me, and pops a few Junior Mints into his mouth.

We're about a third of the way through the movie before either of us does anything to acknowledge that we're together. He's shifting his legs a little, and one knee bumps into mine, pulls away, and then moves back. Then he moves his knee up and down, the seams in our jeans catching with the motion. Despite my nervousness, I like it. I like it a lot.

I decide I'll just relax; never mind the men in cancan outfits; never mind the froufrou pillows all over the gay guys' apartment. Never mind how much trouble they think they have to go to so they'll look presentable to the son's prospective parents-in-law. I try to concentrate on Raj. But this crazy movie is putting me more and more on edge. This isn't me, it isn't him, it isn't how either of us will ever live.

Is it?

Eventually I feel his hand. He takes mine with it, fingers tickling my palm, the underside of my wrist. I close my eyes. And then it's not holding my hand any longer. It's on my thigh.

His fingertip moves forward, back, in circles. And then—God!—then his fingers walk their way along the inside seam of my jeans. Up, but only to a point, and then down. Up again, farther this time, and down. Up. As his nails pull at the crotch-seam fabric, my eyes and mouth fly open. And he stays there.

He works at the thickest part, where the leg seams meet, sometimes scratching, sometimes poking. I can hear my own intakes of breath better than the dialog from the speakers. I look at Raj. He's just gazing at the screen, seemingly not involved in anything else.

Finally I can't stand it any longer. I grab his hand and just hold it, nearly panting now. With my other hand I reach down to calm things. When I'm able, I look at Raj again. He's still gazing at the screen, but he's smiling.

I decide turnabout is fair play, so I work my way up to the thickest seam of his jeans and give him the same treatment. Just as teasing, just as provocative. Gratified, I feel him get hard and hear his breathing quicken. I steal another glance at him. His eyes are closed, and his jaw is set. I go on as long as he lets me.

It was an interesting distraction, but once I focus on the movie again I'm back to wondering what we're doing here. I mean, why this movie? We could have teased each other into agonies just as well in *The Return of the King*. There's one thing that sinks in though. It's a song they do, and the words "I am what I am" keep repeating. It says things like I won't hide just because I'm gay. I won't pretend I'm something I'm not. This, at least, makes sense to me. The question is how much courage I would need to live like that. Especially after what I heard Uncle Steve say.

Maybe these sissies have more guts than I do.

Movie over, Raj takes my hand in the crush of people exiting. I'm behind him, and he pulls our hands against his ass, which both keeps me very close and prevents anyone who's not looking carefully from seeing our hands together.

We go back through the alley, but we don't stop this time. In the car, Raj looks at me. "Ever see that film before?"

"I saw *Birdcage*, but not this."

He nods. "I'd like to talk about it. Would you be more comfortable sitting in the car, or shall we go and get something to drink someplace?"

I imagine myself across a table from Raj, sipping Cokes, talking about homosexuality in general and this movie in particular. "Car."

Raj starts the engine. "That's fine. I'll just get us someplace where we don't have headlights shining in our faces half the time, okay?"

He parks a little way out of town, not far from where Robert had parked us a mere couple of weeks ago and I'd made out with Meg in the backseat. I stare through the windshield at nothing and wait for him to begin. He seems to be waiting for me, but I'm determined. This was his big idea; let him tell me what he had in mind.

Finally he says, "Did it make you uncomfortable?"

I look at him. "You expected that?"

He shrugs. "A lot of guys get the creeps when they see men acting so effeminate."

"So why did we see it?"

"I think it holds a number of lessons. For us, and for heteros. Didn't you see any?"

What does he think, that I'm going to just sit at his feet and hang on his every word? I'm feeling a little hostile at this point. I don't even want to talk about my reaction to the song lyrics—partly because I'm not sure I could live up to them.

"Why don't you just tell me what I was supposed to see? It'll save us some time." I turn back to the windshield, my arms crossed over my chest.

"Fine. First, and most important for you and me, I think we need to see that it will do us no good to pretend that we're something we're not, no matter how compelling the reason, regardless of the situation. Second—and this actually ties in with nonviolence—the gay guys used their very disadvantage as an advantage. Disguising everyone as drag queens not only made them blend in with the club crowd, but it also used the tendency of heteros to dismiss them. To dismiss us."

"How does that tie in with nonviolence?"

"It takes a lot of guts to respond to violence and ridicule with nonviolence and calm. And Jason," he waits for me to look at him again, "it takes a hell of a lot of guts to be gay."

I turn back to the front. "You said some people know about you. Who?"

"Other than my family, there are several people in my classes at school. Some of them respond well to it. Some of them don't. I've had to repaint my own locker more than once this year alone."

He's got my attention again. "Why? What was on it?"

"'Queer.' 'Faggot.' 'Free head here.' You name it." He actually chuckles. "The paint's getting pretty thick by now. I may need a different locker next year."

"Have you ever been, you know—threatened? Physically?"

"Many times."

He stops, stares through the glass of the windshield. I can barely see it, but his jaw is clenched.

Finally I dare to ask, "Worse than that?"

His shrug is almost a challenge. "Sure."

Beaten? Raj was beaten? "Who?" I ask. "When?"

He's quiet so long I'm not sure he's going to tell me. But then, "Most recently, first semester. This year. John Whittier and Brian Cooney. They're seniors."

"What did you do?"

"What could I do? I tried to run, but they cornered me."

"But did you fight back?"

"To what end? That would have served nothing but to enrage them further. When I didn't return their violence, they just got a few licks in and left me there."

"And did you report them?"

"Of course. But they denied it, and it went nowhere."

God. Raj, beaten. I reach out and stroke the side of his face. He claims my hand, and then he pulls me toward him.

His tongue in my mouth feels so sweet. I could have sat there kissing him forever. Except—well, except that he reaches for my belt. And then his tongue feels even better someplace else.

The windows are closed, and it's a good thing. I scream with pleasure.

He holds my hand while I recover, and when I look at him again he's smiling at me. He says, "Did you enjoy that?"

I grin stupidly and nod my head.

"Good. Get used to it."

We sit quietly for a while. Then, suddenly, Uncle Steve is on my mind again. It's like Raj knows. He says, "How are you doing?"

I heave a shaky sigh. "Uncle Steve thinks he's failed me. Failed my father."

"Has he taught you well? Has he taught you to be the best person you can be?"

Well, this isn't quite the response I'd expected. "Sure. I guess so."

"Then he hasn't failed you."

"I've failed him." The words are out before I even know I'm going to say them.

Raj sits up a little. "What are you talking about?"

You just can't say the sort of things out loud that answer that question. They're things like I want Uncle Steve to be proud of me. I want him to want to call me "son." So I translate these into something much less direct.

"He was this big track star."

"Like you're not? But what does that matter? It's irrelevant. If you're good at track, fine. But that doesn't make you the best person you can be. How have you failed?"

"He's ashamed of me." There. That about covers it.

"So you said earlier. But did he? Say it?"

"He said everyone will hate me."

"Lots of stupid people will. He's right."

"He said my life would be awful."

Raj chuckles and says, "It would be, for him. You know, it might help to remember that most heteros don't rub two thoughts together about what it's really like to be gay. They just get this feeling—some of them call it instinctive—that gay is wrong. That gay is bad. If they would add the phrase 'for me,' they'd be right. Trouble is, it usually doesn't occur to them to think of it like that. But, Jason, being straight is wrong, for you. Because you're gay."

I reach a hand behind his neck and pull his face to mine. I don't know how much this will help me, but it feels good to hear him say it.

I beat midnight by five minutes. Raj doesn't just drop me off and split; we sit in the car long enough for some real kisses, and he walks me to the door. Aunt Audrey opens it. Instantly I'm edgy; was she watching us in the car? And is Uncle Steve still up?

Raj, though, seems unfazed. "Good evening, Mrs. Peele. Here's your nephew, safe and sound. Sorry it's so close to the wire."

"Evening it is not, Mr. Burugapalli. But you are correct; Jason hasn't yet turned into a pumpkin, and I guess I don't blame you wanting to get every minute you can with him." She takes my shoulder and guides me inside. "Sleep well."

He nods and is gone. But not gone from my head, from my heart. God! How I love him. I'm sure of it.

"G'night, Aunt Audrey."

"Not so fast, young man."

Her voice sounds stern, but when I turn, I see that she's smiling at me. "Come; sit with me a minute. Would you like some herb tea?" She doesn't wait for an answer.

I wait at the kitchen table while the water's heating. She's leaning against the counter, arms crossed, but her face is soft.

"Did you have a good time?"

I'm sure I'm blushing. "Yeah. I did."

"How was dinner? Did you like his parents?"

Uncle Steve has appeared from somewhere, pajama legs showing under his navy terry-cloth robe. He leans in the doorway and doesn't speak, just listens. And watches.

Aunt Audrey has to prompt me. "Jason?"

I almost can't believe she expects me to go on like nothing's weird here, but I do my best. "Uh, his mom is very friendly. Asked me a lot of questions. His dad was kind of quiet, but I guess he was okay." I'm not going into the relationship between Raj and his dad at this point in time. "I really like his sister, though. She laughs a lot, and she seems like she means it."

"What's her name?"

"Anjani."

"How lovely! Is she older or younger than Raj?"

"Older, by two years. She's finished school, but she's taking some time off to decide what she wants to do about college. I think she's hoping to get married soon, so that might make a difference. That is, where she goes, or maybe even whether she goes at all. It was kind of hard to tell."

Aunt Audrey brings two mugs of chamomile tea to the table. "Someone she met here?"

"Yeah. The guy from India she was supposed to marry crapped out on her. Married someone else, over there. I guess he didn't want to leave India, and she didn't want to go back. It was an arranged marriage; maybe he thought that broke the arrangement. But she really likes this other fellow, also Indian. He's already here. He's a senior in college, so her parents want her to take some time, but I think they like him a lot."

"Really? An arranged marriage? And what about Raj?"

I look down at my hands. I don't know why I feel odd talking about him. "There was this girl in India his parents wanted him to marry, but when he came out to his folks they told her family. They'll find someone else for her."

"That's good. So he's free to date you?"

I look up again. The twinkle in her eye is a giveaway. I can't help grinning in response. I've almost forgotten about Uncle Steve.

"Yeah. I guess so."

"What's the house like?"

I tell her about the open rooms, the amazing Indian furniture, and the ebony elephant I'd seen on the landing, encrusted with semiprecious gems. And I tell her about Raj's room. How it's full of ceremonial stuff.

"What's moksha?" I ask.

"Moksha is—well, simply put, it's when the Hindu soul has achieved enlightenment and is released from the cycle of reincarnation. It's now ready to merge with the primary Hindu god or life force, Brahman. And when it does that, it loses its perceived identity as an individual soul."

"So, you can't say 'I'm in moksha' the way you might say 'I'm in heaven.' Right?"

"It wouldn't be quite the same, no. Most people who believe in heaven think of it as someplace they'll live on forever as who they are, seeing loved ones, that sort of thing. So, no. Not really."

I nod, feeling like next time I'm with Raj, I'll understand a little better.

"What did you do after dinner?"

So much for existentialism. "We saw a film." Even in my somewhat anxious state, I can't help noticing that I've adopted Raj's word, "film," instead of "movie," which I've always said before.

"Oh? Which one?"

I don't want to tell her, but I don't want to lie, either. "*La Cage aux Folles.*"

Her eyebrows rise. "Did you enjoy it?"

"Not really. I mean, I don't feel like I have anything in common with those characters." Take that, Uncle Steve.

She chuckles and then drinks some tea.

Uncle Steve speaks at last. "Good night, Jason. I'm, uh, glad you had a good time."

I'm so stunned I barely remember to say "Good night" as he disappears upstairs.

"Did you use any of your condoms?"

Wow. Okay, Aunt Audrey's got my attention again. Do I tell her I thought about it? But the only thing that happened—only thing, like it was nothing!—was that Raj went down on me. God. I'm still in heaven—wherever—over that. "No. No need. Um, are you going to ask me that after every date?"

"Not as long as you promise me you'll use them if there is need."

"I promise."

"Jason, this isn't just a health issue. It has to do with your own self-respect. You are worth keeping safe. Your life is worth every bit as much as anyone else's and a lot more than a few minutes of pleasure. Do you understand me?"

"Yes."

"And you're only sixteen years old. You may feel like that's almost grown-up, and maybe it is, but you'll have a lot more grown-up years than you will teenage years, and the last thing you want to do is something foolish now that will jeopardize all that time."

I don't respond, so she says, "Are you hearing me?"

I am, actually. I do know what she means. "Yes. I said I promise."

"We love you, Jason. We don't say it often, but it's true. Please remember that."

I sip my tea. It's not that I doubt her. Exactly. It's just that it's registering rather oddly these days. When I can make my face bland again, I ask, "What's with Uncle Steve?"

She sits up straight. "What do you mean?"

"Come on, Aunt Audrey. You know what I mean. You've told him something about me he hates. He doesn't show his face before I leave on my first homosexual date, and then he appears like some ghost and says, 'Glad you had a nice time.' What's going on?"

She stares down into her mug for a minute. Then she says, "He's trying to understand, Jason. It's—well, it's harder for a man. Straight men often have this notion that a gay man isn't really a man." She chuckles. "And, in truth, some gays do seem to encourage that view. But it's hard for your uncle to understand how a man could be a man and want another man sexually. It doesn't make sense to him."

"Why's it easier for you?"

"For one thing, I've suspected you were gay for some time. For another," she reaches over and ruffles my hair, "I know what it feels like to want a man."

Suddenly I don't want to talk about it anymore. I drain my mug. "Thanks, Aunt Aud. For being so cool with this. Think I'll go upstairs now. I'm pretty tired." I kiss her cheek on my way to the sink with the mug.

When I get to the staircase, I see a light on in Uncle Steve's study, and there's a low drone of voices that must be coming from the television. So he hadn't gone to bed when he'd left the kitchen. I stand there for a few seconds, wanting to confront him, wanting to escape. I choose the second.

Once I'm in bed, I know sleep is far away. I try distracting myself by thinking of Raj, by remembering what he'd done in the car. I even manage to get off again just thinking about it. But I'm still incredibly restless. I'm lying there, feet twitching under the sheet, when I hear Aunt Audrey come upstairs. There's the sound of running water in the master bathroom and then silence. I lie there twitching about as long as I can stand it and then throw the covers off, grab my robe, and tiptoe downstairs.

Uncle Steve's study is quiet now, but there's still a strip of light at the bottom of the door. I knock.

At first there's no sound, and I'm thinking he's fallen asleep in there. Then I hear a quiet "Come in."

He's in his recliner, still facing the dark TV screen. I have this odd moment when I'm wondering if my beard growth, when it really comes into its own, will be like his. His hair is as light as mine, but the stubble is kind of dark. How much did he look like my father? I can't remember the difference anymore.

I can feel Uncle Steve's eyes on me as I walk over to a bookcase where I know there's a framed photo of my parents on their wedding day. I pick it up, look hard at my father, and look up at Uncle Steve.

"Was he like you?" I ask. I have to know if my own father's reaction to me would have been anything like his brother's.

Uncle Steve thinks for a minute before he answers. "We were pretty close as boys. There were times we were archenemies, but that never lasted long. As you know, he was a year and a half younger, so sometimes I thought of him as a pest, and sometimes he thought of me as a tyrant. But yeah, I guess we were like each other in a lot of ways."

"You don't talk about him."

"Not a lot, you're right. Perhaps I should, but I'm never sure whether you want to hear it or not."

I set the photo down. "Would he be ashamed of me too?"

At first I don't know if he's going to answer. He just stares at me. Then he gets up, comes over to me, and hugs me. I hold him like I'm afraid I'll die if he lets go of me. But then he does, and I don't. Die.

"Come. Sit down." He goes back to his recliner, and I pull the desk chair out and turn it around. He rubs his face with both hands and then says, "No one is ashamed of you, Jason. And no, your dad would never have felt like that."

"But you—"

He holds up a hand. "I need to be sure I say this very carefully. It's true I'm not your father. But I have always wished I were. And I have always, always been proud of you. It's just that . . ." He stares at the ceiling like he's searching it for the words he needs. "Okay, think of it this way. You've lived with us for fourteen years now. I have a pretty good idea what you're like. What makes you happy. What irritates you. What motivates you. And it may be vain of me to say this, but I've often looked at you and seen little pieces of me, and it's made me glad. And I see how sometimes you react to things the same way I would. So I think I know you, and I think we're a lot alike." He looks at me, making sure I'm with him.

I say, "So?"

"So all of a sudden this thing that is so basic to me, and— I thought—to you, so basic that it didn't even need to be thought about, much less talked about, isn't true. This really basic thing about us is different, and it's different in a way I have trouble understanding. It isn't shame, Jason. Maybe confusion. Maybe even hurt vanity."

"I heard you arguing with Aunt Audrey. You said people would hate me. You said I couldn't be happy."

He sits forward, elbows on knees, and his voice is quiet. "Jason, many people believe this is a choice. I don't know for sure that it can be, but some of those who believe it is will feel like you've got some twisted idea of what feels good and you're going to be in their face about it. Some will even think you're going against God."

I want to tell him about the Vedic attitude toward gays, but somehow this doesn't feel like the right time. So I keep quiet and let him talk.

"And even some people who don't want to judge you will have trouble figuring out how to behave around you. It's like they won't know what the rules are. Men tend to treat a woman in a certain way whether she's eighteen or eighty, and it's different from how we treat men. Because for most of us, there's no possible way any man could ever be a sexual partner. It's like a different set of rules. And when we meet a man who could think of another man sexually, it's like the boundaries have shifted somehow, and we don't know what to do. And women, too, tend to treat other women in a certain way, and they treat men differently. If you decide you're really gay, you'll probably still have women approach you sexually, even if they know."

"You said that to Aunt Audrey too."

"Said what?"

"Like, I might not really know yet."

He looks at me at minute. Then, "The thing is, I can't guide you here. And this is another reason this makes me uncomfortable. I have no idea what it's like to try and figure out what my sexual orientation is, because I've never had to think about it. And I want to help you. But if I try, I can't pretend that I don't want you to be straight. For your sake, and for mine as well. I can't help thinking it would be better all around. But then I think, well, do I necessarily want you to be a teacher just because I am? And the answer is that I want you to do what makes you happy. You should do what makes you want to put all of yourself into it. And I could understand if you wanted to be an architect, or a writer, or a doctor. But this—"

"This makes you ashamed."

"No!" He practically shouts it at me. "No. It isn't shame, Jason. It's confusion. And concern for the difficulties you'd face. It makes me want to tell you to try it my way first. Try to be straight. Try not to go that route. But I don't even know if that's good advice. It might be very bad advice."

He gets up and turns to face the other direction. After a few deep breaths, he says, "I want so much to help you. To do the right thing for you. But I don't know what it is."

I don't know what else I want him to say. Need him to say. I go over to him and hug him from behind, my arms reaching around his chest. I lean my head against his back for a few seconds. And then I leave.

As I'm trying once more to fall asleep, my mind bounces back and forth between the scene with Uncle Steve and—on a completely opposite plane—what it had felt like to be with Raj earlier. And when I remember what my uncle had said about how others would see me—twisted? ungodly?—I get angry. I punch my mattress a few times, but I'm afraid that will be heard in the other room. Then I punch my thigh, but that hurts.

Suddenly my thoughts catch on something Raj said about the film. Something about using nonviolence to win, about having the guts to do it that way. I picture my knife, imagine the weight of it in my hand. It's not enough; I get out of bed, turn on the bedside light, and dig the knife out of my backpack. I heft it, toss it, flip it open, and close it a few times.

I like the solid feel of it in my hand. It's small, only about five inches fully open, so it's legal. Strictly speaking. Not for me, of course, at my age. But the size is great.

I'm thinking back to when I'd decided to get it, just after the first time Jimmy and Dane ganged up on me. When I'd decided I'd had enough.

I don't know how badly Raj was beaten. As for me, I wasn't ever more than roughed up, really; not much bloodletting. It seemed like it happened all the time though. The kids who picked on me did it either because they could and they wanted to make themselves look big, or because I'd shown them up in class and this was how they could show me up.

Mostly I managed to hide it or lie about it (fell off the swing; tetherball came at me out of nowhere), but sometimes Aunt Audrey would haul me into the bathroom for a session with the first aid kit and get the truth out of me. If she thought it seemed like more than a minor scuffle, she'd make Uncle Steve talk to me. But I never got the feeling he was worried. He just wanted to make sure I hadn't started it, that I wasn't in any real danger, and that I was man enough to stand up for myself. He never actually said that; it's just a feeling I got from him.

I was "man" enough. I *am* man enough. But—damn it, I got tired of it. And the older I got, the older the goons got. Older goons do more damage than younger ones. But when older goons know you have a knife, they're more apt just to jeer at you than jump on you. So it did its job. And now that people are starting to call me faggot, now that I'm pretty sure I'm gay, I'm going to need it more than ever.

I haven't practiced with it in some time, but when I did, it felt like an extension of my own hand, closely controlled, nearly invisible. Just after I got it, I used to ride the bus out to a large parkland, find a wooded place where I could be alone, and see how accurately I could throw it. I'd attack leaves on the lower branches of trees to see if I could slice quickly and still get exactly the spot I wanted. I used to be pretty good too.

My knife is like my security blanket. Like a silent bodyguard. It keeps me safe. If I have guts, at least part of it comes from knowing the knife is there. And now, now that I know I'm gay, now that I'm seeing Raj, there's no telling when I'll need it again. But somehow I don't think he'd approve of it. Somehow I can't see Gandhi carrying a switchblade.

I shove it back into its special place in my pack, hooking the pocket clip over the inside edge, and climb back into bed. Before I turn the light out, though, I get up again. I get the knife. I put it under my pillow.

Chapter 8

Another Man's Poison

I get up late on Saturday and successfully avoid having to sit at breakfast with anyone. As I'm spooning cereal into my mouth, I decide to spend some time at the library. Partly it's because I've been so exhausted from all the track practice that I haven't done justice to my homework. Partly it's because I need a distraction so I can stop thinking about my conversation with Uncle Steve. But also I want to do some research on Gandhi. Raj has gone over the guy's life with me; I want to know more about his thoughts.

There's a lot of stuff on his philosophy, and a lot of it is extremely interesting to me. I'd got the idea from Raj that Gandhi was all pacifist, responding to everything by turning the proverbial other cheek. And maybe he did, but that's not necessarily what he expects everyone to do.

Check out this quote: "In life it is impossible to eschew violence completely. The question arises, where is one to draw the line? The line cannot be the same for everyone."

Not the same for everyone. Does that mean I can keep my knife? I feel downright heady. What about the line for sexual orientation? Can that be different too?

Back to Gandhi, Jason.

I'm still browsing through the excerpts when I come across Raj's favorite, about the edge of the sword. I decide to memorize it. I'm sitting there, eyes closed, going over it for the umpteenth time when I hear my name whispered from behind me.

"Jason! I have to talk to you." It's Robert. I slam the book shut, not sure why. I push a chair away from my table with a foot.

"Have a seat."

"Listen, I need your advice. You know so much more about this stuff than I do."

"What stuff? Keep your voice down."

"Sorry. Listen, can we go someplace and talk? I feel kind of exposed here. I only came here because I called your house, and your aunt said you were here."

I suggest Starbucks, but he wants ice cream. So it's Friendly's. Between slurps of his milkshake, he tells me his woes.

"You know I took Debbie out again last night." He waits until I nod. "Well—I just couldn't stop!" Slurp. "It was like—like this huge force just came over me. And she didn't seem to want to stop either. I mean, she never said anything."

"Robert, are you saying what I think you're saying?"

"We did it, Jason. Do you understand?" Slurp.

"Okay."

Sounds like I wasn't the only one on a hot date last night. So both of us are virgins no longer. "So, she wanted it too. Yes? Can we assume she's done it before? What's she using?"

"What?"

"Birth control."

"No. She—she was a virgin, Jason. That's the problem."

I blink. "So, you used a condom, then?"

"No, man! That's what I'm trying to tell you. And afterward she cried and cried, and she said she's right between—
you know. She could get pregnant!"

At least he's stopped slurping. But what does he want me
to do about this? "Let me get this straight. You and Debbie,
both virgins and without benefit of protection of any kind,
had sex last night. And she's worried about the phase of the
moon. Is that right?"

"Phase of the moon?"

"She thinks she's ripe."

"Oh. Yeah."

"Well, it's too late to tell you how stupid that was. But it's
not too late to tell you not to do it again. Get yourself some
condoms. As for your current problem, you have two choices."

I eat a couple of spoonfuls of mint chip ice cream. Robert
can't stand it.

"What? What choices?"

"You can wait a few weeks and see what happens with
her period, or you can help her find a way to get a morning-
after pill. But she might need her parents' consent for that. I
don't really know what the rules are."

Robert sits back and closes his eyes, milkshake forgotten.
He's breathing audibly. Finally he says, "How do I find out?"

I take him back to the library, and we look up local coun-
seling centers. In a way, I feel partially responsible for this; I
wouldn't double with him again, and this is what happens. So
I go with him on the bus to the center. We sit for forty minutes in the waiting room, reading and rereading pamphlets,
waiting. There are a few that talk about being gay, but I don't
dare reach for them.

Finally someone can see us. The good news is they think
they can help. The bad news is her parents need to consent,
and we don't have much time.

On the bench in the bus stop shelter, Robert sounds pan-icky.

"She won't tell them. I'm sure she won't. Then what?" He turns frantic eyes on me.

"You won't know till you ask her. Let's go to your house and call."

"No! Not my house. My little brother will be all over us. Can we call from your place?"

I tell him to keep quiet, hoping no one will see me go upstairs with a boy, but Robert is not the quiet type. Uncle Steve sees us but says nothing. I try not to care what he thinks. What he might think, anyway.

We call from my room. At first Debbie's mother says she can't come to the phone, that she's not well, but when Robert begs for her to say who it is, he's told to wait a minute.

"I think she'll have to talk in front of her mother!"

"Then just ask her yes-or-no questions."

He manages to do this, with a few awkward moments, but the upshot is that she won't tell her folks. So he's back to the waiting option.

"Jason, will you explain to me about the moon thing?"

It's not something I've ever had to worry about, so we get on the Internet and do some research. I've guessed about right; it's going to take two or three weeks, if Debbie told him the truth, to know whether he has something to worry about.

Somewhere between him rolling around on the floor and punching his thigh and then sitting up and wringing his hair, it occurs to me that he's trusted me with something very per-sonal. I'm wondering if it might be time to tell him about me, and maybe about Raj. It could be a good distraction for him. And even if he freaks, it isn't likely he'll tell anyone.

But I need him not to freak. *Please stay with me, pal,* I say inside my head.

I start slow. "Robert, let's talk about something else. Get your mind off this. Is that okay?"

"As long as it isn't about writing. Or reading."

I chuckle. "Nope. Do you remember the first time you were here, and you were worried about what Jimmy Walsh had called me?"

Robert blinks a few times, clearing the fog of self-pity. "I guess so. He called you a faggot."

"You were worried he might be right." I pause, but he's just lying on the floor, knees in the air, staring at the ceiling. I watch him carefully from the chair at my desk. Finally, "Do you, um, do you know any gays?"

He looks at me. "I don't think so. Why?"

"What if you did? I mean, how would you feel about someone who was gay? Would you be, like, afraid of him? Or afraid to be seen with him?"

He scowls, considering this seriously. I'm flattered he's trying so hard, actually.

"No, I don't think I'd be afraid of him. It's not contagious, is it?"

I laugh a little nervously. "No. Not at all. So, you might be able to—you know—be friends?"

I have his full attention now. He sits up. "Jason, do you know someone who is? Hey, it's not Jimmy, is it?"

"No. Not Jimmy." I take a deep breath. "It's me."

His face contorts through about five different expressions and finally lands on squinty eyes, open mouth. It's a good ten seconds before he says quietly, "You?"

"Yeah. I'm gay. Honest."

He's shaking his head. "You can't be gay! I have some idea what you and Meg were up to in the backseat, y'know, after that movie. A fag wouldn't do that."

"Robert, please don't use that word. And it doesn't matter

what I did with Meg. What matters is that it's something I want to do with a boy, not a girl."

He stiffens. "What boy?"

"Not you, don't worry."

I don't feel like I can talk about Raj after all. He may be out to some people, but he might not appreciate me just spilling the beans to someone he barely knows.

Robert moves over to where he can lean against the bed. "Are you serious? But—how come you know so much about girls?"

"I don't have to feel nervous talking to them, because there isn't this layer of sexual tension for me. It's not that I know so much, it's just that I have no fear."

Robert thinks for a minute. "Well, I'll say you have no fear, if you're gay. Christ! I mean, that takes guts, Jason. How do you do it?"

It's my turn to blink. I don't know what to say. How do I do it? "Well, I guess I do it because I have no choice."

"No?"

"Could you choose to be gay?"

He holds up a hand and shakes his head vigorously. "No way, man!"

"Well, I can't choose to be straight. I guess it's just the way I'm wired." Suddenly it occurs to me I should have said that to Uncle Steve. But I hadn't. "It's not something I've known for a long time. I'm just figuring it out this year."

"Okay. And how do you figure it out?"

I chuckle in earnest now. "By making out with Meg in the backseat of your dad's car. And then by—well, by going out with a boy who asked me."

"Seriously?" He sits up straight, all ears now. "Who?"

I'm amazed. He seems so unperturbed. "I can't tell you.

Not yet. Maybe soon; I'll ask him if it's okay. But, Robert—you seem pretty cool with this. Are you?"

He shrugs. "I guess so. I mean, it sure as hell is surprising. Hey, does Jimmy know?"

I shake my head. "No. He was just being an asshole."

Robert nods sagely as if to say there's no denying that. "Right. Well, I mean, I guess I'm okay with it, as long as you don't—you know—try anything. You wouldn't, would you?"

I smile at him, feeling genuine affection for this huge guy who's being so absolutely sweet to me. That is, when you think about how he might have reacted. It wouldn't have been out of the question for him to go screaming from the room, backside first, watching me all the way to make sure I didn't lunge at him.

"No. I promise. You—well, you're my friend, Robert. And that's special enough."

He looks down at the floor. "Yeah. Friends. I like that."

I can't think of anything else I can do to help him with his situation. Except maybe one thing. "Back to your situation though. Do you have any condoms?"

His expression tells me all I need to know.

"Okay, that settles it. We'll have to get you some." I want to add that a second date is not the time to start having sex. But considering my first date with Raj, I decide against giving advice on this point.

When he's ready to leave, I'm tempted to give him a great big hug. I know I can't though; he may be understanding, but I'll bet there are limits.

Dinner that night is tolerable, actually. It's the first time Uncle Steve and I have spent more than a couple of seconds in each other's company since our little chat, and it's like we're both trying to get things back onto something close to an even keel. We need to act like nothing's really different between us, because—really—nothing should be.

I'm kind of hoping Raj will call before the evening is over. By ten, though, nothing. Should I have called him? What are the fucking rules? Are there any? I have to figure this thing out.

Chapter 9

His Royal Highness

On Sunday Robert calls after lunch before I can get my act in gear; I'd planned on some knife practice. It's encouraging, I suppose, that he's feeling comfortable enough to call me, after my revelation yesterday.

"Hey, Jason. How's it going?" Casual enough. Good sign.

"Great. What's up?"

"Nothin' much. Just thought, y'know, we could hang out a little this afternoon. I'm trying to keep my mind off—you know."

I do know. Off whether Debbie is pregnant, and what will happen if she is. The question is, do I want him to see me practicing with my knife?

My silence seems to prompt him to add some entice-ment. "I have my mom's car, if that makes any difference."

That would put a huge dent in the amount of time to and from the park. "The thing is, I have an agenda already. I don't mind if you're in on it, but I need to go to the park."

"For what?"

"I'll tell you when we get here. If you want to go."

"Look, Jason, it's not—it's not related to what you told me yesterday, is it?"

Okay, maybe not quite as cool as he might be. "What do you think, I go there to meet guys or something? No. Nothing along those lines."

So he picks me up around two-thirty. I'm sitting on my front steps, thumbing through a new book on Gandhi I got at the library yesterday. I have sweatclothes on over track duds so I can do a little training after knife practice without coming home first.

At the park it takes me a while to find the place where I used to practice, but I keep looking; it was pretty remote, so no one would be likely to see me. Robert is still mystified, though he seems to trust me.

"What are you looking for, exactly? Tell me, and maybe I can help."

"It's a place I've been before. I don't know how to describe—ah. I think we're here."

And we are. I set down my pack and fish my knife out of it. I flip it into the air so Robert can see it. I catch it just right and flick the blade out. He looks impressed, and I'm feeling good about having him come along.

"Can I hold it? Just for a minute?"

I retract the blade and hand it to him. He holds it a little gingerly and hits the release. He's not prepared for the jerk, and he nearly drops the thing.

"Cool. Where'd you get this, anyway?"

"EBay. It's not exactly legal for me to own it. I'm trusting you, y'know."

He nods, looking serious. "I understand." He hands it back to me.

I let him pick out some nearby targets for me to aim at. Then I choose some, and then I go after leaves. Leaves are useful because I can usually find some about the height an assailant would be, and it's good practice to actually slice something you're thinking of as attacking you. It's a psychological thing.

Robert tries a few moves, but he's not as accurate as I am. "You're good," he tells me, and again I'm glad I've brought him. I'm so vain.

We head back in the late afternoon, talking mostly about how much Robert isn't prepared to be a father. He drops me off at the school yard. I find my way to the cantankerous old gate and let myself in that way. Pack and sweats deposited in a remote corner, I do some stretches and then a couple of warm-up laps before working on my starts, and I move on to dashes after that.

There are a couple of other runners there as well, including Norm Landers from the relay team. Taking a breather, I watch them for a minute. My eyes keep going back to Norm. It's like I'm taking him in for the first time. Maybe now that I'm starting to think of myself as gay, I'm also starting to notice guys in a different way.

And he's worth noticing. First off, he's built for running, like me: lean, just tall enough to get up a good stride but not so tall that he looks like he might topple. His shoulders are a nice balance for the rest of him, and they make an efficient center for his arms to hang from, so they can help in the running. But there's more. There's the thick brown hair, just wavy enough to be interesting. The jaw with clean lines. The straight nose. And, though I can't see them from here, in my mind I can see his gray eyes, framed by long, curling lashes.

At one point he's jogging along in my general direction, I'm looking right at him, and he sees me and waves. The next thing I know, he's close enough for me to confirm my memory of the color of those gray eyes. And the length of the lashes.

"How's it going, Jason?"

"Great. Just getting a little more track time in."

"Wanna work together a little?"

I grin and nod, wondering if he would think I was worth noticing if he were gay. So many ifs.

We do some competitive starts, a few short race lengths, and then we rest for a while, talking about the other guys on the team. Norm says he doesn't like Jimmy Walsh.

"He's so—I don't know. So limited. So Neanderthal. You know?"

I don't feel quite right agreeing with that, so I say, "Plus, he's just out to beat everybody."

"Yeah, or beat up everybody."

We both laugh. I've known Norm for a few years, but we've never actually sat down and talked before.

Norm changes the subject. "It's my seventeenth birthday on Tuesday. I'm getting my new car then."

"Your new car? You already have one, right?" I don't even have to ask; everyone in his group does. Wealthy suburb, umpteen cars. I'm not likely to have a car of my own anytime real soon.

"Yeah, but it's just this old Pontiac my dad got tired of. We're trading it in."

He says something else, but my attention is elsewhere now. Raj is at the high-jump pit, stretching. Norm follows my gaze. "Do you know Raj?" he asks.

Know him? Yeah. In a limited biblical sense. But what do I want Norm to know? "He's helping me prepare for a term paper I want to do on Gandhi," is what I decide to say. It's the truth, sort of, and it accounts for my looking his way. Sort of.

We both watch him for a minute as he takes a few practice runs at the bar, pacing off, analyzing distances and stride lengths.

Norm says, "He's really good." There's a pause. "And he's really good-looking." He turns toward me. "Don't you think?"

Is he pumping me? Does he suspect? I shrug. "I guess so."

Norm's looking at me like he's trying to figure something out. I'm not sure I'm ready for him to do that, so I say, "You practicing anymore today?"

"Nah. Think I'll call it quits. Coach will work us hard enough next week! Hey—d'you feel like stopping someplace for a Coke or something?"

Wow. No one from Norm's clique has ever suggested anything like this with little ol' me. I'm tempted, for the novelty of it and because I'd kind of like to get to know him better. But Raj is here, and I haven't seen him or heard from him since Friday. And everyone else seems to have left.

"Can I take a rain check? I'd like to, but I need to work on a couple of things before tomorrow."

Norm stands. "Let's do that. See you later." He sounds like he actually means it.

I get up and stretch a little, watching to make sure he's gone before I turn my full attention to Raj. He's not actually jumping, it would seem. Just advancing on the bar in kind of a threatening way. I decide to walk over.

I sit on the grass a little ways away from him. At one point, he turns, nods, and then goes back to his attacks. It's like I'm nobody special. I'm not quite sure what to make of this, and I'm almost ready to leave when he comes over to me.

"Come sit under the trees with me?"

Last time we sat "under the trees" we spent most of our time prone. This idea appeals to me a good deal. I fetch my pack.

But we do sit. In a pretty secluded spot too. Raj takes my shoes off and massages my legs, then my feet. It's unbelievable. I would never have thought it could feel so good. The next thing I know we're massaging each other's tongues, lips, asses, whatever.

And then I get an inspiration. Okay, maybe I hadn't been ready to do what Raj might have wanted to that night he came to my house and we went up to my room together. But I've relived in my head what happened in his father's car last Friday night so many times that I'm sure I could do it for him.

I push him down onto his back, pinning his arms with my hands, loving the mild surprise I see on his face. First I tease his lips with my tongue, then flick at the corners of his mouth. He tries to kiss me, but I pull away, smiling at him as lasciviously as I know how. Then I move slowly down his body with my nose, and I let go of one arm so I can use my hand to push down the elastic of his warm-up pants. My fingers walk slowly down while I watch his face. He's breathing through his mouth, eyes mostly closed now.

Good. He's not protesting. I let go of his other arm so I can pull the pants and everything beneath them completely below his hips.

And it's right there, stiff as the wood of the trees, wanting me. That coffee-colored cock that I'd tried so hard not to look at in the showers. And behind it, the almost purple mounds of his balls, looking tender and already bruised. I claim the lot.

His whole body is rigid, legs shaking in tremors, arms out stiff, hands grasping at nothing, jaw pointing to the heaven I want him to feel like he's in. And when he comes, he makes almost no noise. It's like wind in the trees.

He'd swallowed my cum. I'm not quite ready for that. I spit as quietly as I can.

He goes limp. Absolutely limp. It's as if I've extracted from him every ounce of energy he has, every tension, everything that would give him earthbound substance.

Then, eyes still closed, he reaches for me. He pulls my head onto his shoulder and caresses my hair. It feels like hours, or maybe just a few minutes. We don't speak.

Finally we pull apart. He gets his clothes back into order and then lies on the ground, arm under his head, and I lean against a tree trunk and reach for my shoes. We smile at each other like idiots for a minute. Then I remember the book I'd been wanting to show him.

"You think it's something I haven't seen?" he teases.

"They just got it in, that's what the librarian said. So there."

"Where is it? In your pack?" He reaches for it; it's closer to him than me.

I'm pulling a shoe onto my foot when I hear a sharp, hissing sort of noise. I turn just in time to see Raj's hand nearly fling my knife away from him. Like it's burning hot.

Shit.

He looks at me, this ugly scowl on his face. "What in hell is that?"

I blink, shake my head. I don't know what to say. It's a knife, obviously. I hadn't wanted him to know about it, that's true, but I wouldn't have expected this kind of a reaction.

All I can say is, "It's my knife."

"And you do what with it?"

"It's—you know. It's my insurance. My security. It's for when—"

But he doesn't let me finish. He stands, towering over me. "That is not security. That is violence waiting to happen."

"Raj, no! It's to keep violence—"

"Jason, how can you do this? You pretend to me that you care about me, that you care about what's important to me, and yet you have this"—and he kicks at the knife where it lies on the ground, releasing the blade in the process, then jumps back like it's a snake about to bite him—"this instrument of hatred. You carry it with you. You bring it when we are together. You—"

"Raj, will you listen? It's got nothing to do with hatred. Even Gandhi says—"

He's icy now. "Don't you quote Gandhi to me. How dare you presume? And how dare you bring this into my presence?"

I'm angry by this point. He won't listen to me, he won't let me explain, and he's taking this holier-than-thou attitude. As I stand, I'm nearly yelling. "Who the fuck do you think you are, some kind of prince or something?"

Before I can even gauge the look on his face, he's gone. I want to run after him, to get him to understand, to make him see how I fit into Gandhi's philosophy. And I do start, and I call his name. Twice. He ignores me and just keeps walking.

Jesus! What does this mean? I'm still angry, but that doesn't mean I don't hurt. I hurt like hell. How can we have gone from heaven to hell so quickly? I collapse more than sit, lean against one of our trees, feeling like the world is ending.

In a way, it is.

It's dark by the time I make my way home. I must look a mess, bits of twigs and leaves stuck all over me. I didn't care about brushing off once I'd found my knife, closed it, stroked it a few times, and tucked it away.

One sight of me, littered with bits of tree and looking like doom, and Aunt Audrey follows me upstairs. I had kind of thought I'd just curl up on my bed and die slowly, but she's having none of that. She makes me talk.

To be honest, once I start I'm glad. I need to yell at him, but he's not here. So I yell about him. In a way, it's better; he can't interrupt. But I have to be careful. I pretend to Aunt Audrey that Raj and I were talking conceptually, not about an actual knife that I have in my pack this very minute.

"He got all weird. And so suddenly! It was like he's some kind of royalty, and some tiny little thing turns into an offense big enough to go to war over."

She's quiet for a moment, and then she says, "Several years ago there was a new doctor at the hospital. From India. He seemed a little arrogant, which isn't too surprising when it comes to the way some doctors treat nurses, but I know some of the other doctors thought he was unpleasant too. So one day I saw him sitting alone in the cafeteria. He was having a snack or something and reading. I just sat myself down, determined to see if maybe he was just lonely."

"And was he? Or was he really arrogant?"

"As it turns out, I think neither. He was just a little aloof. Reserved, maybe. He was pleasant enough to me that day. Anyway, I asked him a few questions about India, about moving here, and which place he preferred. He told me, 'Oh, India, of course.' I asked, 'What about it, specifically?' And do you know what he said to me? He said, 'Because in India, we have a better standard of living.'

"Well, this puzzled me. So I said, 'Really? Can you give me an example? And he looked at me like he thought I should know. He said, 'In India, we have servants.' "

She chuckles and then says, "I had to stop myself from asking him what the standard of living was like for the servants. But my point is, he was a member of the upper class in India—and remember, India is still very class oriented—and he had servants. Did you say Raj and his sister spent their childhoods there?"

"Yeah."

"And they seem to have money?"

"They must. Their place is huge, and gorgeous."

"So it's entirely possible that they had servants there and

are very accustomed to treating people differently depending on their perception of another person's class."

"Great. So that means I'm like some kind of peasant? And Raj thinks I'm his servant?" As soon as I say this, a couple of scenes come back to me. Scenes in which Raj's attitude toward me had been a little patronizing. I've just assumed it was because he's older and more experienced, but maybe there's more to it than that.

"Jason, I'm sure Raj thinks no such thing. No self-respecting high-caste man would even look twice at someone he thought of as a servant. Or, at least he wouldn't introduce this person to his family but would merely treat him as a source of superficial entertainment. No, I think it might be just that Raj is accustomed to thinking of himself in a certain way, and he was so upset he retreated automatically into that behavior pattern."

"But Aunt Audrey, you should have seen him! He—you know, he actually looked regal. Or maybe just self-righteous. He certainly made me feel like some kind of worthless nobody."

"A worthless nobody wouldn't have been able to upset him like that."

She sits thinking again for a minute, and I let her. I'm going over in my mind the way he'd just assumed I should learn about Gandhi because he wanted me to know. And his professorial patience in the car, when he was trying to get me to guess at lessons learned from *La Cage*. Like I was his kid brother or something, like it was his job to teach me about life from his exalted position.

Finally Aunt Audrey says, "I wonder. I just wonder. There may be something about knives in particular that bothers him. Were you talking about any special kind?"

I lie. "Uh-uh. Just, you know, the kind of knife a guy

might carry for protection, like if he was in a dangerous area or something."

"A gang member, perhaps?"

"Yeah, maybe. That's a good example." Whew. She doesn't seem to have caught on to anything.

"You may just have to wait until you have a chance to talk with him, and you can ask about it. But when you do—"

"He's not going to give me that chance. I don't think he wants to see me again."

"As I was saying, when you do, you'll need to approach it very sensitively. I may be completely wrong, but if I'm not then it will be an extremely touchy subject."

"Didn't you hear me?"

"Yes, sweetie, I heard you. But I happen to think you are too special for him to dismiss that easily. I think you will haunt him."

Chapter 10

Enter Stage Left

Whether I haunt him or not, he haunts me. I'm determined he's the one who owes me the apology, so I act like he's not there. Which, really, he isn't, except during track practice. But since we aren't in any of the same events, it's not an issue there. Except that I have to force myself to stop looking for him. Especially in the shower.

The meet is less than two weeks away, and I need to concentrate. Between thinking about Raj and trying to pretend in front of Uncle Steve that nothing is wrong, I'm off my stride. I have to take action. It almost doesn't matter what it is.

After practice on Monday, I find Norm in the locker room. "Hey. How's it going?"

He seems startled, surprised I've approached him. Is this a mistake? Then he says, "Uh, great. Great. You?"

I'm gonna go for it. "No major complaints. Listen, remember that rain check from yesterday?" I wait, giving him a chance to be really clear with me what his invitation had meant.

He smiles. He actually smiles. "Yeah! You trading it in for the actual thing?"

"Absolutely. Is today good?"

He looks around, but I can't tell for what. "You know, today is just great. Meet me on the front steps?"

While I'm waiting, sitting on a step, I remember that tomorrow is his birthday. He comes up behind me quietly and bends a knee into my back to let me know he's there. I don't know why, but this seems like almost an intimate thing to do. He sits down beside me.

"Looking forward to tomorrow?" I ask.

His grin says he's flattered I remember. "You bet. We're picking the car up after school. Can't wait!"

He leads the way to where his Pontiac is parked, and we head out. I'm not sure if he has a place in mind, but soon it's apparent he does. It's not a hangout where kids from school would be likely to go.

We order some sodas and fries. I'm feeling a little awkward now. I don't really know what to say to a guy like Norm. We've talked about track on the drive here, but that ground is about covered now. Suddenly there's a ringing noise. Norm must have a cell phone. But he doesn't move. It rings again.

"You're not even going to see who it is?" I ask.

He looks at me a minute, then down at his hands, then back at me. "I'd rather talk to you."

There's something about the expression on his face. And suddenly I get it. He's gay. And he seems to know that I am.

How?

I decide to play along until I'm sure. "What would you like to talk about?"

He nibbles a fry, looks at what's left in his hand. "I'm really glad you claimed your rain check. I was kind of thinking you wouldn't want to."

"Why wouldn't I?"

He takes a deep breath. "Look, Jason, please don't get upset if this is the wrong thing to say, but—well, yesterday at the track I was trying to find out if you're with Raj. You know."

There's no doubt in my mind now. But what's the answer? Am I "with Raj"? Sure doesn't seem like it to me. I say, "I'm not. Not in any important way."

" 'Cause it seemed like you might be waiting to talk to him. Yesterday."

"I was, in a way. We do have a little history." Very little. "But I don't think he's that interested. And if he isn't, then . . ." I shrug, letting my words trail off, denying the feelings of guilt, of betrayal. I feel like I'm cheating on Raj.

"Then you, uh, you might be willing to go someplace with me? This weekend? I'll have my car."

I decide to play this one a little cooler than I'd done with Raj. I flash Norm a sideways grin. "Depends. What kind of car is it?"

He's grinning now too. "You'll love it. It's a convertible BMW. The weather's a little cool yet, but we could put the top down anyway, just for a bit. What do you say?"

God. What *can* I say? "Sure. Where d'you wanna go?"

"A friend of mine is having a party at his house. We, uh, you know, we'll have to pretend we just happened to go there together. I mean, you'll be my guest, but—do you know what I'm trying to say?"

I know, all right. It means he's not out. For that matter, neither am I, really. "Sure," is all I give him.

"Anyway, there'll be dancing and food and booze. You'll meet some really rad kids. Plus, we'll take a ride in the car."

I guess he wants to make out in the car. This is feeling kind of weird to me, but everything about my life is a little weird right now.

He's looking really pleased with himself. "Jesus, Jason! This is great. I've—well, I've been watching you for a while. You always seem so cool. Like if someone wants to be friends with you, that's fine, but if they don't, that's fine too."

Cool? Me? Wow. All I have to do is nothing that will spoil that image, and I'll be seen as cool by the in-crowd? Or maybe just by Norm. Raj doesn't think of me as cool, I'm pretty sure of that.

By the time I get home I'm feeling totally overwhelmed. Norm Landers is gay? And he wants to be with me? Maybe nobody else in his group is gay. But—*me*? Ye gods! He's even good-looking. This year isn't turning out anything like I'd thought it would.

I'm careful to make sure Uncle Steve isn't within earshot when I tell Aunt Audrey I'm going out with Norm. But even she seems a little hesitant. "I thought you didn't get along with those boys."

" 'Those boys,' Aunt Audrey? Should I be prejudiced against them because they have money and I don't? Raj has money. That didn't bother you."

She can't come up with any real objections. All she says is, "Just be careful, Jason. You don't know these boys."

Tuesday after school I do a little more knife practice. I just feel like it. I'm in some kind of zone too. My aim is sure, my motions are clean. I like this knife. Hell, I love this knife. Take that, Nagaraju!

But I dream about him. I can't help that.

Chapter 11

Of Knives and Brothers

By Wednesday I'm feeling much better than I had when the week started. Norm asking me out has done wonders for my self-esteem.

In English Lit, Meg seems a little down. I can't imagine I have anything to do with that; I couldn't have been that important to her. I mean, just one date, weeks ago now. But she doesn't volunteer in class like she usually does, and when Williams calls on her, she hasn't been following. She's so embarrassed she seems almost ready to cry.

There's no track practice tonight. I'd been planning to do a little work anyway, but Raj might be there, and as I close my locker I see Meg making a beeline for the front door. I run and catch up with her. I feel I owe her something. And besides, I've told Aunt Audrey about me, and I've told Robert, and they were both fine. And Uncle Steve may have issues, but it did seem as though he was trying his best, just like Aunt Audrey had said. It seems only fair to tell Meg too, and I can't think of a good reason not to.

"Meg? Meg, hang on, will you?"

She stops, but I can tell she doesn't want to. "What do you want?"

"Listen, can we talk? I, uh, I haven't been very honest with you, and I think you deserve better."

The look on her face tells me she agrees with that much. So we walk to this little park a couple of blocks from school and sit on a bench. And not close to each other either. She's not going to make it easy; she's silent as a grave.

"Meg, you probably think I'm some kind of jerk. I wouldn't blame you if you did. But I'm not. I was just confused."

She makes this face, eyes to the heavens.

"No, no, really. Hear me out. When I went out with you, it was really so Robert could go out with Debbie."

Her glare tells me this isn't going well.

"No, wait. That was stupid. And it's not—can I start again?"

She just looks at me. I get up and stand in front of her.

"Robert wanted help meeting girls. I went with him to the mall, and it was supposed to be just for practice, but then he asked Debbie out. And I had just been thinking how cool it was that you enjoyed poetry, 'cause I do, too, and I've always liked you. So I asked you." This was a little better, but not much.

"Plus, I was trying to figure something out. About me. Something that, at the time, I didn't want to be right."

Bogging down now. Silence. Staring.

"I'm gay."

More staring. And then: "Jason, I can't tell you how delighted I am that I was the one who helped you figure that out. You've made me feel like a real woman." And before I can register that she's being sarcastic, she's walking away.

That's not fair! She can't just turn this thing on me like that. I chase after her, dancing backward in front of her as she walks.

"Meg, will you please try to understand? This didn't have anything to do with you. My being gay has nothing to do with how boys feel about you."

She stops moving. "Nothing to do with me? Yeah, I guess that was the problem, wasn't it? It could have been anyone."

"Look, do you think this is easy for me? Do you think I wanted to be gay? Do you think I get any thrill out of telling you this? Almost no one knows, Meg. I've told two people. Three. All right, only a few people know."

"And the only reason you're telling me is because it has nothing to do with me."

"I'm telling you because I feel like a bastard. I feel like I hurt you. And I—I like you, Meg."

She's not saying anything, but she's not walking away either.

I move closer so I can speak softly. "I like you a lot. And I've found very few people in this world I really like. I'm sorry I hurt you. I really am. It's so easy to hurt someone. There's a lot of it going around. I can't stand that I made it worse. That's why I'm telling you."

Her voice is softer now, but she still doesn't sound like she's ready to be my best friend. "Okay, so you've told me. Now leave me alone."

All I can do is stand aside and watch her go.

Thursday after dinner I get a phone call I'm not expecting. Track practice was grueling, I hadn't felt like I was performing well, and my aunt wouldn't let me off doing dishes even though I begged. So I'm half asleep when the phone rings.

Raj!

But no. Close, though. It's Anjani.

"Jason, I have to talk to you. Do you have a minute?"

She has to talk to me? Her brother is who has to talk to me. "Sure. What's up?"

"I—what's up? I'm calling about Raj, of course."

"What about him?"

She makes this exasperated noise. "Honestly, you men! Are you going to pretend you don't care about *him* either?"

"Is that how he feels about me?"

"You know very well it isn't. I know you two had some kind of quarrel on Sunday, because he came home looking like he'd fought a tiger and lost. He's barely come out of that temple he calls a bedroom since. I forced my way in yesterday and made him tell me what was going on. He didn't say much, but he seems to think you've betrayed him in some way. Will you talk to me?"

I'm not really sure why I should, except that I like Anjani. "First, tell me why you think it's me that's upset him."

"Jason, are you serious? You're all he's talked about for three weeks! Jason this, Jason that, Jason is so smart, Jason is so glorious, Jason is—"

"Glorious? He said that?"

"Yes. He's head-over-heels for you. Don't you know that?"

"I—it's a little hard to tell."

There's a harrumphing sort of noise over the line. "I can imagine. But take it from me. And you . . . how do you feel about him?"

Where to start? "Anjani, he wigged out on me, okay? He found something he didn't like, and instead of letting me explain about it, he just made all these assumptions and he—he dismissed me! He acted like he was king of the universe and I had committed some horrendous thing I didn't even know about. It was like my not understanding about it was half of my offense. He wouldn't listen, he wouldn't come back when I begged him to, he just marched off like some high-and-mighty prince."

This is exhausting. And I was tired before I started.

"But how do you feel about him?"

I take a deep breath. "All right, if you have to know, I love him. I don't know why, because when he isn't kissing me he treats me either like some enraptured student kneeling at his feet or like I'm one class up from your Untouchables. And then he confuses the hell out of me and kisses me again. I guess I don't really know how I feel about him."

"Sounds like Raj, all right. But can you tell me what it was that upset him on Sunday? What did he find?"

"If I tell you, I'll have to kill you."

"What?"

"Sorry. It's just that it's—well, it's something I'm not supposed to have."

"Is that why he was upset?"

"No. It would have upset him regardless."

"What was it?" I don't speak, so she tries again. "Jason, please trust me. I'm only thinking of you and Raj."

I have to admit, she's being a pretty wonderful sister. So I say, "Promise you won't mention this to anyone? And I mean anyone?"

"I promise."

"I have a knife. A switchblade."

Her sharp intake of breath sounds so much like the hissing noise Raj made when he found my knife that I nearly drop the phone. More silence. Then, "Now I understand. I'm surprised you don't." Her tone has changed.

"Oh, I understand. He's gone on and on about Gandhi and nonviolence. But you know, Gandhi understood that violence isn't always avoidable. He understood the need to fight. And I think he would have understood the need to prevent violence, and he would have understood why this knife has helped me. I think I'd have been dead a few times if I didn't have it. It keeps the goons off me."

"You—you think this has to do with Gandhi?"

"What else?"

"Oh Jason! Oh my God. He didn't tell you?"

"Tell me what?"

"I guess he doesn't want you to know."

I wait, but she says nothing more.

"Anjani, I trusted you. It's your turn. What is it?"

Her voice is a little shaky. "He'll kill me. Well, you know what I mean. Jason, just as I promised, you must promise. Do you? You can't even tell Raj that you know this. If he decides to tell you, you must act as though you don't know. Do you understand?"

"It's not an issue. He isn't talking to me."

"He will. You're inside him now. Do you promise?"

Inside him, am I? It would be only fair, if I could believe it. He's certainly way deep inside me. "Promise."

"When Raj was eleven, and we were still in India . . . Let me start again. Raj had an identical twin brother. Sampath. When they were eleven, Sampath was killed. He was knifed to death when the boys were playing someplace they weren't supposed to be."

I'm sitting there, blinking stupidly. Images fly before me. Finally I manage, "Did Raj see it happen?"

Nearly in a whisper, she says, "Yes."

Aloof. He's chosen aloof, he'd said. How can you go on after seeing your twin brother knifed to death? On one hand, I'm furious with him for not telling me and then letting it be the reason he leaves me. On the other—how could he talk about it?

Then she says, "Remember at dinner that night, when Dad was awkward about answering your questions? About what he does? He was supposed to stay in India after his brother came here. *He* was supposed to manage that side of the business, not his cousin. But after Sampath was killed, and Raj— well, when he got so withdrawn, both Dad and Mum decided they had to leave."

"Thank you," I tell her. "Thank you for telling me. Maybe someday he'll tell me about his brother himself. But I'm not holding my breath."

"But if he called you, you would talk to him?"

Talk to him! I'd send him a thousand kisses.

But would I talk to him? "Look, Anjani, I can only imagine what that must have been like, what it must still be like. He didn't tell me about it; okay, I wish he had, and maybe he would have in time. But what he did do is hold this against me as though I did know. Or as though I should somehow be expected to know. What kind of a relationship is that?"

"But would you talk to him? You said you love him."

"Of course I love him. Who wouldn't? But he turns against me because of something I can't know."

"Jason, he feels everything so deeply. And that's how he feels about you. Deeply."

"How can you be so sure?"

"Because he hasn't talked about anyone the way he's talked about you. Ever. And because of how far he has retreated since Sunday."

I imagine him holed up in his room, incense clouding the air, with him sitting penance or whatever it would be called and chanting. "Of course I'd talk to him. But he's not going to call. And it doesn't sound like a good idea for me to call him. What about an e-mail?"

"No. Don't call; it will merely hurt you, because it's too

soon. And we all share the same e-mail address, so you shouldn't use that anyway. It will take time, Jason, but he will call. And in the meantime, I will call. I will let you know how he is. Don't you call me, or he'll know. And he can't know; he'd be horrified if he knew I'd called you at all. Do you understand?"

"Oh yes, I can understand that." I can see Raj horrified. All I have to do is close my eyes and remember. "Um, why only one e-mail address? What's going on there?"

"You met my father. Can't you imagine he'd want to know what everyone was up to? Not that he ever uses it, but he could. He could look anytime. And we all know that."

In a lot of ways, I realize as I hear this, I have things pretty good. Almost makes me feel sorry for Raj. And in one way, I do. I say, "Tell me something. Was Raj a loner before Sampath died?"

"The two boys together were like one loner. Sampath was the sun, and Raj the moon. Raj went into a sort of trance when Sampath died. Wouldn't speak for weeks. He didn't speak until we had moved over here, and it was like he hadn't even realized we were moving until it was done."

So he retreated after losing Sampath. And now he's retreating after losing me.

"Is that why you moved?"

"A number of things happened at once, but certainly it was the deciding factor."

"What did he say? When he spoke again?"

"He—he called my name. It was night, and from his room he called me and called me until I heard him and went to him. And then he cried."

I take a shaky breath. This must be the "medical problem" he'd mentioned to Uncle Steve.

"Jason, please don't give up on him. He's worth so much. And he loves you."

It's me whispering now. It's all I can manage. "I love him too."

So I don't tell her I'm going out with Norm on Saturday. I don't tell her I curse Raj while I slice at leaves with my knife. But I've told her what she needs to know. I guess the rest is up to him.

Chapter 12

False Impressions

Norm picks me up at seven-thirty on Saturday. The BMW is this frosty shade of pale blue, and the top is down. Aunt Audrey is watching out the window, and her face tells me she disapproves. And then he honks his horn.

She turns to me.

"I know, I know." I go out to the car.

"Hey, handsome," Norm says quietly.

"Hey. This is some car."

He jerks his head toward the passenger side.

"Norm, can you come in for just a minute? My Aunt Audrey is really looking forward to meeting you."

He looks kind of blank. "Why?"

"Why what?"

"Why does she want to meet me? She doesn't know, does she?"

"Know what? That I'm gay? Yeah. She knows."

In a kind of fog, he turns off the engine. "Jesus, Jason. You didn't tell me that."

"Your folks don't know?"

"Are you shittin' me? No way."

"Just come in and say hello, and then we can leave."

He's recovered pretty much by the time we get inside, and he's sweetness and light. But I'm freaked out, because it isn't just Aunt Audrey now. Uncle Steve is there too. And he insists on Norm telling him exactly where this party is. I grab my jacket and start to follow Norm out the door when I hear Aunt Audrey say, "Eleven o'clock, Jason."

I step back in. "It was twelve with Raj."

"We knew a little something about Raj."

I don't say ah, yes, or boo, just look at her and then leave. She's not being fair. I decide not to tell Norm; we'll see how the evening goes.

We leave the top down. Norm takes a direction away from the Oakwood development, where the party is, and heads out of town on a highway. I don't know where he's going, but I'm not going to ask. I'm going to be cool.

Soon it gets too cold driving with the top down, so we pull over at a rest stop and put it up. When we get back in, Norm doesn't turn the key right away. He just sits there, looking at me like he's waiting for something. Finally I get it: I have to take the lead.

"Y'know," I tell him, lowering my voice, "this gearshift thing is in the way."

"I think you'll find it's worth working around it."

Man, does this kid know how to kiss. My whole face is wet, and I can't get enough. But I'm wearing a snug pair of jeans, and my hard-on is testing the seams. And then Norm's hand makes it worse.

I'm groaning now, and he's still kissing me and kneading my crotch. Something's going to explode.

"Wait," he says.

Wait! Is he fucking kidding? I massage myself while he fetches something from the rear compartment. Then he undoes his pants and tells me to do the same, and he hands me a small towel like the one he has on his legs.

Now he's looking at me, hard, and he flips open this plastic bottle. He takes my left hand and oozes something into it, and then into his right. Then he reaches for me, and with his left hand he guides mine onto him, and suddenly there's this marvelous mutual thing going on.

Moksha. Nirvana. Heaven. I don't care what you call it. I am in another world. I'm just barely with it enough to remember what the towel is for when the time comes. When I come. Norm comes right after me.

We sit there, panting in unison for a few minutes, and then he kisses me again. It's less frantic now, but still very, very sexy.

Once we're zipped up again, we're too out of it to do anything else. So we recline the seats a little, hold hands, and veg. I doze off once or twice; don't know if he does or not.

When we're finally alert enough for speaking, Norm digs in the back again and comes out with a bottle of vodka. He looks around the rest stop and then takes a swig and hands it to me, and I do the same. It burns. I can't remember ever sucking this stuff from a bottle. Once when I was maybe ten I snuck some of Uncle Steve's, but I put it in a glass. Then I stuck the tip of my tongue into it and decided to add a little water. I didn't like it then, and I don't much like it now, but I don't see a good way to avoid that swig without seeming like a little kid. If I'm gonna hang with guys like Norm, aren't I gonna have to be at least a little cool? I won't change who I am—not for anybody—but this is the first time I've had a chance like this, and I'm not gonna blow it over something that might not matter very much. I'll just make sure I don't overdo this stuff. And that Norm doesn't either; he's driving.

He says, "So how come you told your aunt and uncle?"

"How come you don't tell your folks?"

"You are kidding, right? They'd fuckin' freak. I'm just trying to keep my grades up so I can get into a really great school where I can be who I am. Till then, I'm not rocking any boats."

"D'you think they wouldn't pay for college or something, if they knew?"

He sucks at the bottle again. "They'd kick me out."

"So, who does know then?"

"Only guys like you. A few guys I've been with, you know. Raj."

"Raj? Raj knows?" Has Raj gone out with Norm? I'll kill him.

"I approached him. A lot like I approached you. So that only someone who had an idea what was going on would know what I meant. And he knew, all right."

"So you went out with him?"

He hands me the bottle and shakes his head. "No. He's pretty stuck-up, really. You?"

"Just once." I sort of have to admit this. I swig and hand the bottle back.

We sit in silence a minute or so, contemplating life. Sex. Vodka. Then Norm caps the bottle and hands it to me to resettle in the back. He starts the engine, and back on the highway he finds an exit. We're off again, this time to Oakwood.

So Raj wouldn't go out with Norm. And I will. Guess that puts me in my place, huh? And what would he think, if he knew? Do I care?

Yes. I do care. Suddenly this whole thing feels like a big mistake. I hardly know this guy, and I feel slutty. I even brought condoms with me.

We ride in silence for another several minutes. I'm hoping Norm thinks of it as companionable silence. He breaks it.

"You do dance, don't you?"

"Yeah. I love dancing. But I've never danced with a boy before."

He clears his throat. "Um, look, maybe I wasn't clear the other day. We can't actually dance together at this thing. D'you get it?"

I get it. But I'm cool, so I just make a face that I hope says, "Chicken."

The house, when we get there, is like a small palace. All the cars are along the lines of Norm's, or even more expensive looking. I'm out of my element, and I start to panic. What the hell was I thinking? There will be kids from school here who know I'm not cool, who know I'm just the smart kid who gets good grades and doesn't know how to have fun.

But I remind myself I'm with Norm.

And I am, right up until we're inside. Then suddenly I'm on my own. Not knowing what else to do, I find the food table and try to look as though I don't really want any of it. I've put a few things onto a napkin when Norm is there suddenly, with a girl, and a beer for me.

"Jason, this is Kathy. She's from Wilson High."

"Ah, our nemesis." I figure she'll know what this means; our school and theirs compete like warring siblings at everything from concert band to football teams. But she looks blank.

So I try for a recovery. "Norm and I are racing against your track team and two others in a week."

"So you're on the track team? What events?"

Okay, now we can talk. But it never goes much deeper than that. Norm winks at me and disappears again, and Kathy and I dance for a while. At some point this guy comes along and cuts in, and I'm a free agent again.

I decide it's time for a breather, so I go on a hunt for a

door that leads outside. The house is big enough so that this is harder than you might think. I finally manage to get out onto a deck, where there are a few couples necking and some kids smoking. As it happens, one of them is Norm.

"Jason, come on over."

It's cool out here, but manageable. Norm introduces me to a couple of guys. One of them, Evan Soucie, actually lives here. He just nods at me, as his hands are occupied with the rolled cigarette he's inhaling from. But it doesn't smell like tobacco.

In a flash it dawns on me what it is. I've never been offered marijuana before, and I don't want it now. Call me a control freak, but I don't like the idea of letting some substance change my behavior for me. I didn't even drink the beer Norm gave me earlier; the swig or two of vodka in the car was enough.

Evan hands the roach to Norm, who takes a drag, holds his breath, and holds it toward me. I smile and shake my head. He jabs it at me, so I take it, but when I don't use it, another guy takes it.

Norm exhales, keeping his eyes on me, and then says, "What's the idea?"

"Training. You shouldn't either. Not a week before the meet." I have absolutely no idea whether this is a logical thing to say or not, but it seems to have the right impression on Evan.

"You're really dedicated. What's the matter with you, Norm? You don't care about the school's good name? You'd let your pleasure-seeking jeopardize our chances for victory?"

Or maybe it's not the right impression. I can't quite tell how facetious he's being. Then he removes any doubt. "I suppose this also means you're not having any ass tonight either, eh?"

For some reason most of the other guys think this is hysterically funny. I guess you have to be stoned. I stand there a minute, watching Evan, contemplating how much fun it would be to ask if he really knew what kind of ass Norm wants. Finally I clap him on the shoulder, and as I'm walking away, I say, "Have a ball, boys."

This has more of an effect than I would have expected. All the laughing stops, and suddenly Norm is at my elbow.

"Jason?"

I don't stop walking. I'm headed for the backyard, where there's drug-free air. All I say is, "Yeah?"

He doesn't say anything, so I turn to look at him. We stand there. I'm waiting.

Finally he says, "See, this is what I meant. You don't care what everyone else is doing, you just do what you think you should do. I—I don't know how you get away with it. I wish I could do it."

There's this pity that comes from nowhere, pity for the poor little rich boy who's as much a victim of his background as he is a beneficiary of it. He's always been on the "in" side, and he feels terrified to do anything that would put him "out."

"Stick with me, kid," I tell him. I'm still in my cool mode, and it seems the right thing to say. I move forward again until I find a tree I want to sit under.

Norm is still standing where I left him, unsure whether to come "out" with me or go back to his crowd. He decides on me, but he just stands at my feet, hands in his pockets, kicking at nothing.

"You don't want to sit with me?" I prompt.

He shakes his head. "Can't do that. It will look like—you know."

I wait about as long as I can stand it. If he'd sit down, we might have a nice conversation. Or if he'd go away, I could sit here on my own for a while. But I get up and go back into the house, Norm at my elbow again.

The feeling I have is so weird. Like I'm someone else. It's like I'm floating through this scene where everyone else seems desperate to care about nothing. Their eyes are too bright and unfocused. They laugh too loud, at nothing. I'm not used to feeling above this crowd.

There's one girl sitting on a chair, alone. She's watching me. Have I seen her before? Don't think so. I ignore Norm and walk over to her. Her eyes get bigger, maybe wondering what I'm about to do.

"My name's Jason. Would you dance with me?"

She stares at me a minute, and then she stands up. I take her hand, and we move to where there's some room. I ignore the fast pace of the song that's playing, and I hold her close and just sway back and forth. She's with me. She gets it. We're both outsiders, and we're ignoring what's going on around us and doing what we want to do.

I want to ask why she's here. I want to ask her name. I want to know what it is about her that makes me feel like we're the same. But if I do any of those things, she could think I'm interested in her in a way I can't be. I'm not going to do that to a girl again.

Eventually I take her back to her chair. "Thank you," I say. "That was perfect."

In a way, I'm thinking to myself as I head for the kitchen to get a glass of water, that was just as bad as talking to her. I kind of swoop in, make her feel wanted for a few minutes, and then disappear.

Like Raj did to me. This is so fucking complicated.

I decide to take the glass of water to her. And then we both go out into the backyard and share it. We sit under the tree. Her name is Elaine, and she's Evan's cousin. She's visiting for the weekend, and she couldn't think of a way not to be at this party.

"I feel so out of place here," she says, handing me the glass. "I don't know any of these kids, Evan's not doing anything to help, and I hate the smell of beer, and I think I smelled pot."

"You did. I was offered some."

"I don't think I want to do that."

"I know I don't. At least, not here. I mean, if the circumstances were different, if I were with someone I trusted, then maybe. But not like this." I don't want to seem totally uncool.

"Do you know where you're going next year?"

"Next year?"

"Which college?"

Wow. "Did you think I was a senior?"

"Yes. You aren't?"

"Nope. Be another year yet."

"Oh."

I take a sip from the glass I'm holding. "Where are you going?"

"Oh, I'm a junior too. I just thought . . ."

"Thanks, I guess."

"You just seem older than most of the guys here."

"I'm not drunk."

Her laugh is pretty. "I guess that's the difference."

Norm is headed our way now, and he has a girl in tow. They sit on the grass near us, giggling about the possibility of earthworms being under them. The other girl, Tammy, doesn't shut up. I wish they hadn't found us. I'm not here to bolster Norm's nongay reputation, and I liked talking to Elaine. Conspicuously, I look at my watch. It's only ten o'clock, but—what the hell.

"Elaine, you've been the best part of the evening for me. I'm kind of sorry that I need to leave now."

I look at Norm, who's got this startled look on his face. I don't say anything, and finally he says, "Can we talk over here a minute?" We walk away and stand with our backs to the girls.

"Just what are you doing?" he wants to know.

"I'm ready to leave. Are you going to drive me, or should I call a cab?"

"Jason, Jason. Please, man, I want to take you home, but not until we've had a little more time together." His breath smells like stale beer, and the smell of pot hangs over him. I don't really think I want any more time with him tonight.

"Norm, tell you what. If you want to do something sometime that will give us a chance to talk, to get to know each other, let me know. But walking around pretending I'm someone I'm not, with someone who's pretending he's something he isn't, is not getting me off."

"You're embarrassing me, man."

"In what way?"

"How can I leave early just to take you home?"

"Fine. I wouldn't want that. But I can't embarrass you. You have to do that for yourself." I turn and walk away.

"Jason, fuck you!"

I just keep walking. Elaine catches up with me on the deck.

"Jason, um, this may be a little awkward, but if you need a ride, I can give you one."

In my fury at Norm, I'm about to turn her down, but then she adds, "And you'd be doing me a favor. It would get me away from this crowd. Please?"

I wait out front while she fetches the keys to Evan's car, and Norm finds me.

"Jason, look, I'm sorry. It's just that I had this whole idea of what tonight would be like, of how we'd be together afterward, and you're leaving."

"How would we be together, Norm? Were we going to have sex?"

"Keep your voice down. It's not like you don't want to." He pulls me into the shadows and stands very close, reminding me again of how he smells.

I want to tell him I don't want him at all like he is now, but I don't want a scene either. "It's like I said a minute ago. When you're sober and not stoned, I like you. If you want to spend some quality time with me, let me know. But right now I'm going home."

He steps closer still and pushes his fingers into my hair. And now, behind him, I can see something I hadn't before. I think it's the guy who had cut in on me with Kathy, the girl from Wilson High. He's watching Norm and me pretty closely.

Just then Elaine comes out of the house and Norm steps hastily away from me. He walks past her and back inside.

"Ready?" I ask, sounding more chipper than I feel.

The car is penned in rather badly by others, and she's nervous about getting it out. So I do that part for her and turn the wheel over to her. I make a point of noting landmarks so she can find her way back again as I direct her toward my house. In between, we talk a little about her school, her parents, her relationship with Evan. Then she floors me.

"My parents want me to marry him."

"But—you're cousins. You aren't supposed to do that, are you?"

"I'm adopted."

What does one say to that? "I'm sorry" seems all wrong, as does "That's okay. I'm an orphan." But guess what I say?

"I see. I'm an orphan myself."

"What?"

"I live with my uncle and aunt. My parents died in a car crash when I was two."

"I'm sorry." At least it was appropriate for her to say it.

"So, are you going to marry him?"

"Evan? I don't like him any better than he likes me. I only agreed to this visit because my folks promised me my own car if I came here and made nice to him."

"Where are his folks tonight, anyway?"

"They're there. Upstairs."

"Do you think they know there's pot?"

She shrugs. "As long as the noise doesn't get too loud and nobody gets raped or murdered, they probably don't much care."

And Aunt Audrey wanted me home by eleven.

"Why was Norm so mad at you?"

I don't know this girl from Eve. I can't tell her Norm is gay; it seems like some kind of unwritten law, or it ought to be, that you can't out someone else.

"He gave me a ride over, and he wasn't ready to leave. I'm not sure why he thought anyone cared if I left with someone else."

"And a girl, at that. Maybe that was it. He's jealous." I glance at her profile, and the smile I see there worries me a little. Does she know? Who might be jealous, and why? Then she adds, "Maybe he wants to leave with a girl too, and you did it first."

Whew.

We're at my house, and Elaine pulls into the driveway.

"Do you think you could write down directions for me? So I can find my way back better?" She fishes a pad and pen out of her handbag and gives them to me. I talk while I'm writing, so she can understand the turns and landmarks we passed on the way. When I hand her back her things, she has this sweet smile on her face.

"Thanks, Jason. It was a treat getting away, and you're a great guy to talk to." And before I really know what's happening, she pulls on my arm and kisses me. I have to admit, it's a nice kiss. Then she does it again, and I'm getting into it.

Panic sets in. I pull back.

"What?" she wants to know. "What is it?"

"Elaine, I—" If I tell her, will she react like Meg? And I was enjoying it! What was that about, when I'm supposed to be gay? "I can't. I'm sorry."

"You're already with someone else?"

That's it. "Yes."

She nods. "Okay. Thanks for telling me. Not everyone does."

"You're a terrific girl. If circumstances were different . . ." Very different. "Thanks so much for the ride. You're a lifesaver." I give her one more light kiss and get out. She waves as she drives off.

As I turn toward the house, I see Aunt Audrey at the window. I open the door, close the door, hang up my jacket, and sit on the sofa. I know she's going to make me anyway. At least Uncle Steve is nowhere in sight.

"Interesting evening, Jason?" She sits in a chair across from me.

"You could say that."

"That didn't look like Norm's car. In fact, it didn't look like Norm."

"Norm was in no condition to drive. He'd had too many beers."

"How many did you have?"

"None." She didn't ask about vodka.

"And the girl?"

"She's the cousin of Norm's friend, the guy whose house it was. She wasn't having a good time, so she offered to drive me home. It was either that or call you."

"And did you show her a good time?"

"What?"

"I saw the way you were kissing. Are you playing both sides of the fence now?"

"Aunt Audrey, she kissed *me*. We sort of hit it off. Both outsiders at that place."

"And she didn't mind that you're gay?"

"She doesn't know I'm gay. I didn't see a good way to tell her that without giving Norm away, and he's not out."

"This should be an interesting relationship."

"Why are you giving me a hard time? I'm home early, I'm not drunk, I haven't done anything illegal, and I haven't even needed any condoms."

She sits back and rubs her face a minute. "I'm sorry, Jason. You're right. It's just that I felt sorry for that girl, afraid she might think a terrific boy like you might be available to her. And seeing you go off with that boy earlier put my back up. I didn't like him. I'm sorry if that hurts you. He just didn't seem honest to me."

There's that word again. Honest. Honesty. Honestly. Honor.

"Then you'll be delighted to know he's pissed at me. Seems I embarrassed him, not seeing the huge benefits I could reap as a result of him bringing me to that shindig, not wanting to stay and get wasted like they'll probably be soon."

"Are you hurt? Upset?"

I shrug. "No. Disappointed. He's nice, when he isn't under the influence of people he has to lie to just to be around. I might see him again, but not like that. And I don't know if he's ready to let someone get to know him. So . . ."

She nods, sighs, and then grins at me. "I got some ice cream while you were gone."

We go into the kitchen and attack the stuff like we're five years old. It's a side of her I don't remember seeing. I like it.

Lying in bed later, I'm troubled by a couple of things. One is the kiss. Elaine's. My aunt has a point, and in the interest of honor, honesty, I will do my best to avoid leading anyone on. Girl or boy. But am I gay? Is Uncle Steve right? And is it possible to be less than 100 percent gay? I decide not to mess around with girls until I've figured this out. After all, I've never lost any sleep over a girl. I lose lots of sleep over Raj.

The other thing is, I don't know if I'd go out with Norm again or not. What I said about him to Aunt Audrey reminds me of one of the lessons I was supposed to get from *La Cage*. One of the lessons from Raj. About pretending to be something you're not.

Plus, something in me—heart or head, I can't tell—feels like shit, going out on Raj. Another part argues with it. Raj took himself out of the picture, after all; what do I owe him?

But then that other voice comes back. It says, *Fine, but what do you really want?*

What I really want is Raj.

I settle in, prepared to lose a little more sleep.

Chapter 13

Jason on Hold

I must be really off my stride. Coach says he wants to talk to me after track Monday afternoon. With Norm acting so formal, and Raj so aloof, it's no wonder my performance isn't making Coach happy. I'm not exactly happy myself.

After I shower, I knock on Coach's office door.

"Come in, Jason. Thanks for stopping by. Close the door, will you? And take a seat."

Close the door. Sounds serious. I wait for him to speak.

"Remember the day I asked you about Meg?" He waits; I nod. "Remember you promised to let me know if there was something you needed to talk about?"

I'm confused now. "Is there?"

"Cute. Don't be cute; it doesn't suit you. You led me to believe that you and Meg were going to work something out. But she's moping around, and you're not focusing. Now. Is there anything you want to talk about?"

"How do you know she's moping?"

"Her father and I are good friends. I used to date his wife." He grins. "Just a little humanizing character development, if you like. The point is, what is it that needs to be worked out?"

"Has she said anything about me?"

"Not a word. Except to get all stony when I asked about you over the weekend. My wife and I were over there for dinner."

"You asked about me? Why?"

"I was under the impression you were dating. Or is that what she's upset about?"

I just shake my head. "Coach, we had one date, okay? And then I didn't call her again, and I guess I didn't say hi often enough, and she'd been left with the impression that we'd had a really good time. She'd just told me that when you saw us. Up in the bleachers."

"Was she right? Did you have a good time?"

What can I say? "Yes."

"Did you have sex?"

"What? No! Of course not."

"So she's all mopey over not being called for another date when she thought you both had a good time. That's possible. But that was a while ago. And what about you? You're acting rather odd lately as well. So I'm going to ask again: is there something you'd like to talk about?"

If I say no, he'll hammer at me. We'll go round and round. But if I tell him I'm a little mopey myself over a troubled love affair, how will I explain that?

He gets tired of waiting for me and prompts, "Are you having love troubles in another corner?"

I stare at him. Does he know? How could he? "Another corner of what?"

"Another girl. Because you're acting just like someone suffering from unrequited love. Is there another girl?"

I grind my teeth. Can I do this without going too far? I decide to try. "There is someone else. And yes, it's a little difficult right now. We aren't speaking."

"What happened?"

"Coach, I don't think—"

"Jason, whatever this is, it's affecting your form, your concentration, your ability to win for us. Now, if talking about it will help, great. If it doesn't, then there's no harm done. Is there?"

"What if I don't want to talk about it?"

"Obviously you need to talk about it with someone. Why not me?"

I scowl at him. It doesn't help. "I don't know what to tell you."

"Why aren't you speaking?"

"The other person feels like I betrayed them. I didn't, but they won't listen."

"Is she a student here?"

She, she. They always think she! "The person is a student here, yes."

"So you see her all the time, and you still don't speak. That would tend to make anyone feel burdened enough to have it interfere with all kinds of performance. Have you tried to start a conversation?"

"No."

"Why not?"

"It's too soon."

"Too soon for what?"

"This person needs to think about things a little more. Then we can talk."

"Why do you keep saying 'this person'?"

We stare at each other across his desk. Finally I can't take it. I get up and pace around the room. I'm nearly shouting as I round the chair for the second time. "You don't understand! It's not something I can talk about. It's not something you can help with. It's not something—"

"Jason, is there a pregnancy involved here?"

I slam my hands down on the back of my chair. "Christ!" He just looks at me. "Why does everyone always assume the same thing?"

"Just say no, Jason, if that's—"

"No, then! No, no, no! No pregnancy!" I pause. I look right at him. "No girl."

"No . . . no girl?"

"No girl. 'This person' is a boy." I let that sink in. It doesn't go far enough, it seems; his stare is still pretty empty. So I add, "I'm gay."

"Please sit down."

This is it, I'm thinking. I'll be off the team before he can remember how many *t*'s there are in faggot.

"Tell me about it."

"What?"

"You're pretty angry, and I don't think it's all at the other boy. You sound angry about being misunderstood, about having people assume things about you that you know aren't true. And unless I miss my guess, you haven't told many people what the truth is."

Well, this isn't quite what I expected. So I ask, "Did you understand what I just said?"

"I think so. You're gay, and you're having a lovers' quarrel with another boy who's a student here. You're angry at him, you want to call him, but you don't think you can do that yet, or maybe your pride is in your way, and you're tired of people assuming you're having girl problems. Have I come pretty close?"

"Yes."

"Good. Now. Are you trying to keep this a secret?"

Secret. Secret? Yes. No. "I'm just learning how to deal

with it myself. I don't know how to get other people to deal with it, so no, I'm not telling many of them."

"You live with an aunt and uncle, is that right? Do they know?"

"Yeah. My aunt even likes the other boy."

"Good. Is he out at all?"

"Sort of. Not in a big way."

"Do I know him?"

"What's going to happen if you do?"

"What do you mean?"

"Am I off the team?"

"What? Off the team? Why?"

I blink. "Because I'm gay."

He chuckles. Chuckles! "Not unless you're accosting the other boys in the showers, no. Are you doing that?"

I just shake my head. Not me; Raj.

He says, "Now, what's that got to do with—wait a minute. You're telling me he's on the team."

"I didn't say that."

"No, that's true, you didn't. And ordinarily I wouldn't try to guess. But there's another boy, also a star, who's suddenly not doing so well either."

I can't help it. I close my eyes, just for a second.

He looks almost smug. "Now this is making some sense. What can I do?"

"You know who it is?"

"I'm pretty sure. But what I want to know is if I can help. Do you need an intermediary? A counselor? Wait! You asked for a counselor the last time we talked. Did you mean it?"

I shake my head. "It was just a wisecrack. We, um, we sort of have one. His sister wants us to make up. She's doing her best." I can't believe I'm telling him all this.

"Interesting. So, do you think there's any chance you two will be over it before the meet this Saturday?"

I have to grin. "Probably not. But I know what you mean about my focus. I think it will be better this week."

"I need for his to be better as well. What do you think I should do? Should I talk to him about this issue with you?"

"What? No! No, please don't do that. It will only make things worse."

"So how can I get him to focus?"

I think about Raj, about what he's like, about how much it would upset him to let someone down if he could avoid that.

"Have you asked him to? Focus?" I ask.

"I haven't, not yet. He's next on my list. He'll be here in a few minutes."

I stand up so fast my chair flies away behind me. "Raj is coming here? He can't see me! Really. And don't ask him questions. Just tell him you've noticed his performance is a little lower than usual; ask if you can help in any way. He'll say no. Then leave him alone. He'll do the rest."

"Jason, wait. Have you talked to Meg?"

As I'm opening the door, I say, "Yes. I told her. About me. I don't think she took it very well. See you."

As I dash out of Coach's office, I realize with a start that he hadn't said a name, and neither had I, until the very end. What if it wasn't Raj he thought he was talking about? Well, he knows now. I take up a position where I can see the door but not be seen very well and wait.

Sure enough, there's Raj. It's everything I can do not to call out to him. Anjani said he was hurting too, and she was right. For him to let his performance slide, he must be in bad shape. He's so proud, and so controlled.

Good.

Not good. God, I want him! I want to hold him, to bury

my nose in his neck and inhale, to feel his lips anywhere on me at all!

He goes inside, I hear Coach say something, and then the door is shut. I wheel around so fast I bump smack into just about the last person I want to see right now.

"In trouble with teacher, are you, pet?"

"Buzz off, Jimmy." Still reeling from my anger at Coach and my confusion from having him be so—well, understanding—and wanting desperately to talk to Raj, I'm in no mood for this creep in front of me.

I make a move to walk around him, since he isn't moving, but he grabs my arm.

"Hey, pretty boy. I'd like an apology."

"Fine. I'm sorry you're such a jerk."

I yank my arm free and turn away again, and the next thing I know he's jumped on me, raining blows wherever he can. We crash to the floor, knocking over a metal trash can as we go, and I'm trying desperately to get a hold on him someplace that will hurt.

Then it seems like something's pulling Walsh away from me. I roll face up and see him, bright red, eyes glaring, teeth bared. He's spitting more than he's speaking, but he's saying, "Faggot! You faggot!"

Norm has one of his arms, and in a matter of seconds Coach has the other. Behind Coach stands Raj. He just looks at me a moment, no expression on his face, and turns away.

It's like he's hit me. It's like he's condemned me, like he's so sure I started this fight, violent person that I am.

Raj has disappeared. I'm groveling on the floor, something screaming in my head. It has no words. I can barely hear Norm say to Coach that Jimmy started the whole thing. Then the only feet I can see are Norm's. His hand appears in my vision, and I take it. He pulls me up.

"You okay?"

My breath is coming in short panting noises, and my vision is blurred. Through clenched teeth I say, "I have to hit something."

Norm takes my arm in his hand and steers me toward the gym. In the corner there's a punching bag suspended from the ceiling. He stands behind it. And I hit it.

And hit it. And hit it. My hands hurt, my knuckles are bleeding, and I can't even breathe anymore. Finally I'm on the floor. Again. Only this time I'm shouting these wordless screams, pounding the floor with my fists.

Norm sits beside me and waits till I'm a little quieter. I feel his hand on my shoulder, gently moving across my back, returning to the shoulder. On one hand, I'm barely aware of his touch. On the other, it feels like the best kind of friendship.

We're still on the floor when Coach finds us. I work my way to a sitting position, and he reaches down and helps me up. "Are you hurt anywhere, Jason?" I shake my head. But he grabs my chin so he can see my face. "Let's get some ice on that cheek. No danger to the eye, anyway. Come back to my office. Norm, come too, if you like."

Coach calls the house while I sit in the same chair I was in earlier, a frozen sports-injury packet pressed to the side of my face. When he hangs up, he says, "I spoke to your aunt. She'll be here shortly. Now, can you tell me how it started?"

"I'm not sure. He was right behind me and I didn't know it, and I turned and bumped into him. He called me teacher's pet and then demanded an apology. I wouldn't give him one, and he jumped me."

Coach looks at Norm. "Is that how you saw it?"

"I'd say so, yeah. I actually think Jimmy was sneaking up on Jason, and that's why he was so close when Jason turned. But I couldn't say why."

Coach lets out a long breath. "I may as well tell you both, he'll be suspended from school for two weeks for instigating a fist fight on school grounds. And obviously he's out of the meet this Saturday. And off any team I'll ever manage."

He stands up. "Norm, I'd like to thank you for helping here and for staying with Jason. Could I have a word with him alone?"

At least I have the presence of mind to turn to Norm. I hold out my hand, and he shakes it.

"Thanks, Norm. For being there."

When he's gone, Coach says, "I heard what Jimmy was saying to you. The name he called you."

Through clenched teeth I say, "I hate that word."

"You *should* hate that word. There are a few theories about how it came to apply to you. Want to hear one?"

I nod my head. It's starting to hurt.

"The original meaning of the word 'faggot' is the kind of twigs you would use for kindling when making a fire. In the Middle Ages, when it was common to imprison witches, it was also common to imprison men caught having sex with other men. When it was time to burn one of the witches, the imprisoned men would be taken out under guard and forced to gather kindling for the fire. If they couldn't find enough, and sometimes even if they could, the men themselves would be tied up and thrown onto the fire. As kindling. As faggots."

I don't know what I was expecting, but it wasn't this.

"Jason, if I ever hear anyone call anyone else that name, they will be very sorry. I didn't tell you this earlier, because you were in such a hurry to leave," he throws me a grin here, "but my brother is gay. And I'm very proud of him, of the life he's made for himself, of the courage he's shown. If I can do anything to help you along that road, I'd welcome the chance. I hope you'll let me know if there is."

"Thanks. I will." I'm at a complete loss as to what else to say. But he doesn't seem to expect anything. But then something occurs to me. "Um, do you know if Raj knows what happened? Does he think I started that fight?"

"He knows it was Walsh I dragged into my office and not you, so it seems unlikely he'd think that. Why?"

"I just—the reason we—shit."

"What is it?"

"He's mad at me because he's got this idea I'm a violent person. He's committed to nonviolence. Gandhi, that sort of thing."

"And how did he get that idea?"

"I like knives." What else could I say?

"Of course you're violent. I mean, look at those hands! You must have absolutely pulverized that punching bag. I'll bet it's bleeding from every pore."

I look up at him, not getting it, and see his grin.

"Jason, I think you know whether you're violent or not. And if Raj thinks you are and you don't agree, then I'd say he needs to be very specific about his points and give you a chance to explain them. Have you tried that?"

"Not yet."

He laughs. It feels good to hear it. "You boys. Honestly. Get your act in gear, Peele. Tie him up, if that's what it takes to get him to listen to you, but don't stop communicating as long as you think there's an important misunderstanding. Got it?"

I try to smile; it wobbles, but I guess it's good enough.

"I'll just go out and see if your aunt is looking for the office." He lays his hand on my shoulder briefly on his way out.

I almost wish he hadn't left. Alone, I feel like I'm going to start crying. I lean my head back and try to take a few deep breaths, but they're so shaky they scare me.

Tie him up. It's actually a little amusing to picture this, and I play with the idea. I tie him to one of our trees, and slowly, with my knife, I cut every scrap of clothing away from his body. Then I take bird feathers that I find among the pine needles and tickle him, anywhere I feel like it, until he agrees to listen to me. This image sustains me until I hear footsteps outside the door. But it's not Aunt Audrey. It's Uncle Steve.

He waits until we're in the car before asking any questions. Seat belt on, he turns the key in the ignition and says, "So what happened?"

Where to start? I decide to stick to the bare facts; no embellishment, no background info, no character development. "Jimmy Walsh jumped me from behind. I hit my face on the cement floor as I fell. Coach pulled him off me, and now Walsh is off the team."

"Jimmy jumped you? Are you sure he wasn't just fooling around?"

"He's off the team, Uncle Steve. Coach wouldn't have done that if it was horseplay." I get a jolt of unholy glee as I add, "If it was just boys being boys."

"So what was it then?"

"Look, I don't know why he jumped me."

"Didn't he explain himself?"

"Coach took him into his office. I wasn't there, so I don't know what he said." I steal a quick glance at Uncle Steve's profile. He looks as though he's forcing patience.

"And, Jason, he said nothing to you at all?"

"He called me teacher's pet."

"Why would he do that?"

"He didn't mean that. He meant something else."

Uncle Steve's voice is tense now. "You really are going to make me pull teeth to get the story out of you. What *did* he mean?"

I don't want to tell him. It would be like handing him permission for that "I told you so" that no one ever wants to hear. I grit my teeth, but that makes my battered face hurt, so I stop. "He called me a faggot."

At least that shuts him up. No more questions, Uncle Steve?

At home Aunt Audrey satisfies herself that my injuries aren't fatal and then puts me to bed with a fresh ice pack, ointment, and Band-Aids on my hands, a handful of ibuprofen in my stomach, and a bowl of ice cream beside me. She tries to feed it to me, but I draw the line there.

"You know, Aunt Audrey, you may regret those unpleasant things you said about Norm Saturday night. He was like my knight in shining armor today."

"I'm listening. I like to give people a chance to redeem themselves."

"He's the one who pulled Jimmy Walsh off me, before Coach got to us, and he stayed with me. He took me into the gym so I could attack the punching bag in there. I was—I don't think I've ever been so angry. I was screaming mad. He held the bag for me, and when I couldn't even hit it anymore and just went on screaming, he calmed me down and stayed with me till Coach came to get me."

She's silent a minute as I take a spoonful of ice cream, and then she says, "You're right. You said he was a nice boy when he wasn't drunk or trying to lie about who he is."

"And he did all this despite the fact that Jimmy was shouting 'faggot' at me." Somehow it's much easier to say this to Aunt Audrey than it had been to Uncle Steve.

She blinks. "And how does Jimmy know you're gay?"

"I'm not sure he does. He's called me that before. Before I knew, even. So—I don't really know."

"And where was Raj? Did he see any of this?"

I set the bowl down. I'm afraid of dropping it if I have to

talk about Raj. "He was in Coach's office. He came out behind him, so he only saw the tag end. So he probably thinks I
started it. He already thinks I'm a violent idiot anyway."

She takes my hand. She hasn't done that in years. "Jason,
I'm sure he thinks no such thing. Isn't it about time the two
of you talked?"

I free my hand and reach for the ice cream again. "I don't
care. I don't care what he thinks of me."

Aunt Audrey just watches as I finish the ice cream and
then takes the bowl. "See if you can get some sleep now. I'll
see how you are in a bit, and we'll have dinner."

"Aunt Audrey? Does Uncle Steve know about Raj?
About—how we're not seeing each other anymore?"

"I haven't said anything about your argument with Raj to
anyone. Now, sleep."

Maybe an hour later I'm dozing when Aunt Audrey comes
in. "Jason, do you feel up to a call from your friend Norm?" I
sit up quickly and look at my phone. Why hadn't I heard it?
"I turned off the ringer. Believe me, if anyone important had
called, I'd have told you. Like Norm. Do you want to pick it
up?"

Of course I do. "Norm?"

"Hey, bud. Just wanted to see how you are."

"I'm okay. Just a bruise on my face and some cuts on my
knuckles. And my neck is stiff."

"If a pack of horseshit had thrown itself on my back, I'd
have a stiff neck too!"

I laugh, but it hurts a little so I have to stifle it. Then,
"Norm, listen. I really appreciate what you did. Everything
you did. Just coming over took guts."

"Sure." He sounds a little sheepish. "I just—well, you
know how I feel about that Neanderthal. And I hope you
know how I feel about you."

I take a few breaths. "I'm sorry I left on you. Saturday night. It's just that I felt so out of place there, and I couldn't really be with you, and it was all bumming me out in a big way."

"I know. And you're right, that wasn't much of a date. But it's the kind of scene I think of as a good time. Or I have in the past. But I didn't have a good time there either. I dunno. It's—it's what I know."

"And you're not really ready to go on dates, are you? With a boy."

There's silence. "No. Are you?"

"I don't know. I wish I could say I am. I want to. It's just . . ."

"Yeah." More silence. "Well, I just wanted to make sure you're all right. Will you be in school tomorrow?"

"You kidding? School might actually be an okay place without Walsh!"

We laugh and hang up. I turn the ringer back on, and immediately the thing rings.

"Hello?"

"Jason? Oh Jason, are you all right?"

"Anjani?"

"Raj said you were in a fight. He said this troublemaker jumped on you."

I nearly faint with relief. He doesn't think I started it! "I'm okay, Anjani. Really. I have a bruise on the side of my face, and my knuckles are a little skinned, that's all. The other guy is the one who's getting kicked off the team, and he'll be suspended for a couple of weeks."

"Thank God."

"He, um, Raj—he talked about me?"

"I make him. I go into his room every day and ask him, 'Did you see Jason today? Did you talk to him? How does he seem?' And sometimes he tells me something, and sometimes he just says, 'Leave me alone now, please.' "

"Do you—do you think he's ready to talk to me? To listen to me?"

There's a pause, and then, "Almost. But not quite. It won't be much longer, Jason. If I had to guess, I'd say he's deliberately not changing anything in his life until after Saturday. He gets so concentrated on things, you know?"

I'm numb. "Yeah."

"Plus, you know, he'll have to admit he was wrong, and almost no one does that easily. Raj less easily than most. He can be so stubborn! After Saturday, he'll be ready to consider getting back to his life again. I'm thinking that would be a good time. But you know I'll tell you."

I'm pretty touched at how hard she's trying, even though I feel sure it will come to nothing. "Thank you. I don't know how to thank you, but thank you." I'd told Aunt Audrey I didn't care. It wasn't true. But it's kind of hard to take second place to a track meet. Or even get put on hold for one.

But we wouldn't want Raj to have to put his pride aside, would we?

What about *my* pride?

Whatever.

Chapter 14

Everybody Out, Now

Tuesday lunch is the first time I see Robert that day. He takes one look at my face and says, "Fighting again, Peele? Can't keep you out of trouble, can we?"

I throw him a dirty look but don't speak.

"Seriously, what'd you do, fall on the track or something?"

"Nope. It was our friend Mr. Walsh again. Haven't seen him in school today, have you?"

Obediently he looks around the room. "I haven't, you're right. Where is he?"

"Suspended. And off the track team. Fighting on school grounds."

He sits back in his chair, impressed with this news. "So if he was fighting with you, how come you're here?"

"Dummy, he jumped me. As a matter of fact, I didn't even get one lick in."

"What made him mad enough to do something stupid like that?"

"No idea. I bumped into him by accident, and I guess my insincere apology irritated him. The next thing I knew, he was on top of me. Norm Landers and Coach pulled him off."

"Norm, the guy on the relay team with you?"

"Right." Among other things.

"Wow."

"So I'm thinking I want to get in some more practice with my knife. He can't get me here for a while, but his sub-goons could, and he might ambush me someplace else. I want to be prepared."

It's a conclusion I'd come to on the walk to school. My aunt had made me promise to ride the bus, but she leaves before I do, so . . . I think better when I'm walking, and I needed to think what it meant that Raj hadn't done anything to find out whether I was hurt yesterday or not. What I decided is that whatever Raj thinks of me, whether Anjani ever gets him off his high horse enough that he'll deign to see me again, I am going to be who I am. If he has a problem with that, he can just go back and watch *La Cage* again until the lesson sinks in. And who I am is someone who doesn't get pushed around by bullies.

Robert's eyes brighten at the idea of knife practice. "Can I come? Tell you what, if you let me work with it a little, I'll see if I can get my mom's car. How's that?"

That, I tell him, is just fine.

In the park, I let him work with the knife enough to get a little better than last time, and actually it helps me; I can see some of the things he's doing wrong that I might be doing as well.

I'd told Coach I was going to be more focused this week. I am. Damn Raj anyway. If he is putting me aside for the sake of the meet, I can do the same with him. So just watch me focus.

Robert has had no news from Debbie, he tells me on the ride back from the park. We go over some of the same ground as before; his worries haven't changed much. But it's harmless to listen, and it keeps me from feeling guilty about not talking to him about Raj, Norm, anyone. I'm glad I've told him about me, but that's all I can do. And to his credit, he seems perfectly normal with me. Doesn't seem skittish or uncomfortable.

As I'm getting out of the car at my house, I tell him, "Robert, you're okay. See you tomorrow."

He calls to me as I walk to the front door. "Hey! I finished that character sketch of Santa. I'll e-mail it to you tonight!"

He's a character himself.

I check my e-mail and read Robert's character sketch before I start my homework. He's no Jeffrey Eugenides, who wrote that amazing book *Middlesex* about this boy whose genitals didn't show, so he was raised as a girl. But for Robert, this is head and shoulders above where he was. I send a reply.

"I hope you're proud of yourself. You should be! Williams had better be prepared to reassess your skills. Great job, my friend."

Almost immediately I get an IM from him. He must have been sitting there waiting. It says, "Thanks. For all your help, and for being my friend."

I don't reply again. Partly it's because we've said it all. Partly it's because my eyes are a little moist, and I can't focus on the screen.

Wednesday after school I decide I feel like putting in some track time. Raj is there, of course, but I pretend he isn't. I barely look at him, actually, and I'm pretty proud of myself. Norm is there, and we work together for a while and go and get some sodas after. This time, though, I insist on going someplace close by.

"We aren't going to be holding hands, Norm. We're just a couple of track-team members getting some refreshment after a hard workout." He has to admit that's harmless enough.

"You look like the poster child for the 'Stop Domestic Abuse' campaign," he tells me from across the table. "How are you feeling today?"

"Better. Aunt Audrey is a firm believer in the powers of ibuprofen, and I've eaten a lot of it. Neck is still a little stiff, but it's easing up."

"Guess you won't have to worry about him for a while."

"Yeah. I just wonder if I'll have to worry about his partner in crime."

"Dane?"

So Norm knows that as well. "Dane indeed."

"You know, I've, uh, I've heard something about Dane."

"Something terrible for him, I hope."

"Well . . . maybe." He just sits there.

"C'mon, Norm. Fess up. What?"

"He wasn't in school today. Did you notice?"

"Can't say I did. But I don't look for the guy."

"He lives near me, you know."

"Dane? He's from Oakwood?" Somehow that had escaped me.

Norm nods his head. "The news is that something happened at his house this past weekend. Seems a friend of his older brother's took a liking to him. The wrong kind of liking."

This makes no sense to me. "What are you talking about?"

"His brother's in college now. A sophomore. And I guess he's been hanging out with kind of a rough crowd. One of them is this friend who's a junior. I can't remember how he met Dane. But anyway there was this incident, and I don't have any details, but the friend and some other college kid decided it would be fun to play with the kid brother. You know."

I'm sure I'm supposed to know, but I don't. I shake my head.

Norm looks around and then leans as close as he can over the table. "You know. They took him. They had him. They did him."

"Did what to him?"

In a hoarse whisper, Norm says, "They fucked him, man!"

Something deep inside me shivers, and my ass feels funny. "You're not serious."

"I am! And either he told Jimmy or somebody else did. So now Jimmy's on this crusade against what he calls faggots, because he's so fucking confused in his own head he doesn't know you don't have to be gay to do that sort of thing."

I lean back in the booth; I need support. "So that's why he was so ready to jump me. But—do you think he knows?" I lean forward again. "About me?"

Norm shrugs. "Maybe. He knows about Raj, so if he so much as saw you talking to him, he'd assume you were."

I think back. The first time Jimmy had called me that, it was the day I'd gone over to Raj when nobody else did, after his jump.

"Norm, I think it's time to get serious about something. I think we all need to come out. Every one of us. This is insane! Do you mean to tell me that kids don't talk to Raj because he's gay?"

"Duh. Just figure that out? And if a lot more guys figure it out about you . . ." He just lets that hang in the air.

"You'd stop talking to me?" He looks down at the table. I drum my fingers. "So you won't come out, is that what you're saying?"

"Are you crazy? It's a death sentence! And you'd better not either, if you know what's good for you."

A death sentence. So Norm probably agrees with Uncle Steve's assessment of what it would be like to be gay. I'm starting a slow burn. "Who else?"

"What?"

"Who else do you know who's gay?"

He's actually squirming. "Jason, I can't tell you that, man! You know that."

"I wouldn't out you to a straight person who hadn't figured it out, but do you mean to say that if I meet another guy next week who's gay, I can't tell him you are?"

The hoarse whisper is back. "Listen and listen good, Peele. You say nothing about me to anybody. Do you hear that?"

I throw myself backward, arms crossed over my chest. "This is sick. This is just sick. How are we supposed to make any progress here?"

"I'm not on a crusade, Jason. I'm just trying to survive."

"Well, surviving is not living. For Christ's sake, it's not like we have leprosy!"

"No. That can be cured."

We stare at each other across a few feet of empty air that seems like a much greater distance.

"Look, Norm, I like you a lot, and I'm really grateful for what you did yesterday. But you need to find some guts. You need to be who you are, if you've figured that out. Do you want to be hiding and afraid the rest of your life?"

He's getting angry now. "I've already told you. I'll come

out when I get to college, when I don't have to worry about everybody talking to my folks. I need them to foot the bills until I can be on my own."

"Why are you so sure they'd hate you?"

"Ha! You don't know my old man. Ex-marine." He deepens his voice: " 'Suck it up, marine!' " He shivers. "I still get that all the time. Like I'm in the service just because he was. Still is, in his head."

"That doesn't mean he'd hate you."

"Oh, whatever he'd do, it would be for my own good. You can count on that. Tough love, you know?"

Suddenly I sound like some kind of hypocrite to myself. Hadn't I assumed Uncle Steve, and maybe even my father, would hate me? Or at least be ashamed of me? And I remember how Aunt Audrey had received my news. Maybe I should go easier on Norm; at least I can be who I am, more or less, at home.

"I'm sorry. I can't know what it's like for you. But I do know that as long as most of us are hiding, the few who stick out are going to get more grief than the whole lot of us would if we were all out. They'd have to learn to deal, if there were enough of us out. Do you see what I mean?"

He nods, looking down at his hands. "Yeah. But that's not going to happen in my lifetime." He sits forward again. "Look, Jason, I want you to know something. I really am going to do this, as soon as I can. I hate this. I hate pretending and lying and not being able to be with you the way I'd like to. And I'll do my part. I just can't do it yet."

We sit in silence for a minute or so, contemplating life. Jesus, but it's complicated. And it doesn't help when something like this thing with Dane happens. I wonder if he'll feel up to jumping in the meet. And I wish I could talk to Jimmy, get him to see that this isn't a gay thing. But that's not going to happen.

"Is Dane gonna be okay?" I ask finally.

"I guess. I don't have any details, but I don't think we'll see him for a week or two."

"So, no jumping on Saturday."

"Don't think so."

There's little else to say, it seems, or nothing we can think of. Eventually we come to a silent agreement to leave, to go home. Norm gives me a ride.

"Listen, do you want to come in? Aunt Audrey would love to thank you for helping me out."

His head turns sharply toward me. "Does she know? Did you tell her?"

Shit. I thought he'd understood that. "I didn't exactly tell her. But I think she knew that Saturday was us going out, like. On a date, sort of."

He pounds once on his steering wheel.

"Norm, I'm sorry. I didn't know how strongly you felt. But it's not like she and Uncle Steve ever see your folks. And they wouldn't just blurt that out to anyone. Not to anyone, really. It's okay."

"Whatever. I'll see you tomorrow."

Guess that means he isn't coming inside. "Norm—" But he's turned away from me.

I'm trying to do homework after dinner, but in my mind I'm picturing what it must have been like for Dane Caldwell. I keep feeling antsy, and I have to get up and move around, think of something unrelated, but it doesn't help much. I'd almost told Aunt Audrey, but I didn't know if it might worry her.

Just before nine o'clock, the phone rings. It's Anjani. Her voice is sharp.

"Jason, what do you think you are doing?"

"Doing about what?"

"Are you out of your mind? Here I am trying my hardest to smooth the way for you, and you have to go chasing after someone else! What's the matter with you?"

"Anjani, I don't know what you're talking about. Please say something that makes sense."

"Raj saw you. Talking to some boy—he wouldn't say a name—he knows is gay. He says you've been talking to him a lot. Today was once too many, and now Raj is furious. Why couldn't you be patient?"

She means Norm. And even in his anger, Raj won't say his name. But what the hell am I supposed to do? "Anjani, this is way out of proportion. This guy is nothing to me compared to how I feel about Raj. He's a friend, and as a matter of fact, he"—I can't tell her exactly what he did; the boy who helped me yesterday may have been named to her. I hate this.—"he stuck his neck out for me when I needed his help."

"Well, Raj thinks—"

"This is going to sound harsh, and I'm sorry for it, but I'm not sure I care what Raj thinks."

"What did you say?"

"I agree with everything you've said about him. He's wonderful, he's worth five of anyone else, he's honest and true and honorable and stubborn and arrogant and has way too tight a rein on himself. I get all of it, okay? But that doesn't give him the right to treat me like this. I'd have come to him in a second, not a thought to focusing on some stupid track meet, if I'd thought it would help. But he leaves me alone, letting me think the worst. He doesn't know you're calling me, so for all he knows I think he hates my guts."

"You're giving up."

I heave a breath. "It has nothing to do with giving up. First, I haven't replaced him with someone else. Second, it would serve him right if I did. If he thinks I'm being disloyal—well, he doesn't want to know what I think of him right now!"

"Jason, you're making me feel stupid and useless."

"I'm sorry. I'm really sorry. But what exactly do you expect from me?" And suddenly it dawns on me what she expects. She probably has this idea in her head about how I ought to behave if I were an old-fashioned girl. Raj is the boy, and he's allowed to be pig-headed and mean, but I'm the girl, and I must wait patiently for my man to come back to me. Well, I don't like that for anyone. Girl or boy.

"Anjani, you need to remember I'm a boy too. I can't act like an innocent farm girl waiting at home for her sailor to return from the sea even though he's been gone five years and hasn't written. Do you know what I'm saying?"

"I guess I want you to love him. It doesn't seem as though you do."

This is getting us nowhere. "Look, I really appreciate everything you're trying to do. I think you're a wonderful sister. I wish you were *my* sister. But right now, Raj is looking for reasons to keep me in the wrong, and that makes me crazy. I don't take that, not from anybody."

"Not even for love?"

"If Raj really loves me, that will have to be more important to him than his pride. And if that's not the case, then it's not a love I want."

There's not a lot more to say. As I hang up the phone, I realize how much Anjani has helped me. Talking to her has made me figure out how I really feel about this situation. I don't see that there's anything I can do about it. And that means I don't avoid Norm just because Raj wants to think the worst. Of course, Norm may be avoiding *me* now.

When I go to sleep, though, I dream about Raj. And in the dream, he's crying.

Chapter 15

What Are the Rules?

My own life may not be going so well, but Robert's is looking up. At lunch he tells me Debbie is not pregnant, and he's so jubilant I have to remind him to keep his voice down. Then in English Lit he gets a chance to show off his recent work.

Williams has us do a character sketch about once a week, though he changes the day. This week it's Thursday, today, and Williams says the subject is up to us as long as the character is mythical. I look at Robert, who's looking at me. I shrug.

I busy myself on Satan (who may not be mythical to everyone, and sometimes I think he's alive and well and going to my school) and hope Robert has the sense to re-create his Santa. Ha! All the same letters in both subjects! It's irresistible, and I work it into my sketch even though I may get points detracted for adding unnecessary complexity. Sometimes gifts have a little of Satan in them, after all. Consider Raj.

Williams always has one student read aloud before class ends. If no one volunteers, someone is chosen. Sometimes Williams chooses someone other than the volunteer, and I don't blame him; I almost always volunteer. Today I don't, hoping Robert will.

He does. His face is shining, and his hand is in the air. I shoot psychic instructions at Williams: *Choose Robert. Choose Robert. Choose Robert.* Whether I'm good at this or Williams is so startled to see Robert's hand that he can't resist, I can't tell, but he chooses Robert.

Robert sure has everyone's attention. And as he reads, a little haltingly but still confident, I can tell he's done a pretty good job at remembering what he'd done. This is a gift for me, whether from Santa or the gods, I don't know, but I can't stop grinning. Still, I decide the next step is to get Robert to do this a little more spontaneously. I start lesson plans in my head.

I clap Robert on the back as soon as the bell rings. "Great job, bud! You're ready for the next step." He just looks at me, puzzled, and I go back to my desk and collect my things. The final official track practice before the meet is today.

Too much haste . . . how does the saying go? I drop about half my things on the floor, and several papers go shooting under desks. But it gives me a chance to witness something that does my ego some good. Meg, who has informed me she never talks to Robert unless she's on a double date with me, goes over and tells him what a great job he's done.

"Thanks, Meg. I've been working on it. Jason's been helping me."

I glance up at them when I hear my name, and they both turn to look at me. Meg's eyes are—well, they're not harsh, they're not soft, but there's something good there. For me. I just nod and go back to my litter cleanup.

Sure enough, there's no Jimmy Walsh at track practice, and no Dane Caldwell. I would have expected to feel good about Jimmy, and maybe I would have if it hadn't been for

Dane. But it's like Jimmy was standing up for his friend in an odd, misguided sort of way. It's not me he's doing it for this time, but I can't bring myself to gloat. As I'd put into my paper, Satan himself has a few redeeming characteristics, even if they aren't easy to see.

Norm is friendly enough and even offers me a ride to the meet on Saturday; guess he's forgiven me for spilling the beans about him to Aunt Audrey and Uncle Steve. Coach doesn't have us complete a relay; we just practice handoffs and starts. It's a little frustrating, but psychologically I guess it makes sense. It may give us that much more will to run on Saturday.

I ignore Raj. He ignores me. I'm tempted to stand someplace he can see me as he does his practice approaches, but I decide that's too mean. And I'm not sure I could take it.

We have a final group hug sort of thing before Coach lets us go. He gathers us all around to give us his pep speech. Norm and I stand together as Coach tells us all on peril of failure not to run, jump, throw, whatever, until we're warming up at the meet on Saturday. He's going on about getting lots of sleep and what a great team we are and how we're going to teach Wilson High—and the other two schools, but Wilson is our main competitor—a lesson they won't forget, or some such propaganda, and I'm looking around as inconspicuously as possible. Where's Raj?

Finally I see him. He's standing alone on the outskirts of the group, and he's looking right at me. All sound except my own breathing goes away. This has happened before; when? Oh, after Paul Roche had dropped the baton, and I'd won anyway.

Coach must have stopped speaking, because suddenly I can hear clapping, and everyone is starting to move. The spell is broken, and I look away. Then I look back, but Raj is headed for the locker room.

The last thing I want to do right now is see him in there. Or in the showers, God forbid. I head for where Coach is standing.

"Can I talk to you for a minute?"

"Sure, Jason. Are the bleachers okay?" I nod and follow him to some spot he seems to choose at random. "What's on your mind?"

"I heard something about someone, and I just want to know if it's true." I hadn't planned this, but it makes sense to me now. I do want to know.

"What have you heard?"

"About Dane. About what happened to him."

Coach looks at me hard. "What have you heard?"

"He was raped. By some college kids who know his brother."

Coach looks across the field at nothing. "And you heard that where?"

"I'd rather not say. It's someone who lives near him, though, so that's how this person knew."

"Let me ask you this. If something like that happened to you, who would you want to know about it?" He looks back at me.

"No one, I guess."

"Exactly."

I guess that's all I'm going to get out of him, but in a way it's an answer. We sit there for a minute, and I'm about to thank him and get up when he says, "Any changes in your situation?"

He means with Raj, I guess. I shrug. "I dunno. I'm trying to convince myself it doesn't matter."

"Why?"

" 'Cause I'm not sure it's worth saving."

"I can't help you with that decision, but I still think it's important for all of us to be clear with each other. What's going to be important to you, whether the relationship continues or not, is what he thinks of you. How many times have you said to yourself, 'I don't care what so-and-so thinks of me,' and how many times did you actually mean it? And this time, it's someone who really got under your skin. Do you know what I'm saying?"

"Yes."

"I hear a 'but' in your voice."

"It doesn't help. In fact, it's worse. If I can just put him aside, if I can convince myself it doesn't matter"—my voice is starting to crack, and I have to clear my throat—"then maybe I can go on."

Coach has the good grace to look away. But he reaches a hand out and pats my knee a few times. "You've got it bad, kid. You need to get out of this limbo, one way or the other."

"Yeah." Limbo. Satan looms again.

We walk toward the locker room together. It makes me feel a little better when he tells me that my focus has improved.

"You're going to do really well on Saturday, Jason. And however it goes, I want you to know how proud I am of you." He squeezes my shoulder and then heads toward his office.

It surprises me that his saying that means so much to me. But it does. It makes me feel like maybe there's hope for my life.

On the walk home I'm thinking maybe I should be counting my blessings. Robert is a good friend who is doing better at school because he asked for my help and I gave it to him. Norm is going to be a good friend, I can tell, even though we may have a few rough spots. Coach is on my side, and that seems to be worth a lot. And Anjani is trying her best to help me, though really she's doing it for Raj.

And Aunt Audrey—well, she's the best. Positively the best. Even when I don't want her to be. Somehow I feel sure she's doing her best to bring Uncle Steve along too.

She's waiting for me, actually, when I get home. "How did practice go, Jason?"

"Great. It was really good. I think I'm ready."

"Your uncle and I are looking forward to Saturday too. We'll drive you over. I know it'll have to be a little early, but he loves to think he's still in the thick of things. Makes him feel like a kid again, reliving his own glory days." The smile on her face is so sweet, like she really cherishes him. And I know she does.

Damn. No ride over with Norm then. I'm heading up-stairs to phone him and change clothes when Aunt Audrey calls to me again.

"You had a phone call."

I spin around. Raj?

"I left the number on your notepad next to your com-puter. It was a girl. I think the girl you went out with a few weeks ago. Meg?"

"Meg called? What did she want?"

"Well, Jason, she's not about to tell me. But I have a ques-tion for you . . ."

"I know. Have I told her. Yes. She knows."

Aunt Audrey just smiles at me, so I dash up to my room. Meg? Meg called me? I punch the numbers and wait. She an-swers the phone herself.

"Oh, hi, Jason. I, uh, I forgot you had track practice this afternoon, so I spoke to your aunt."

How do you ask a girl what she wants without sounding rude? "I was wondering why you'd called me."

"Yeah." She sort of giggles, but it's just a nervous thing. She's not a giggly girl. "I guess I just wanted to say I understand. Better than I did, anyway. About what you told me the other day."

"You mean, about my being——"

She interrupts before I can say the word. "Yes. That. I wasn't very nice to you, and what you did took courage. Telling me that. I want you to know that I appreciate your being honest with me."

I don't quite know what to say. You're welcome? "Sure. It seemed only fair to let you know, after—you know."

"Yeah. And then Robert, in class today. He said you'd been helping him. That was really sweet. And it seems to have worked!"

I chuckle. "It was an uphill battle sometimes, but he really wanted to do better." I decide not to say that he'd already written that sketch before. "He's actually enjoying reading now, I think. At least, some of it."

We chat for a while about nothing in particular, and when we've run out of that, she says she has to go help get dinner ready, and we hang up.

I sit on the side of my bed for a while, just thinking. Adding to my list of blessings.

And then I'm sad again. If only I could add Raj. I jump up and start stripping. I'm just changing clothes, but you'd think the cloth was burning me or something. I don't know if I'm angry or hurt or what, but there's something in me that wants to explode. Down to my underwear, I throw myself on the bed and scream into my pillow.

"Fuck! Fuck! Fuck!"

My poor pillow. I've drenched it, pounded it, and now I'm shouting obscenities at it. And it's always there for me. Ridiculously I feel guilty, like I'm ignoring its friendship, taking it for granted. I pound the bed for a change.

Lying there, trying to calm down, it occurs to me that I'm being a real idiot. Here's Coach telling me that I need to do something about this misunderstanding, me telling Anjani I'd throw away my focus on anything if I thought it would help, and I'm not calling Raj. And the only reason I'm not calling him is that Anjani, the old-fashioned girl, told me not to!

Okay, there's another reason. My pride. But—hell! What's that, in light of what I'm going through?

I sit up and check my watch: about half an hour till dinner.

Holding the phone, I try a few opening lines. "Raj, you need to stop being such a jerk."

No.

"Raj, get down off your fucking high horse . . ."

I try again. "We need to talk. You don't understand something very important about me, and—" But does he care?

I care, damn it. I dial.

His mother answers. "Oh." That's all she says when I tell her it's me.

"Is Raj there?"

"Well, he—"

"May I speak with him, please? It's important."

There's this pause, and then she says, "All right, I'll ask." And she sets the phone down.

So I wait, trying to see her in my mind's eye as she goes up the stairs and down the hall to his room, knocks on the door, and opens it to the smell of incense. My breathing is very shallow, and everything inside me is shaking. I try taking some deep breaths, but it doesn't help.

"Jason, I'm sorry. He can't come to the phone."

Can't. Won't. I want to challenge her. I want to beg her to please, please tell him it's important. Tell him it's killing me! But all I say is, "Thank you."

Thank you. For what? For confirming my worst fears?

At first I think I'm going to cry again. But I'm too numb. This worries me a little, so I try to work myself into a state.

"How can he do this to me?" I demand of my sleeping computer screen. "How can he treat me like this?"

I'd send him an e-mail, but Anjani told me the whole family shares the account.

So?

I'll never know whether he actually sees it, is "so." Anjani could see it and delete it because she told me not to contact him without her approval. His father could see it and think maybe his son won't be gay anymore if he deletes it. His mother could see it and decide Raj has suffered enough and delete it. Raj himself could see it and delete it without even opening it. I'd never know. That's worse. So I don't do it.

After dinner, though, a sullen affair for which I'm fully to blame, I do sit at the computer. I've got some Mozart on the CD player to help get me into a writing mood. And I compose an e-mail to Raj. I just don't send it.

"Raj, it's me. Jason. Remember me? The one you dragged to that drag queen movie?" I delete that. Just had to get it out of my system.

When I'm finished, it looks like this: "I love you. At least, I think I do. I've never loved anyone before, so I'm new at this. And maybe that's why things are so screwed up. I don't know what I'm supposed to do. Are we having a lovers' quarrel, or don't you feel anything for me? If we are, what's the next step? What are

the rules? I don't know any of the rules for this kind
of relationship. I didn't even know who was supposed
to pay at the movies. You seem to know everything,
and I know nothing. So please. Please! Tell me what
comes next. Because I've tried everything I know
how to do. Help me. I love you."

I store it in my Draft box.

Well, now I'm at a loss. Without anything specific in mind,
I send my browser over to Google. At first I enter search
terms about Gandhi, but I've already read most of the stuff
that comes up. And I'm hardly still working with Raj on that
imaginary term paper. Then I do a search about the Vedic tra-
ditions about being gay, but the results are kind of daunting—
too much information all at once on a topic I haven't even
scratched the surface of before.

I sit back, just kind of doodling on the keyboard, and my
mind goes—of course—to Raj. And then Gandhi, and things
Vedic, which takes me back to . . . how did Anjani put it?
That temple he calls a bedroom. The smell of incense. And
when he held me, the smell of Raj.

Into the search field I enter the string "+homosexual
+scent," and then, just before I click on search, I move the
cursor to the "I'm Feeling Lucky" button.

Man. Lucky is putting it mildly.

It goes right to this article that talks about how homosexuals give off certain pheromones that are sexually attractive to
other homosexuals.

There's a printer icon at the bottom of the screen. I turn
the printer on and click.

I do a full search this time. And no end of results. I'm not
sure whether I'm more amazed to think that this orientation
is a naturally occurring phenomenon with a perfectly reason-

able explanation or to see how many irrational denials there are from people who have decided not to believe it. These people seem to be so tied to their conclusion that gay equals bad that they can't tolerate a whiff—pardon the pun—of anything based in provable fact.

And the facts roll in. According to this Swedish research project, the gay men they studied had the same responses in their hypothalamus to male scent as women did. And since the hypothalamus controls sexual behavior, this is a sexual response. Arousal. And although no one is saying what causes what, the test results all point to the same thing: gay men respond to men—and probably even more to gay men—in this natural process over which no one has any control. They've even shown it to be true in animals!

Wow.

And I'm supposed to be able to sleep now?

By the time Uncle Steve knocks to point out that it's bedtime and watches while I turn off the computer, I've printed out reams of paper. Everything from the National Academy of Sciences to bloggers' rantings on both sides of the debate.

But I know which side I'm on.

Chapter 16

Lucky in Friends

Robert is all excited on Friday. At least someone is in a good mood. Seems he spent a good chunk of last night doing another character sketch. He's very mysterious though. Won't say who it is.

"Debbie?" I guess. Then I name all the sports figures I can think of. Then, "Your dad? No, wait. Your kid brother." He just grins at me, as if to say I'll never guess.

"I'll send it to you after school. You can read it tonight."

That was between first and second periods. I'm really dragging, and I don't know how I'll get through the rest of the day. Let alone be mentally up and ready for the meet tomorrow.

Coach has arranged for his track team to be excused from phys ed for the day, so we all have study hall instead. On the way in I see Norm, and I realize I'd forgotten to call him last night.

"Norm!" He looks my way and nods. When he's near enough, I say, "Listen, I can't ride with you tomorrow. Aunt Audrey and Uncle Steve want to go over early with me. I'm sorry."

He looks a little miffed, but then he says, "It's okay. My dad wanted me to ride with him and Mom anyway. It'll make his day." He throws me a sarcastic smile. "What are you doing Saturday night?"

"No plans. Why?" Is he going to ask me on a date?

"I was thinking it might be cool if you could come over. I'll introduce you to my folks at the meet, and we can rent a movie or something. I have a DVD player in my room." He looks around and then lowers his voice. "Maybe we could even—you know. Fool around a little."

I can't help smiling. I'm not sure I want to fool around in his bedroom, but the evening could be fun. "Sure. We can lick each other's wounds if we've lost our race."

He raises his eyebrows two or three times in quick succession and grins.

We allow ourselves to be separated by the crowd going into the room. Thank God I'm not in the same PE class as Raj, so I don't have to pretend I don't see him in here. I do a little homework, but it's hard to concentrate.

I'm pretty tired of myself by this point; I've been a misery-guts all day. So first I pull out one of my Internet articles and read through it again; I have a few of them in my pack. And then I start a list. Call it a thanksgiving list.

1. *Aunt Audrey and Uncle Steve. They took me into their life when they didn't have to. They bought me clothes, shoes, books, a computer, gave me a room of my own. They feed me, and they even love me. They care who my friends are whether I want them to or not. And even if Uncle Steve is confused, he still wants to do what's right for me.*

2. *Darin. He was my best friend for years and probably gave me the first hint of who I am. Hell, he practically*

made love to me. I need to tell him I'm gay. I need to know if he is.

3. *Rebecca. She's helped me in ways she may never know. I have to call her. I have to tell her about me.*

4. *Robert. He saved my ass that day with Jimmy and Dane even though it wasn't his fight. He accepts me for what I am and teaches me as much as I teach him.*

5. *Coach. I don't think it's too much to say he cares about me. He wants me to win for his team, of course, but he also cares how I feel. He wants me to be happy. He's proud of me.*

6. *Williams. He's one of the only teachers who's ever made me really work, and I've learned more in his class about what I can do than in all the others combined. Except maybe track.*

7. *Norm. A mixed blessing, perhaps, but he's a good person at heart, and he cares about me. He's willing to risk at least a little to help me. I can't ask him for too much, but I know his limit, because he's honest with me.*

8. *Writing. I don't know what I'd do if I couldn't write. If I couldn't get things out of me where I can see them.*

9. *My knife. Knowing it's there makes me feel safer than I used to feel. Protected. Like even if there's no Robert and no Norm and no Coach around, my knife is there. My knife is part of me. It's an extension of my hand, of my thoughts, of my motion. Of my life.*

I think I'm done, and then I have to add two more. One is Raj. The number ten looks lonely and stark for a few minutes, my pen hovering over the notebook. And then I write.

10. *Raj. Without Raj, I wouldn't know who I am. I wouldn't be so sure of my destiny, of where I will have to look for*

happiness. I wouldn't be so sure of what's important to me. The problems I'm having with him are teaching me what not to do in a relationship.

There's probably more to write about Raj, but I leave it for now.

11. Dane. Nothing like what happened to Dane Caldwell has ever happened to me. And it never will. See #9.

I figure I'll stop before I start feeling like some kind of Pollyanna. I go back to my homework, and it's a little easier now.

For dinner that night we have steak. I can't believe it. I love steak! We almost never have it. "What's the occasion, Aunt Audrey?"

"You need protein. You're going to need a lot of it tomorrow. And you're going to win." She stands there smiling at me, and I can't help myself. I give her a big hug.

It's Friday, and ordinarily I'd be watching TV or a movie or hanging with a friend or something, but I decide to read. It isn't until nearly ten o'clock that I remember Robert was going to send me another sketch. I don't really feel like reading it, but he's on my blessings list, so I feel a certain obligation.

I turn the computer on and fire up the Internet connection and then my e-mail package. Something flashes across the bottom of the screen before I can read it, but I'm focused on bringing messages in. And sure enough, there's one from Robert. It's entitled, "Character Sketch: Jason Peele."

Me? He's done a character sketch of me? I click it open.

"Jason Peele is someone anyone should be proud to know. Being about the smartest guy in class doesn't make him conceited and stuck-up. He uses his brains to figure out the best way to help someone else who is not as smart. He takes the time to figure out what they need, and who they are, and then he shows them what to do in ways that make sense to them.

"He is not easy to intimidate. He is not big or powerful, but he does not back down from a threat, whether it comes from competition on the track team or from the bullies who wish they were as good as he is.

"Most important, Jason is honest. He is gay, and he is not afraid to say so. He is not afraid of the prejudiced people who call him names. He is not afraid that people will not like him, because he knows the value of people. His own honesty helps him see it, or see when it is not there, in other people, and he knows that the honest people will be fair. He knows the people who will not like him because he is gay are not the honest ones, or the fair ones, and he will not pretend for them. He will not pretend he is someone he is not.

"Jason Peele is someone anyone should be proud to know. I am very proud, because he is my friend."

Through the mist in my eyes I scour the page for a contraction of any kind, and I see he's been excessively careful to avoid them. I laugh, and it comes out a kind of sob. He tries so hard. He almost certainly used spell-check; the word "conceited" might have given him some grief.

I'm still half laughing and half crying as I wonder how long this took him, how many drafts he deleted, when the word "draft" gets stuck in my brain. I remember the flash across the bottom of the screen as I opened the e-mail package.

Deadly serious now, I cursor to my Draft box.

It's empty.

Jesus Fucking Christ! How could it be empty? Was there a blip in our service or something? My hand shakes as I cursor over to the Sent box, praying out loud, "God, oh God, please don't let it be here. Please. Please. Please."

It's there.

Frantically I search though the Help function, looking for some instructions about how to get a message back, knowing even as I do that it's hopeless. The message is gone. Who will pick it up? Who will see it first?

Who will delete it first?

Will they delete it? Whoever "they" is—will they? Or will Raj actually see it? What did I say, anyway? I open the sent message and read it again. Thank God I hadn't put anything in there about him going down on me. I almost did. In fact, I did, hoping to inspire some of the passion he must have felt for me at one time; then I deleted it. But all those I love yous are there. The repeated "please." The desperation, the hurt. It's all in there.

I'm still staring at the screen when my aunt knocks on the door.

"Jason? Don't you think it's time you got some sleep?" She looks at me. "What's wrong? You look like you've seen a ghost."

Maybe she'll know. Maybe she'll have some idea what's likely to happen to my message. To my heart. I point to the screen. She bends over my shoulder and reads it.

When I think she's finished, I say, "I didn't mean to send it. I put it in the Draft box. Or I thought I did. But when I logged on, it went out automatically. Aunt Audrey"—and I turn my chair to face her as she sits on the side of my bed—

"the account isn't just his. It's the whole family's. Anyone might see it. What do you think will happen to it? What if someone else sees it first?" I can hear the fear in my own voice.

"Oh, sweetie, we can't predict that. You never know how anyone will react when they come face-to-face with this kind of honesty. This kind of feeling. Do you want him to see it?"

I squeeze my eyes shut and rub my face. "I don't know what I want anymore. I tried calling him. He wouldn't come to the phone."

"Tonight?"

"No, no. Yesterday. A couple of days ago. I forget." When was it anyway? The days are blurred.

She pats the bed, and I sit beside her. She takes my hand. "Jason, no matter what happens with Raj, I want you to remember something. You have been true to yourself, and you have done nothing to hurt anyone. What's more, you have done everything you could to try and understand what happened and to resolve it. If this situation gets no better, it's not because of you. Raj may have reasons you'll never know—"

"I know them. Or some of them anyway."

"What are they?"

Putting aside my promise to Anjani, I tell Aunt Audrey what happened to Raj in India. To his brother. And how he was when he moved here.

"When did he tell you that?"

"He doesn't know I know. In fact, I'm not even supposed to tell you. His sister has called me a few times. She wanted us to get back together, and she was trying to work on Raj. But it wouldn't seem she's had any success."

"So she told you this to help you understand?"

I nod. "So I guess I shouldn't feel so sorry for myself."

"I have a feeling, Jason, that if he lets you go, one day he'll realize the mistake he's made. I think it's going to cause him a great deal of pain. And I hope you won't be angry, but I feel much more sorry for him than I do for you."

She kisses the side of my head. And suddenly I want her to see Robert's sketch.

"Remember my friend Robert, who needed help writing?"

"Of course."

"He's quite full of himself now, and he wrote a terrific character sketch in class yesterday and read it aloud. And then tonight, he sent me this."

I get up and click on his message to open it, then send it to the printer. She reads it once, and then she reads it again out loud. Toward the end her voice gives out, and she starts crying. She stands and pulls me to her.

I can feel tears dropping onto my shoulders for a minute or so, and then she wipes her face off and smiles at me. "See?" she says. "Much more sorry for Raj." She hugs me again and says, "Off to bed with you. Track stars need their sleep."

I'm actually in bed, sure I'm not going to be able to fall asleep, when I realize that I've left Robert hanging. Here I was so concerned that I wouldn't know how Raj received my message, and I didn't respond to Robert. The time he'd sent me his Santa sketch, he'd been waiting on his computer, for God's sake, so what must he be doing tonight? I pray he's out with Debbie or Carol or somebody.

I can't call him; it's nearly eleven o'clock. But I can send him a message. Maybe he'll log on in the morning. As I'm waiting for the computer to boot up, it occurs to me that I might have a response from Raj. Or Anjani. Or one of his parents.

But no. So I just write to Robert.

"Hey, bud. I don't know what to say. That is about the greatest thing anyone has ever done for me. Thank you."

I fall asleep pretty quickly, actually.

Chapter 17

Blue

My aunt lets me sleep most of the morning and then makes pancakes for a late breakfast. I love pancakes. I load them with butter and maple syrup, the real stuff. The orange juice tastes sharp and almost metallic, but it makes the next mouthful of syrupy pancake taste even sweeter. Uncle Steve seems to be acting more or less normal. He's been doing his best lately, but the strain usually shows. Today, I guess, the track meet has leveled the playing field. So to speak. We're on equal footing, all us track stars.

The timing is just about perfect. By the time I've digested breakfast, warmed up with some stretches, and walked hard for a couple of miles, it's time to leave.

In the car, Aunt Audrey asks, "Are you excited?"

I have to admit I am. "Yeah."

And from Uncle Steve, sounding like a motivational speaker: "Are you going to win?"

"You bet."

I actually feel pretty good. I'm in good shape, I have energy, and the adrenaline is starting to pump. We're meeting at

Wilson High because they won the overall total last year. I'm determined it will be at home field next year.

I walk Aunt Audrey and Uncle Steve to the bleachers in spite of them insisting I should just go find my team. It works out well, because Norm is just getting there with his folks. I see them first.

Do I say anything about how there should be no mention of homosexuals? That Norm's folks don't know? I steal a quick glance at Uncle Steve.

Hah. No way is he going to spoil his own good time. He needs to think of me as no different from the other boys, except that he wants me to be better at track. He's not saying a thing. And Aunt Audrey wouldn't spoil it for him. No danger.

Norm's dad looks just like the ex-marine Norm described. The hair on his head is cut to stubble, the jaw is square and firm, and his handshake nearly crushes my bones.

"Good to meet you, son," he says to me. "Norm here's been telling us how fast you are. I wanna see you prove it!"

"Yes, sir!" I say, and salute. He salutes back and then grins. He might not be the first person I'd tell I was gay, but he might be an okay guy anyway.

Norm and I head for the part of the field where our colors are hung, and I assure him his secret is safe.

"Whew. Thanks."

"Your dad seems okay."

"Yeah. Right. You've seen the tip of the iceberg."

I look to see who's already there, trying to pretend to myself that I'm not looking for Raj. He's there, all right, sort of off on his own as usual. It's starting to dawn on me that I don't really like that. Why can't he be a little more friendly? Once he'd told me that he doesn't like secrecy, but something about him sure inspires it. He looks at me, but only briefly. I can't tell whether he's likely to have seen my e-mail or not, but right now my energy is really going into the team anyway.

Coach gathers everyone and goes over the order of events. Foot races alternate with other competitions, with the relay races near the beginning of the meet and the short dashes the very last. So I have to wait all the way through for my last event. The challenge will be to stay limber after the relay without getting tired or being on my feet too much.

Denny Shriver, Rich Turner, Norm, and I take a lap together as we're waiting for the official start. We're feeling great, it seems. We're confident. We're going to win. It's a rush being with these guys, they're so positive. And I know they're good.

We sit through the first event, an endurance run, and then stand and move around during the shot put. We're next, and we're nervous, but we're ready.

We draw the second start, which means we don't have the inside lane, but we don't have the outside either. There are four teams competing, one from each school. Wilson draws third start.

As we're all jogging to our positions, I'm thinking the starter from Wilson looks familiar. From my position I take a hard look at him, and even from this distance I suddenly recognize him. He was the guy at Norm's party who cut in on my dance with Kathy. And the one who saw Norm touch my face in the shadows. Well, well.

The starters crouch, and the folks in the bleachers get quiet. The whole world is silent for a few seconds. And then the runners launch.

God, I love this. I'm watching Rich gain on the team on the inside lane, getting really excited, until I notice the Wilson runner. He's flying. There's no way Rich is going to get to Denny before this guy gets to his second. And if he's that fast, what the hell should I expect from his anchor?

Christ. Am I *sure* I love this?

So we're behind Wilson by the first handoff. But then the unbelievable happens. Actually, two unbelievable things happen.

First, the handoff from Wilson's second to their third fouls, and the baton is on the ground. It's incredible! In my peripheral vision, I can see the Wilson starter punching the air. He yells something I can't hear.

The second thing isn't something that actually happens. It's that the team on the inside lane has got a guy running third who may be Olympic material. Why he's not on anchor I can't figure. I'm not so worried about Wilson's anchor now; I'm worried about the inside lane. And the guy hands his baton off to their anchor about two seconds before Norm gets to me.

We're good though. We're very good. Norm and I are so in sync. It's like the day of the tryouts. Two well-oiled pieces of the same machine. And the look on his face tells me what he expects me to do.

I run. I run so hard. I'm grunting and whistling breath in and out so fast it's like one continuous motion. There's no one else on the track. I have to believe that. I can't think about the other runner. I have to think about nothing. That finish line has to get bigger and bigger and bigger.

For the last one hundred feet or so, there's a body next to me. It's grunting and heaving a lot like mine, but I'm going to grunt and heave more. That line isn't big enough yet.

About three feet from the finish line, something disappears from my side vision. Once I'm across, I know it's the other runner. I hear Coach shouting. I hear a couple of guys call my name. I jog forward, baton held high.

And I look for Raj.

Nowhere.

So I look for Uncle Steve. He's standing, shouting something victorious and clapping furiously. As soon as I recover enough, I grin and wave, and Aunt Audrey waves back. Robert is there. He's sitting right beside her, fingers in his mouth, making this ear-splitting whistle. And on the other side of Robert is Meg.

Of all things.

She's smiling at me and clapping for all she's worth.

As I'm turning away from the bleachers, I see Raj's parents and Anjani. Should I wave? Should I smile at them? I just keep turning.

I jog back to my team, and we do a group huddle and a lot of high fives. Coach shakes everyone's hand and slaps us all on the shoulder. It's a great moment, maybe even greater than at the end of the day when the ribbons will be handed out.

The four of us walk a little to work out the energy and keep our muscles from cramping, and we pass near the Wilson team. Their starter looks hard at me, and then at Norm. I'm sure he knows where he's seen us before. I have to ignore him though. It's not like I can tell Norm about him here, and maybe it wouldn't be good to tell him at all. I put it behind me.

Rich Turner is also in the hundred-yard dash. Coach had asked him to run after Jimmy was suspended. There are two runners from each school, and the race will be divided into two races, so four runners compete in each dash. Rich will be in the first; I'm in the second.

Rich and I hang around together through the other events. He's standing next to me during the high jump, and I'm just as glad it isn't Norm. Norm may not know the full story about who Raj was to me, but he knows something, and it's easier being with Rich right now.

I don't know why I hadn't noticed this before—too into my own world, I guess—but Dane is here. And he's jumping. He must have worked out something special with Coach. It looks like his performance isn't up to his usual standard, but I have to give him credit. A hell of a lot of credit.

Raj is stellar. He does everything perfectly, and no one can touch him. He just sails over anything they put in front of him. The crowds oooh and ahhh every time he goes over. And he always lands just so. I think that's what really gets to me. It's like no matter what goes on before, he knows what to do. And he always lands just so.

Rich says to me, "Do you know him at all?"

"Sort of. Why?"

"He's always off on his own. I've heard he's—you know."

"No. What?" I want him to say it.

"Well, somebody said they thought he might be gay."

"He might be. Anybody might be. Does it matter?"

Rich shrugs. "I guess not."

I can't go up to Raj this time, to tell him how well he's done. Or, at least, it would be less than satisfactory. But I can go up to Dane.

He sort of flinches as I approach; maybe he's just skittish about everything right now. So I decide not to hold my hand out, just talk to him. "It's good to see you here."

He sneers over his shoulder, his side to me.

"No, really. I mean it. I'd heard you were sick or something. But I'm glad you could make it."

I can't exactly tell him how well he's done; he'd know that was false. But in any case, he won't speak. He looks hard at my face, probably scouring it for sarcasm. I let a long breath out.

"Look, Dane, I know we haven't been best buddies. Probably never will be. But I don't wish you any harm, okay? And I think it took a lot for you to be here today. I'm impressed. That's all."

His face has changed, sort of a begrudging acceptance of what I've said. He says nothing, but he raises his chin at me before walking away.

We do what we can.

At long last it's time for the dashes. Rich and I head over to the starting line. He's in the first race, along with that Olympic guy. Not a good sign. I slap him on the back and head over to watch with the other runners in the second race. As I approach the group of guys, I see that one of them is the Wilson relay starter.

Great.

Okay, I've ignored a lot of things today, this week, this life. Here's one more. I pay no attention to him as the first four runners crouch. There's no lane issue, so all four guys are next to each other in a line, and it's interesting to compare their starting techniques. Rich is good. He's ready. I'm glad he's the one Coach went to for Walsh's replacement.

The signal goes, and Rich springs forward. He's really focused. The Olympic guy is ahead, but he's limping! I'm shouting Rich's name and the word "go" in quick succession. And he does.

But in the last couple of seconds, the second guy from Wilson's relay team squeaks ahead. Rich wins second place, and that's an honor, but it won't help us regain home field for next year. By my count, we're tied with Wilson right now. If I don't finish ahead of Wilson in my heat, we've lost it.

After these first runners have had a chance to take their bows or cover their shame, the other four of us are told to move up. The Wilson guy from the party, their relay starter, is on my right. I'm wishing I'd thought to look up his name. It's sure to be on the event sheet, just like mine is, but I didn't. Maybe it's better this way. He means even less.

I crouch, fingers pricked by the grit of the track surface. I'm waiting for the signal. Nothing else exists. And then, just before the signal, coming from my right, I hear it.

So quiet.

"Faggot."

The signal pops, and I explode. I'm going to beat the hell out of that guy. I don't care how fast he was on the relay. He's gonna eat my dust.

The other two runners are nowhere in sight, but the Wilson creep and I are neck and neck. I haven't saved anything for the last few yards, but I'm counting on my anger.

Close to the finish line, I'm about out of steam, and I'm sure I've lost. And suddenly my mirage is back. The one that helped me beat Walsh in that qualifying heat weeks ago. Only this time it's not my imagination.

Raj is standing there. He's in the group of people facing the finish line, but he's definitely visible. His eyes are on me, and his face seems as intent as when he's jumping.

So it isn't anger that wins me that ribbon. It's Raj.

By the time I've recovered enough to look for him again though, he's gone. I see him when he steps forward for his own blue ribbon, but then he disappears once more. He's nowhere in sight when I collect my ribbons for the relay and for the dash. I love the cheers, the applause, Aunt Audrey's huge smile, Robert's arm pumping the air, all for me.

But I miss Raj.

I'm not up for fooling around with Norm. It won't be easy to tell him this; he looks so euphoric. His dad shakes my hand and claps my back, says I'm a "real company man." Makes it even harder when I pull Norm aside.

"Listen, I need another rain check. I don't feel up to going out tonight."

"Jason, Jason, what are you saying? You're just exhausted. Let me get you some water or—"

I catch his arm. "No, really. I'm sorry, honest." And it is honest, I suppose, though it doesn't feel much like it. Especially since I've decided not to tell him what the Wilson runner said; he'd be worried sick about being found out. It may happen, but it won't do him any good to worry about it.

Norm looks concerned about me, which is kind of nice. "Hey, you all right? You're not sick or anything, are you?"

"Nah. Just need a little time to myself, I guess."

I don't really get any private time though. I hadn't told Aunt Audrey I was even considering going to Norm's, so she's invited Meg and Robert over for dinner. Talk about the odd couple.

"How come you don't have a date tonight, big guy?" I ask Robert when he arrives at the house ahead of Meg.

He shrugs and grins. "I guess I was kind of hoping we could hang out. Get some of that star dust to rub off on me, y'know?"

Friends can be better than lovers, I decide.

Meg arrives with a salad, and somehow without my knowing it, Aunt Audrey has made my favorite cake: devil's food with burnt sugar icing. The dinner is so much fun I almost forget my dark mood at the track. It makes me feel really good to know that Meg and I are going to be friends after all.

But when I'm upstairs alone again, about to go to bed, admiring my two blue ribbons, I can't conjure up any joy.

That night, in my dreams, unbidden, David Bowie comes to me. It's a little different this time though. It's not really a wet dream. He doesn't speak. He just wraps me in his arms and holds me while I cry.

Chapter 18

Resorting to Nonviolence

If I was in a funk after the meet Saturday, I'm in two of them on Sunday. My aunt even offers to let me take the car to go clothes shopping. It's an interesting irony, this suggestion. She's a woman, but shopping doesn't cheer her up; yet because I'm gay, she seems to think it will help my mood. Maybe if there were something I was itching to buy . . .

There's something I want. I just can't buy it.

After lunch I go up to my room and flip the computer power on. Maybe a little writing will clear my head. And maybe, just maybe, there will be a message from Raj.

No.

And writing doesn't help. Usually I love a blank screen, a blank sheet of paper. Not today. So I open a saved version of one of those articles on scent to see if it can perk me up any. Again, no.

In disgust I turn from my desk, and, almost without thinking about it, I pick up my phone and dial.

Anjani answers. She doesn't sound too thrilled to hear from me, and who can blame her? Last time we talked, I practically accused her of thinking I was a girl and of giving me bad advice. And I'm calling, for the second time now, so I'm ignoring her advice, good or bad.

"Jason. Hello. You did well yesterday." No enthusiasm, but at least she's polite.

"Thanks. So did Raj. Um, is he there? Would he—"

"No, actually. He isn't."

Not there. I wrack my brains; would he go to the track? Hell, I'll just ask.

"Do you know where he is?"

She pauses and then says, "He went to see a film."

My stomach clenches. Is he with someone? All I say is, "Oh. The retro theater, do you know?"

"I think so. But Jason—"

"Don't worry. I won't embarrass him, and I won't tell on you." I hang up before she can say more, and she doesn't call back.

I throw myself down on my bed, trying to think. Trying to sense any real thoughts through the sulk. So what if he's on a date? So what if he's found someone else already? He's let me know in so many ways that it won't work with me, even though he keeps sending me mixed messages. Like that look from the crowd yesterday when I was racing the Wilson runner.

And to be honest, I'm a little tired of his superior attitude. One can carry aloof too far.

Fuck him. I'm going for more knife practice. I tuck my knife into the fifth pocket of my jeans and thunder down the stairs.

"Aunt Audrey, can I borrow the car after all?"

"Thought of something you'd like?"

"Yeah. Is it okay?"

She hands me the keys. Briefly I contemplate calling Robert, but I think I want to be alone today.

I'm halfway to the park when I pull a U-turn in the middle of the road and head for town.

Pretty close to where he'd parked with me, I see Raj's dad's car. There's a spot across the street, so I park the VW. Then I just sit there, breathing hard, trying to think and failing.

What the hell am I doing?

It's like the feeling I'd had watching Raj and Anjani through the boutique window before I'd met her, before I knew she was his sister. I went into that store because I had to know. If she'd turned out to be his girlfriend, then at least I would have been able to pick myself up and go on. The feeling I have right now is like that, only twenty or thirty times more powerful. I get out, slam the car door, and sprint across the road.

I go through our alley—ha! "our alley" indeed; he probably takes all his dates in here. At the other end, I stop and look at the theater. Today it's *Harold and Maude*. I've heard something about this movie. It's a cult film too, like *La Cage*; what is it with Raj? If I remember, it's about a young boy who keeps faking his own suicides to get his mother's attention, and he ends up falling in love with an old woman who teaches him how to live and then kills herself. What's the lesson in this one, oh my guru?

Damn, but I wish I didn't love him.

Looking as casual as possible, I cross the street and examine the showtimes. If he's in there now, he's in a show that will end in about half an hour. Maybe less.

I decide to duck into the music store next door to the theater. It'll be open only another ten minutes, but what the hell. I walk up and down the aisles, not really seeing anything, and somehow I find myself in the section for musicals. My watch tells me I have six more minutes, so I scour the headings until I find it. *La Cage aux Folles.* And it has that song, "I Am What I Am."

Now I'm in a little bit of a rush, 'cause I want to buy it and take it back to my car in time to watch the theater door. I fumble with my wallet, the guy behind the register eyeing me suspiciously; probably can't figure out why I seem nervous.

I dash back through the alley, throw the bag into the trunk, and make it back to the theater in plenty of time; still no one coming out.

I walk up the street a little, pretending to window shop but really looking for a good place to wait where I can see without being seen. I find one and position myself there and watch.

I'm there maybe fifteen minutes, shifting from foot to foot, keeping an eye out for anyone who might actually care that there's this delinquent-looking kid loitering, and then a few people leave the theater. Then a few more, in groups and an occasional single. I'm shrinking against my wall, hoping to blend in with the cement between the bricks, when I see him.

At first I think he's with someone, as there's a guy walking close by, and I can barely breathe. But then the guy turns to wait for a girl. They look like college students.

So Raj is alone. Now what? All I can do is watch.

He looks both ways, crosses the street, and heads into our alley. I feel like I can still call it that, for now. Part of me wants to tear myself away from the mortar I've psychologically merged with, and part of me is hanging onto it stubbornly. I decide that the last thing I want, really, is for him to know I was watching him, or that I even care enough to do that.

I tell myself it's enough to have seen him. Maybe I don't know a lot more than I did, but at least I know he isn't on a date. I stand there until there's no one else coming out of the theater, and for that matter no one else on the street. It's late on a Sunday afternoon, after all, and everything's pretty deserted. I'm starting to feel a little foolish now, hanging onto this wall, but I want to be sure he's through the alley, maybe even in the car and driving away.

No need to look both ways now; there are no cars to dodge. But as I'm at the alley entrance, I hear sounds coming from farther in. Thudding noises and some kind of guttural language. Cautiously I move forward.

"Stinking brown faggot," is what I hear, and I can barely see someone plunge his fist into the stomach of another guy who's being held by someone else.

Brown? Faggot?

Christ, is that Raj?

I sneak farther in, until I can make out what's really happening. Three guys are in there, most of the way through the alley toward the other end. There's just enough light coming in from above that I can make out the face of John Whittier in his green varsity football jacket. He's the one doing the punching.

And it is Raj.

Automatically my hand goes to my knife.

It isn't there!

Fuck! I don't know whether to be more upset that I don't know where it is or that I don't have it, so I can't save Raj.

But I have to save Raj! There has to be another way. Irrationally I think, "See Aunt Audrey? I told you I needed a cell phone!"

If I run out of the alley, I can get help. But will there be anyone there? And how long will it take to find someone willing to help? Raj is in trouble right now.

Think, Jason. Do you have another advantage?

I can run. So what?

I'm smart.

And I'm gay.

I walk farther in, trying to pretend I hadn't seen or heard anything yet. When I'm pretty close, Whittier looks up at me.

"Oh! My heaventh!" I breathe, my voice a high falsetto. "What are you boyth doing? Oh, oh!" I cover my cheeks with my hands and try to look like some kind of demented prostitute. They've stopped beating Raj, and he's fallen forward, semiconscious. It's as bad as I'd feared. Now they're both staring right at me.

"Oh!" I repeat. "Oh, thith ith terrible! I mutht get help! Oh!" And I turn, doing my best to sashay quickly back through the alley, desperately hoping they'll take the bait. At the other end, I take one deliberately frantic look back down the alley and see Whittier chasing after me.

Excellent. I mutter one more helpless "Oh!" and throw my hands into the air.

And then I'm off.

I dodge in and out of doorways, each time letting Whittier pass and then doubling back, until I have him totally confused as to what I'm doing. Then finally I make a mad dash for the next street, turn the corner, and fly. When I'm sure he can't see where I've gone, I stop and wait. I hear running footsteps, then "Shit! Fuck!" between panted breaths, and then he gives up looking and goes back where he came from.

I run around the block to the other entrance and wait behind a car, watching. And sure enough, emerging from the alley I see first the other guy, Brian Cooney, and then an exhausted John Whittier. It's obvious he's a tackle; no quarterback, this. He can't run to save his life.

As soon as I'm sure they're gone, I dash into the alley. Raj is there, on his side, clutching his middle and groaning quietly.

"Raj! It's me, Jason. I have to get you out of here."

I think he knows what's going on; it's a little hard to tell. But he does his best to help me help him up.

Outside the alley, I have a choice to make. Do I take my aunt's car, which is smaller and farther away, or do I search for Raj's keys? I prop him up against his car, and he decides for me.

"Here."

He's fishing in his pocket, but he's too slow. I move his hand and reach in myself. I get the back door open, and he kind of falls across the seat. From the driver's seat, I see a phone. I dial.

"Aunt Audrey? Listen, I have an emergency. Raj has been beaten. What's the best thing to do?"

She doesn't even have to think, and she doesn't ask any stupid questions. "Go to the hospital emergency room and ask for Dr. Watson. I'll call ahead to let them know you're coming."

I almost laugh. Dr. Watson, really? As in Sherlock Holmes? I'm feeling a little giddy.

She adds, "I'll be there as soon as I can."

Next I punch the numbers to his house. His mother answers.

"Mrs. Burugapalli? It's Jason. Jason Peele." As if she didn't know. "I need to tell you Raj has been hurt. I've got him in your car now."

I give her the name of my aunt's hospital, and she says she'll be there as soon as possible. She must be a lot like Aunt Audrey, or maybe she's just used to Raj being hurt. She doesn't ask anything either.

Aunt Audrey's name carries weight, that's for sure. As soon

as I've said she's told me to ask for Dr. Watson, a couple of or-
derlies follow me out to the car with a gurney and bring Raj
in. He has almost no color in his face, which is pretty spooky.
But he's conscious, barely. We don't wait long for the doctor,
thanks to my aunt's call, but while we do he holds my hand.
The side of his face is all bruised, and I'm getting angrier by
the second. Those bastards!

Then he squeezes my hand and says, almost in a whisper,
"I know what you did. And what you didn't do."

"Didn't do?"

"The knife."

Ah. But he doesn't know why.

Then he tries to smile. He can't, but he says, "You used
your secret edge."

Dr. Watson turns out to be a woman, so it's not as funny as
it might have been. Or maybe it's even funnier. I'm feeling
like it would be easy to laugh hysterically right now, or to
cry; it would be one and the same. She says she's taking Raj to
X-ray and to examine his wounds, and then he's gone.

I'm waiting nervously when the Burugapallis get there.
All three of them. I've just started my story when Aunt Audrey shows up with Uncle Steve in tow. I hadn't expected
him, but I suppose it makes sense that he'd come. I feel awkward though, both sets of parents—in a way—meeting each
other for the first time, all knowing what Raj and I have been
to each other. Or having some idea, anyway.

I begin the story again. I don't really talk about my little
playacting; I just say I'd run the guy senseless and then lost
him so he and his friend would leave, thinking someone
would be coming. And I mention that I'd put Raj in his car
because it was closer and has a bigger backseat.

So now we're all waiting for Dr. Watson to come back, no
one really knowing what to say, and thank God no one asks

me how I happened to be where Raj was. I hadn't thought of a good answer for this. I'm sure, though, that Aunt Audrey will want to know.

And then a horrible thought occurs to me. She and Uncle Steve have to drive me back to the VW, and—what if my knife is in the car? What if it's sitting right there on the driver's seat, in plain view, and she wants to ride back with me? It would be just like her.

Shit.

At least this worry keeps me busy until Dr. Watson shows up again. She greets Aunt Audrey cordially.

"He'll be fine," she tells us. "Minor facial abrasions, and a couple of ribs are cracked, not broken. We've wrapped them. The really good news is that there's not much internal bleeding, which is what we worry about in cases like this. We'll keep him overnight for observation to monitor that, but I expect he'll be able to go home tomorrow."

His mother asks, "Is he conscious? May I see him?"

They all want to go. I do too, but also I don't. So I don't. Just before they disappear, I call out, "Hey! I've got your car keys."

There's a moment when everyone looks blankly at me. Then Anjani comes back to where Aunt Audrey and I are standing, takes the keys, and returns to her folks. Aunt Audrey and I are turning toward the door when I hear, "Wait!" It's Raj's mother. She comes to us and takes me in her arms. I try to pretend it's Raj. But it isn't.

All the way back to the VW, I'm wracking my brain. Am I sure I put the knife in my pocket? Did I put my hands in my pockets while I was waiting for Raj to come out of the theater, and was it there then? I just don't know.

At the VW I say, "I'll drive, Aunt Audrey. I have the keys anyway."

But, as I'd predicted, she's getting out of Uncle Steve's car. "Jason, I'll drive. You're not exactly calm."

I stall for time and peek in through the driver's side window. Nothing. Think fast, Jason. Where might the knife be? And then it hits me.

"Okay, but I need to check something in the trunk. I bought something earlier, and I want to make sure it's there."

She waits at the driver's door while I open the trunk.

And there it is. It must have got caught on the key ring when I pulled that out of my pocket to put the CD in here. It's so small, I didn't notice at the time. Even now it's nearly hidden under the bag. I grab it quickly, shove it into a pocket, slam the trunk, and climb into the passenger seat.

Christ. Close one. But it did keep my mind off Raj, at least a little.

Aunt Audrey has questions now. "Why were you here, Jason? I thought you'd gone to the mall."

I think for a few seconds and finally decide that honesty is the best route here. At least, relative honesty. "I called Raj before I left. I really wanted to talk to him. Anjani said he'd gone to this theater. I wasn't going to come here. I didn't know when I left the house that I'd do this. It just came over me as I was driving how much I needed to see him. So . . ."

"So you waited for him to come out?"

"Yes."

"What if he'd been with someone?"

The sixty-four-thousand-dollar question. "I guess that's something I needed to do too. To know that."

A minute passes. Then, "It was very brave of you, Jason. Letting those boys know you were there so they'd follow you. If you hadn't stopped them when you did, Raj's injuries might have been much worse. I'm very proud of you."

I don't know whether to feel good about what she's said or feel bad that I'm still deceiving her a little. But I say, "Thanks."

We haven't been home very long when the police show up. It's actually just one detective. He's already been to the hospital, he says, and he got Raj's statement. Now he needs mine for corroboration, and he can nail those two assholes (not his words). I don't tell *him* about the knife either. But I do end up having to tell him something else I'd rather not.

He asks, "Why were you in the area?"

My aunt and uncle are sitting right there. Thank God I've already told Aunt Audrey, and thank God I've been honest. But that makes it only a little easier to tell the detective, who doesn't look as though he's likely to have a soft spot in his heart for gay teenagers. And of course I have no idea what Raj has said. Or Anjani; she'd be the only one who really knows why I was there, and they may have talked to her. So I guess it's just going to have to be truth again.

"I, uh, I knew Raj was at the theater. I was waiting for him to come out." Will that do?

Evidently not. "Why were you waiting for him?"

Aunt Audrey intercedes. "Detective, why do you need to know that?"

"Ma'am, we have no reason to believe that Jason would be involved in helping the alleged attackers. It certainly looks like the opposite is true. But we need the whole picture in order to make that case." He turns back to me, and Aunt Audrey says nothing else. My turn again.

I take a deep breath. "I wanted to talk to him." The detective is just staring at me. "All right, we've gone out. And I wanted to see if he was with someone else, okay?"

He barely blinks. "Was he?"

"No. He was alone."

"If that's true, then why did you wait so long before following him?"

"I—I didn't want him to know I was there. That I'd
watched for him. I was trying to let him get back to his car
and leave."

He scribbles a few things. "When you entered the alley,
what did you see?"

So it all comes out. My little act. Knowing Raj, he will have
been scrupulously honest. Which means I have no choice.

My story has an effect I hadn't anticipated. I don't know
whether it's stress or tension or what, but by the time I'm finished, Uncle Steve is having trouble containing his laughter.
This gets Aunt Audrey chuckling, and even the detective
looks like he's fighting to maintain a cool demeanor. He has
to clear his throat once or twice before asking me any other
questions.

I'm the only one not laughing.

Before the detective leaves, Aunt Audrey makes him
promise that the two "alleged attackers" will not be anywhere
near the school this week.

On Monday, not only is Jimmy Walsh not in school, and
of course Brian Cooney and John Whittier are missing—not
that I ever see them anyway—but Raj is also absent. It's not
like I used to see him all the time, but there was always a
chance. Now I know he's not there. It seems I have a way of
making people disappear.

Not that Raj not being there makes any difference. He
doesn't want to see me, certainly. I'm sure by now he knows,
or will know at some point in the very near future, that I fol-

lowed him to the theater. He'll hate that. It will seem so demeaning to him. I'll have proven myself to be of lesser quality than he is, yet again.

Coach catches up with me as I'm pawing through my locker after English Lit. "I heard what happened to Raj," he says. I look at him and nod to acknowledge him, but I don't speak. He adds, "Are you going to visit him?"

I exhale loudly. "I doubt very much that he wants to see me."

"But you rescued him."

I heft my pack onto my shoulders. "If he wants to see me, he can let me know. Until then, he's on his own."

I can feel Coach's eyes on me as I walk away from him. It's like I've disappointed him somehow. Too bad. I'm feeling pretty disappointed myself.

During dinner I barely speak. I'm not rude; the consequences wouldn't be worth it. But I'm no fun either. Afterward I'm about to head upstairs when Uncle Steve says, "Jason, is there anything troubling you? Can we talk for a minute?"

"I'm okay. Really. I just—"

"Can we talk anyway?" He turns toward his study and sort of beckons me in.

Well, this is tense. I'm incapable of speech, and he wants to have a chat about what's troubling me.

We take our accustomed seats, he in the recliner and me in the desk chair. He's silent for so long I'm beginning to wonder what this is all about. Then he says, "I am so Goddamned proud of you. I'm proud of the way you acted yesterday, how brave you were, and how quickly you thought of the best way to help your friend. And I'm proud of your performance Saturday too. There were so many things that went wrong, so many obstacles, and such great runners against you, and you exceeded even your past efforts. You were terrific, Jason."

I can't help at least half a grin. "Thanks." But in my head I'm echoing, ". . . your *friend.*"

But he's not done. "Especially that last heat." *Sure,* I'm thinking, *short dash was your thing; of course you'd want me to be great at that.* But then he goes on, "That Wilson runner was huge competition. And I confess, there was a moment near the end when I thought you'd lost it. It looked like you hadn't held onto any reserves, that you'd thrown everything out all at once. But I should have known better."

He's smiling, like he's taught me this thing that made me win. And I almost don't say anything. What would it hurt to have him believe that? And he has given me some great coaching from time to time. But I'm not in a generous mood.

"That wasn't it."

"What wasn't it?"

"I really had blown it all. I was angry. Hell, I was furious. Do you know what that Wilson guy did?" Uncle Steve shakes his head. "Right before the signal? Like, microseconds before? He called me a faggot."

And suddenly I'm breathing hard. Angry all over again, racing again. Racing—what? Something. And then Uncle Steve's quiet voice deflates me.

"I'm sorry."

The anger was better; this makes me feel like crying, and I will not do that. I may be a faggot, but I'm no sissy. So I say, "It was Raj."

"What?"

"Raj? Remember Raj? Burugapalli? The high jumper. My lover." I see him flinch at that one. "The one I rescued last Sunday. Remember him?"

"Jason, of course I know whom you mean. But what are you talking about?"

"He knew. Somehow, he knew. Probably because he's had that word thrown at him so often. Maybe even by that runner. And he was standing right at the finish line, right where I could see him, knowing that I'd run like hell to get to him first. And he was right."

Silence.

"So I didn't do everything right. I didn't pace myself. I didn't think. I didn't give a fuck."

"Jason, don't use that word . . ."

"And now he's gone again."

Damn. He's got it out of me. He'd wanted to know what was wrong, and I've told him. I get up and pace around the room.

Uncle Steve is quiet for a minute, and then he says, "Gone where?"

"How do I know? Away from me, that's all I know. And I want him back. I want him back!"

The only sound is my feet hitting the floor. I'm in a cage, and I feel just about as murderous as a tiger. Then Uncle Steve says, "You really are sure, aren't you?"

He sounds so sad. It deflates me all over again.

"Yes."

"Can you tell me how?"

I sit down. I tell him the story Coach told me about the witches being burned with human faggots to coax the flames along.

"Would I *choose* to be treated like kindling?" But that's not an answer. I just feel like shocking him. It works, and now I feel like shit. He actually looks like he's about to cry. I don't think I've ever seen that, and I don't want to now.

So I tell him something else. I tell him this.

"They've proven it, you know. That it occurs naturally. They've even discovered that some animals are homosexual. Sheep. Penguins. Lots of animals."

He blinks and then stares at me. I have his attention.

"It has to do with pheromones, or whatever it is humans have like that. Women give off female pheromones, and men give off male ones, and they even believe that gay men give off their own variety of male ones. And our hypothalamus detects this and starts the arousal process. Automatically. Without us even knowing about it."

He's stunned. He's just sitting there, mouth hanging open a little, scowling like he's trying to understand, like he's thinking really hard.

"You want to know how I know? Because when I'm with Rebecca, or Meg, I can force a response, but it's like— well, it's kind of like black-and-white television next to when I'm with Raj. Then it's like virtual reality."

Uncle Steve finds his voice. "Where did you see all that about pheromones and animals?"

"On the Internet. All these really high-end science institutions are doing research on it." He's shaking his head. "You don't believe me?" I'm about to get up and fetch some of my printouts.

"No, wait. It isn't that. I'm just—I guess I'm a little stunned. It's . . . it's really *not* a choice, is it? And it's not something anyone has done. This is who you are."

"Yes. This is who I am. The real me." I take a deep breath. "You didn't fail me, or my dad. And I didn't fail either of you. Because there's nothing wrong with being who I am."

He rubs his face. Hard. Then he sits back in his chair and gives me this wobbly smile. "So, young man, what are we going to do about Raj?"

Well, really, there's nothing to be done about Raj. Nothing Uncle Steve can do anyway. One day maybe I'll have to face that I can't have Raj.

For now, it's enough that Uncle Steve understands. It's enough that we both understand.

Chapter 19

Friends and Lovers

It rains on and off for most of the rest of the week. I swear if I hear one more person say how lucky we were it didn't rain last Saturday for the track meet, I think I'll scream.

Norm asks if I'll come to his house after dinner on Friday. I do, but thank God his younger brother wants to see the movie he's rented, so we don't spend much time alone. When his brother finally leaves us, Norm already knows that I'm not exactly in a chipper mood.

"You've been a pain in the ass all week, Jason. Won't talk to anyone. What's up?"

Should I tell him? I decide there's no point in keeping secrets, as long as I can level with him without hurting him. I sit on the floor in his room and lean against the bed. "I wasn't completely honest with you."

"About?"

"About Raj." I look at him, and there's a sideways, sardonic grin barely showing.

He says, "I thought so."

I blink. "You did?"

"Jason, it seems every time I look at you, you're looking at him. Or for him. And then you played the shining knight for him last Sunday. You're in love with him, aren't you." It isn't really a question.

"Yeah. I guess so. But he's not an easy person to love. He's been furious with me for something he doesn't understand, and he won't let me explain. And it's really coming from something he doesn't even think I know about. Something I found out about only after he threw a fit."

"What? Does it have anything to do with what happened on Sunday?"

"No. I'm sorry. I shouldn't have said that much, 'cause I can't talk about the rest of it. But he wouldn't answer e-mails or phone calls or anything. He's avoided me for weeks now. Am I in love with him?" I throw my hands into the air. "How the fuck do I know?"

"Can you tell me what happened Sunday?"

"I called him, but his sister said he was at the retro theater. I had to know if he was there with someone, so I waited for him to come out. He was alone, and I didn't want him to know I'd followed him there, so I waited while he went down this alley back to where he'd parked. I'd left my car in about the same place, so I waited a few minutes for him to get clear and then started in. That's when I saw them. Cooney was holding his arms behind him, and Whittier was punching him."

"Jesus. What did you do?"

I leave out the part about not finding my knife where it should have been. "It seemed like it would take too long to go and fetch someone, like Raj would be too hurt by then. So I figured I could outrun them and make them worry that someone would come, you know. I, uh, I got their attention." I'm chuckling now, which of course peaks Norm's curiosity.

"What? What's so funny?"

I fall sideways onto the floor. "You're gonna love this.

They were calling him faggot, right? So I pretended to be this really swishy queen type, screaming 'Oh, Oh,' and lisping, talking to myself about getting help. You better believe they couldn't resist that!"

"You didn't! Jason, you're too much. And did they chase you?"

"Whittier did, and he's the one who was hitting Raj. I ran him a merry race, I can tell you. Had the poor guy so turned around I don't know how he found his way back to the alley. But it did the trick, and he collected his partner in crime and fled. So I picked Raj up and took him to the hospital."

"Wow. Jason, that's so cool. If he doesn't love you after that, he's an idiot."

I'm not laughing anymore. Norm is grinning at me, but it's kind of a sad grin, like he knows what this means for us. I reach for his shoulder and pull him to me, and we lie there like that for a while.

Finally he says, "I know we can't be lovers, Jason. But I hope we'll be really good friends."

I nod. "And you know, sometimes friends can be better than lovers."

Saturday looks gloomy again, though it's not raining anymore. Uncle Steve is holed up in his study, correcting exams. Aunt Audrey and I have a late breakfast, and I'm helping her clear the table when the phone rings. She jerks her head toward the phone for me to get it.

"Hello?"

"Jason."

Raj.

"Yeah?" I don't know what he wants, but I'm not going to make it easy.

"It's Raj." He sounds awful. Weak, breathy.

"I know. What's up?" I don't even ask how he is. He never asked how I was, after Walsh jumped me. I know this is petty, but I can't help myself.

"I was wondering . . . I know this would be an imposition. But—would you consider coming over sometime today?"

Coming over? Does he want me to sign his cast or something? Not that he has one. I want to tell him he's right, it would be an imposition. I want to tell him he can wait until it's convenient for me. Maybe I consider my options for too long, because he speaks again.

"Please?"

"Any time in particular?" I struggle to keep my tone even and cool.

"No. I'm pretty much trapped here, so whatever is good for you. Just call first, so we'll know you're on your way."

" 'Kay. Later."

When I set the phone down, I realize I'm not breathing.

Aunt Audrey says, "Who was it, Jason?"

I take a shaky breath. "Raj."

She turns to look at me. "Really. What did he say? How is he? You didn't talk long."

"Sounds kind of weak. He asked if I would go over." I don't tell her what I expect. He wants to thank me, I'm sure, but then he just wants closure. He can't write me off as long as he owes me, so he has to express his gratitude first. That would be Raj, all over.

I can tell she's trying to be cool, just as I had. She says, "I don't think I'll need my car today. Just let me know what you decide to do."

"Thanks."

She doesn't hound me, doesn't pump me for information. She knows I'm hurting.

I lie on the sofa for a while, trying to read up on European history for an exam next week, taking notes that mean nothing to me after I've written them. Around one-thirty I give up and ask Aunt Audrey for the car keys. I call first so His Highness won't be unprepared for the command performance. Anjani answers.

"Oh, Jason! I'm so glad you're coming over. I didn't get a chance to thank you properly, and I felt so awkward calling you after—well, after our last conversation. I'll tell Raj you're on your way."

I think I changed my shirt. It's a bit of a blur. Getting into the car is a blur. Driving over to Raj's is a blur. The only thing that isn't a blur is something I couldn't even have explained at the time; I picked up the bag containing that CD from *La Cage*. A farewell shot at Raj, perhaps? Like saying, *You could have been with someone who understands you. Someone who actually takes you seriously.*

When I get there, Mr. Burugapalli answers the door. "Come in, Jason." He's in the process of saying something about how grateful he is when Anjani shows up, her mother right behind her. Anjani hugs me first, and then her mother does. Seems everyone in this family likes me except the one who brought me here in the first place.

Mrs. Burugapalli says, "I'm sure you want to go right up and see how Raj is doing. Anjani, would you go up with Jason?"

I'm not sure why this is necessary, but it doesn't matter. Maybe a chaperone is a good idea. Maybe he and I will be more civil to each other in front of Anjani.

The blurriness is gone; all my senses are on the alert. On the way upstairs I notice every color in the oriental carpet, every grain of wood in the banister, each flash of reflection from the bejeweled ebony elephant on the landing.

Raj's door is standing open, but Anjani knocks on it anyway.

"Raj? Jason is here." She grins at me and then turns away and heads back downstairs again. I gaze after her stupidly for a moment, and then I go in. It feels like entering a lion's den, or a snake pit, one of those places where you have to do everything right or you die.

He watches me from where he's propped up on pillows on the bed. The whole side of his face is one gigantic bruise. I drop the CD bag just inside the door.

"Please, sit," he says. There's a chair beside the bed, facing Raj, already positioned for a visitor. I sit, but I don't speak.

He doesn't waste time. He doesn't ask how I am, he doesn't say how he is. He says, "Jason, I've behaved very badly toward you." And he stops.

I just nod once, more in acknowledgment than agreement.

He tries again. "I'm sorry."

I take a deep breath. This is something, at least. So I give him a little advice. "For future reference, you might want to remember that the more time that went by, the less I wanted to talk. The less I even wanted to see you."

His attempt at a grin with his injured face makes me think he hasn't understood. It's like he's trying to be—sexy or something. He says, "And why is this for future reference?"

"Well, for when you're with someone you want to stay with for a while. Your next—I dunno, boyfriend. Is that the right word?"

"Next boyfriend, Jason? Why should I be thinking about my next boyfriend?"

Is he going to make me say this? "Why are you making this harder?"

The look on his face now says he doesn't know what I'm talking about. "Jason . . ."

I'm nearly shouting so I won't cry. I hate this. "Didn't you ask me over here to say thanks for saving my ass, and now good-bye? Didn't you delete that e-mail I sent you without even reading it?"

He just blinks at me. And then he starts shaking his head. "No. No, no, no. No." His head drops back onto the pillow, and his eyes squeeze shut. I can barely see a tear in the corner of the one nearer to me. "I am such an asshole sometimes."

Well, gee, I've wanted to say that to him for a couple of weeks now. I decide not to contradict him.

When he opens his eyes, the tear falls. "I read the e-mail, Jason. And I love you too. Please forgive me."

Forgive him? He loves me? This is too sudden. I can't quite accept it. I stand and walk across the room, my back to him.

"Jason?"

I wheel on him. "You hurt me really badly, do you know that? You made me feel like shit, like you thought you were some kind of god and I was the scum of the earth. And now all of a sudden you love me. Why should I believe you?"

Slowly he moves himself away from the pillows, grimacing in pain, and then swings his legs over the side. He manages to stand, but he's wobbly and looks like he's in agony. I want to go to him, but I can tell it's not the right thing to do.

With one arm he supports his weight as he lowers himself onto the floor. And he kneels.

He kneels! What a weird thing to do. But this is Raj.

Still, it's too much. "Raj, please! What are you doing? This has to be bad for you."

"I'm begging you," he says, teeth clenched, "to forgive me. And I'm begging you to believe that I love you. You have humbled me."

Suddenly the ridiculousness of this scene grabs me, and I

start to laugh. I laugh harder and harder, holding my sides. I can hear Raj saying, "I can't laugh! Don't make me laugh!" But he can't help a snort or two, and it sounds so funny it sets me off again.

Finally he lets me help him back onto the bed, and when I sit on the chair again, he reaches out a hand. I take it.

Then he closes his eyes and says, "I meant what I said. You have humbled me." He tries to smile. "And I don't humble easily."

I'm out of the chair and on the floor again, but I'm the one kneeling this time, beside the bed, still holding the hand Raj gave me. I ask, "Did you mean what you said?"

"About forgiving me? Yes. Please. Say you will."

"I will, if you'll tell me again that you love me."

"I love you. I love you! And I beg you to tell me you can forgive what an idiot I've been."

I don't let go of his hand, but I sit on the floor. I want more. "What kind of an idiot have you been?"

He nods. "You're good for me. You don't let me get away with anything. Very well. I was an idiot for not telling you why the knife upset me so much and for being angry with you about something you couldn't understand. I was an idiot for thinking that you should be a certain way just because I wished it. I was an idiot"—and here he reaches with his free hand for a book beside him that I hadn't even noticed before—"not to allow you to focus on Gandhi's teachings in your own way."

He reclaims the hand I've been holding so he can open the book and find a place he's marked. "I was rather hoping you'd be willing to teach me." He hands me the book.

"Teach you?" I take it, but I don't know what I'm supposed to do.

"Just read the places I've marked in pencil."

"Aloud?"

"Please."

Back in the chair, I go to the yellow sticky marker on which I see the numeral one, and I read.

" 'I do believe that, where there is only a choice between cowardice and violence, I would advise violence.' " I look up. Raj's eyes are on me, intent. He nods once, so I find the second marker.

" 'Nonviolence in its dynamic condition means conscious suffering. It does not mean meek submission to the will of the evil-doer, but it means the putting of one's whole soul against the will of the tyrant. Working under this law of being, it is possible for a single individual to defy the whole might of an unjust empire to save his honor, his religion, his soul, and lay the foundation for the empire's fall or its regeneration.' "

Raj says, "In our case, one of these unjust empires is a world where you and I are not allowed to love. We must defy this. Do you agree?"

I just nod. How can I not agree? It's what I'd said to Norm, really. Maybe Norm can't join us yet. But he will.

"Will you read the next one?"

The next one says that only a worm crawling at the bidding of a bully will be afraid or unwilling to use violence to defend family and loved ones if nonviolence doesn't succeed. I like this one. A lot.

When I finish reading it, Raj is smiling at me. "You were very clever, taunting those bullies the way you did, and you managed everything without resorting to violence. But I know that if you had no other choice, you would have used your knife." He leans back and shuts his eyes. "You have taught me much."

Do I tell him? Do I let on that I reached first for the

knife, and that it was more a question of resorting to nonviolence rather than the other way around? Maybe someday I'll
tell him. Not today.

He says, "Please read the next one."

At the next sticky, I read, " 'In life it is impossible to eschew
violence completely.' " I look up. "I know this one! It's my favorite, like the one you love about the edge of the sword."

He smiles at me, and I read on.

" 'The question arises, where is one to draw the line? The
line cannot be the same for everyone. Although essentially
the principle is the same, yet, everyone applies it in his or her
own way. What is one man's food can be another's poison.' "

That was the last marker, and Raj knows it. He's about to
speak, but I beat him to it. Raj, for all his professed humility,
is still Raj, and he still thinks he's controlling everything. He's
also still lecturing me. So I close first the book and then my
eyes, and I recite.

" 'I know the path. It is straight and narrow. It is like the
edge of a sword. I rejoice to walk on it. I weep when I slip.
God's word is: "He who strives never perishes." I have im-
plicit faith in that promise. Though, therefore, from my weak-
ness I fail a thousand times, I will not lose faith, but hope that
I shall see the Light when the flesh has been brought under
perfect subjection, as some day it must.' "

Raj has covered his face with his hands, and my guess is
he's trying not to cry. That would probably be painful, if
laughing is, but in even more ways.

I decide the time for revelation has come.

"Raj." I wait until he's wiped his face and is looking at
me. "I know about Sampath."

"Anjani." He looks away.

"So I understand about your reaction to the knife."

"Your knife is only a knife. Everything depends on how it

is used. And I hold things too close to my chest." He shakes his head, as if to correct himself. "No. I have held things too close to my chest. You are helping me to be open."

He rubs the unbruised side of his face. Then he looks at me. "Jason, will you be my friend?"

Something catches in my chest. Perhaps I've misunderstood how he loves me. Am I a Norm to him? "Is that everything we will be?"

"No. I hope not. I want us to be that and much more. But I must begin there. I am learning trust. A hard lesson. And sometimes it's easier to trust a friend than a lover."

He's right, there. I already trust Robert in ways I don't trust Raj. So I guess he's not the only one who has to learn.

"And Jason?" He pauses, then, "I meant what I said. I love you."

I glance down at my feet, not sure what to do. Is there a rule for this, and is it different for gays? Do I tell him I love him too?

Fuck the rules.

"I love you too." I smile, but it's a little wobbly, so I try to lighten things up. "How long will it be before you can laugh again?"

He blinks, not sure where this is coming from. "From what the doctor said, though it wasn't about laughing, I'm guessing a couple of weeks. Why?"

"If you can laugh, I can hold you. And maybe more. Do you think we could be really good friends in a couple of weeks?"

He reaches his hand out for mine. "I'm sure of it."

I squeeze his hand once and release it. All of a sudden I know why I brought that CD. I go over to where I've dropped it, locate Raj's player, find the right track, and adjust the volume. Not loud—but I still want it to fill the room. Then I go back to my chair and take Raj's hand again.

We sit there, not speaking. The words speak for us: We will be true to ourselves, and we will not hide. We will not pretend.

So many things go through my head. But the most important is the list I make. It's a two-part list, and on one side of it are the people I know who've been mean, or who've proved themselves to be untrustworthy. On the other side is a list of people who understand or want to, who help or at least try, who offer support and maybe even love.

No matter how many times I start over, each time the list of people like Aunt Audrey and Robert and Anjani and Coach and Norm and Meg—and even Uncle Steve—is lots longer than the one with John Whittier and Brian Cooney and Jimmy Walsh. The unjust empire Raj and I will battle is so much weaker than ours.

How can we lose?

A Secret Edge

ROBIN REARDON

ABOUT THIS GUIDE

The suggested questions are included
to enhance your group's reading of
A Secret Edge.

DISCUSSION QUESTIONS

1. Jason gets a switchblade when the bullies who've terrorized him all through childhood get big enough to do some real damage. He says that what counts is that he knows he has the knife, that the knowledge alone will help keep him safe. In what ways might this be true? Is Jason fooling himself? What are some of the instances in which Jason demonstrates confidence or bravery when his knife is either nowhere near him or wouldn't help him if it were?

2. The first two of Jason's friends we learn about in the story are Jimmy Walsh and Robert Hubble. Although these two boys turn out to be adversaries, what do they have in common that attracts Jason's friendship? What does it say about Jason that he made friends with each of them?

3. The first time Jason notices Raj, Raj is performing a perfect high jump. After he lands, he stares back at Jason, and Jason has the feeling Raj is encouraging admiration. Once we know more about Raj, is this assessment still viable? Is it part of Raj's personality to want admiration—or do we learn things about his personality and his life experiences that allow us to interpret apparent arrogance differently?

4. The first time Jason dreams about Raj he gets the impression in the dream that Raj is standing at a distance, and that Raj would come to Jason if he could. How does this image play out in the story? What's holding Raj from moving toward Jason? Is he arrogant out of a sense of superiority, or is his stance—physically and emotionally—defensive?

5. In the mall, when Jason sees Raj with his sister in a store and he goes in, how would you describe Jason's behavior? He doesn't know whether Raj is gay yet, but isn't he flirting with Raj? Do you think Raj knows this? How does he respond? If you'd been a shopper in that store, not knowing Jason or Raj, would you have picked up that they were attracted to each other? How, or why not?

6. A few times over the course of getting to know Raj, Jason wonders what the rules for romance are when it's between two boys. This implies that he thinks he knows what romance between a boy and a girl constitutes. Where would he get that understanding? Why wouldn't he get an understanding of the rules between boys from the same source? Are the rules different when the two people are the same sex? If so, should they be? Should the rules between two boys be different from the rules between two girls? Should there be rules at all? What purposes do they serve, and/or what barriers do they create?

7. Uncle Steve tells Jason that there's a set of rules that men apply to men, and another that men apply to women. Do you agree? If so, what might these rules be, and why do they exist? What about women? Do they have one set of rules for men and another for women?

8. After he tells them he's gay, Jason gets reasonably good reactions from Robert and, eventually, from Meg. His Uncle Steve has a harder time hearing the news. If you were good friends with someone you believed was

straight, someone you had known a long time, and then you found out he or she was gay, would you find that confusing? If so, how much of that confusion do you think would come from not knowing what the "rules" were anymore? Do you think you'd feel betrayed in some way? What if you had thought they were gay and they turned out to be straight? In each case, how would your thinking about that person change? Would you act differently once you knew the truth? Do you think it would affect your friendship in either case? In both cases?

9. When Uncle Steve learns that Jason is gay, he tells Audrey that he has failed Jason and Jason's father, Steve's brother. Why would he feel that way? What might Steve have felt he should have done differently? Is there anything Steve or Audrey could have done to force Jason into one sexual orientation or another?

10. Most young boys, including many who will prove to be gay, spend their formative years trying to prove they're male. They adopt tough-guy behavior, avoid girls, and hang around only with each other. Some of them could easily pass for girls if they wanted to, almost right up to puberty. Why is being seen as male so crucial to most boys? Do you think the importance of this struggle could affect how adult men of any orientation view homosexual men? Do we see girls go through similar struggles to prove they're female?

11. Raj tells Jason that the more violence a man shows against gays, the more he fears them. Why? Is there

something about homosexuality, or homosexual men in particular, that society finds threatening?

12. While watching the film *La Cage aux Folles*, Jason speculates that he may not have the courage to be honest about who he is. Afterward, in the car, Raj says that it takes a lot of guts to be gay. Do you think this is true? If so, why is courage necessary?

13. When Jason meets Elaine at the party he attends with Norm, he feels like he and Elaine have something in common. They dance their own dance, ignoring the music. It turns out they're both orphans. Neither is into drugs or excessive alcohol, and in this environment they're on the fringe. Jason feels sorry for Norm, who believes he has to do what his crowd does or be alienated. Which of the boys do you find more interesting: Norm, who has a good heart but has never tested himself by going outside the lines; or Jason, who has had to develop aspects of his character that allow him to live outside those lines? Is it possible that lack of acceptance by the standard "crowd" gives a young person space to develop his or her own character; or is it better to have the support of as many people as possible, even if you feel you have to fit a certain mold to get that support?

14. When Jason finds Internet articles about the responses of male homosexuals to pheromones, he also finds material from people who refuse to believe it. The research findings are real; they were not made up for this story. The results of the first study on humans were re-

leased publicly in 2005. Why might some people refuse to believe them? What have they got to lose?

15. There are four "edges" in this story. Can you name them?